An Afterlife for Rosemary Lamb

A Mystery

Louise Wolhuter

The poem on page 155 is an excerpt from 'The Lesson of the Water-Mill' by Sarah Doudney, from 'The Psalms of Life', *Sarah Doudney Selected Poems and Hymns*, © Charles J. Doe, published by Curiosmith, 2017.

Originally published in 2022 by Ultimo Press,
an imprint of Hardie Grant Publishing.
This edition published in 2023.

Ultimo Press	Ultimo Press (London)
Gadigal Country	5th & 6th Floors
7, 45 Jones Street	52–54 Southwark Street
Ultimo, NSW 2007	London SE1 1UN
ultimopress.com.au	

  ultimopress

All rights reserved. No part of this publication may be reproduced, stored in a retrieval system or transmitted in any form by any means, electronic, mechanical, photocopying, recording or otherwise, without the prior written permission of the publishers and copyright holders.

The moral rights of the author have been asserted.

Copyright © Louise Wolhuter 2022

A catalogue record for this book is available from the National Library of Australia

An Afterlife for Rosemary Lamb
ISBN 978 1 76115 171 2 (paperback)

Cover design Andy Warren Design
Cover photographs Sky by Raychel Sanner / Unsplash; Mangroves by Ravigopal Kesari / Unsplash; Mosquito by Antagain / iStock
Text design Simon Paterson, Bookhouse, Sydney
Typesetting Bookhouse, Sydney | Typeset in Mrs Eaves
Copyeditor Ali Lavau
Proofreader Pamela Dunne

10 9 8 7 6 5 4 3 2 1

Printed in Australia by Griffin Press, an Accredited ISO AS/NZS 14001 Environmental Management System printer.

The paper this book is printed on is certified against the Forest Stewardship Council® Standards. Griffin Press holds FSC® chain of custody certification SCS-COC-001185. FSC® promotes environmentally responsible, socially beneficial and economically viable management of the world's forests.

Ultimo Press acknowledges the Traditional Owners of the Country on which we work, the Gadigal People of the Eora Nation and the Wurundjeri People of the Kulin Nation, and recognises their continuing connection to the land, waters and culture. We pay our respects to their Elders past and present.

For Valda Mary Williams 1905–1999

PROLOGUE

Meg

It was a meat-and-potato town that Rosemary Cole grew up in. Winifred, Carney County, up around the middle part of Queensland's coast, beyond the theme parks and koalas and the dry ginger stretch; through the sugar cane, and past the smelters and rum distilleries.

It was a pretty town when I knew it. At its centre was a wide lake, a tidy park running around its reeds, peppered with picnic benches and four or five coin-operated barbecues. Children fed ducks from the sandy lip of a playground, though there was a sign that told them not to.

Winifred may have changed since I was there, but I doubt it. I expect you would still find the buildings on the main street crackle-white from the sun—the post office, the police station, the library that doubles as an information centre. There is a small cinema with slung chairs, and a stretch that holds (or held when I was there) a cafe and a clothes shop and a chemist. The nicer houses fan out from the lake and are painted pastel colours: apricot and tangerine, lemon and lime, caramel and toffee. Colours you can almost smell and sort of taste, like when you look out at the ocean on a scorching afternoon and think of mint and cool and wet, but not of salt.

When I was a child, my grandmother used to read aloud at bedtime from a thick, cloth-covered storybook with pages the colour of cheese. Stories set in litter-free streets, where apples shone on trees and jam tarts cooled on windowsills. Cooks were fat and ruddy-faced, and boys and girls wore buckled shoes and long white socks that were never dirty or fell down around their ankles. The farmer's name was Mr Pod or Barley, and the baker was a Sally Bun or Treacle. I always felt the town of Winifred would have settled well, between those pages.

The butcher's name—as if he'd made it up (although I know he didn't)—was Tom Lamb, son of Thomas, son of Thomas Senior. They were all Lambs, and they were all butchers. Men were expected to follow their fathers and their fathers' fathers. Women were expected to follow the men.

The local paper made news out of nothing. People slept soundly, and safer than they imagined they would in Brisbane or Rockhampton or Mackay. (Except for a while, when Jessie Else went missing. Locks started turning then.)

It was nothing like the town where I grew up, where grass grew way past windowsills, houses weren't painted at all, and yards were packed with rusted hulks of cars and stoves and hide-and-seek refrigerators.

But I would not have left it if I could have stayed.

God's own country, my grandmother called it, and she'd come a long way to find it. Travelling all by herself on a steamer full of post-war refugees, welcomed in New Zealand for their willing hands and hips. A Catholic, of course, with a trunk of shame, an angel on her shoulder and a life led in the torchlight of an all-seeing God.

'He's watching you,' she used to say, 'every minute of every hour of every day and night,' until my brother and I were too afraid to steal or lie or take our clothes off.

It rained often where I grew up, and the rain came down cold and sideways. It fudged the sky and stung like bees—not like the rain that fell on Rosemary Cole. The rain in Carney County is soft even when it's pouring down, even in February when your tank fills time and time and time again. The Wet, Australians call it. In New Zealand it's just the weather: the earth takes it all and everything grows. In Carney County, the earth takes its time and muddy brown water spills through the town. Then comes winter, with its blue-sky mornings and sharp-lit afternoons, its pelicans and its butterflies, its months of mangoes and avocados and lilac-golden sunrises.

At the edge of Winifred, on the far side of Lake Carney and hidden by trees, is a chocolate factory grown up from the milking shed it was in the way-back when Winifred was a simple dairy farm. At the bottom of the high street, what was then a farmhouse is now a pub, though they call it Carney's Grand Hotel. Named after Nathan Carney, who built the dam they call a lake; who bought and raised the cattle and built the now-a-chocolate factory. Tourists order battered lunches from a chalkboard on what began as Nathan Carney's porch, and locals sit and sip and chatter in the same pink light that I imagine Nathan Carney must have sat in, back in his day, in a rocking chair perhaps, smoking a long and spindly pipe, and looking out across the water to his milking sheds. He could have seen them then, before the council planted trees to hide the buildings; years before the barbecues and picnic tables, before the town was a town with a name at all.

No one knows what became of Nathan Carney in the end. One year there came more rain than any other and the flooding was so great that history left it capital letters. The Great Flood of 1936 changed kilometres of coastline and sent his cattle slipping and a-sliding. Leathery legs were broken, and when the skies cleared Mrs Carney woke to find her husband gone and only a scatter of cows in an early morning mist, on a carpet of brown where sweet points of grass may have been only days away from thrusting through. Still in her nightdress, she wandered out among them and put a bullet through the roof of her mouth.

But the Carneys left the makings of something to be built upon—the wash of a county, paddocks, barns and milking sheds, a farmstead and a chapel, a willing if thinned workforce—and after a while (after the war) came Winifred, a rich Scottish widow with a knowledge of chocolate-making and a business plan that evolved into Winifred's Finest. You will have seen it in your local supermarket, in its plum-coloured boxes with curls of gold. Dark and milk assortments, soft centres and truffles, hollow rabbits past Australia Day, and Santas come September.

People were proud to say that they were Winifred born and bred. It was a claim that rode in on a full chest, tipped hats, and lay a trail of breadcrumbed expectation that fathers would be followed, as the butcher had followed his father, who'd followed his own. But times change, and on the butcher's wide window the arc of *Lamb and Sons* was shortened. A single letter taken first, when the eldest moved away, then *Son* scraped off completely when it was clear the youngest would not take the road expected.

A cousin followed, in the end. The son of a brother of Mrs Lamb, so not a *Lamb*, but a son of the town, and family, Tom was quick to reassure his customers. It was the son of a son of a sign-writer who re-stencilled the window—*Lamb & Coulter Quality Butchers*—and I imagine it was the son of a panelbeater who resprayed their big refrigerated van.

Eddie may not have wanted to be a butcher, but he remained 'the Butcher's Son', and though Rosemary Cole became Rosemary Lamb the day she married him, to the town she would always be a Cole. Every peg had its place. The Butcher, the Baker, the Troublemaker.

Winifred's storybook pages were rarely turned. It was a town of known beginnings, but it was not a place for beginning again.

It was a plate of meat-and-potatoes expectations that rested the bitter barrel of a gun on Mrs Carney's tongue, I think. Her husband left her somewhere she never would or should have found herself without him: lost and all alone, in a place she saw no path away from and with no way of continuing on as the woman those around expected her to be. Without a farmer, without a farm, how could she go on being the Farmer's Wife?

'You can leave, you know,' I would have told her. 'You can go somewhere else and start again. There are other ways. There are other places.' And there are other people. There are people like Rosemary Lamb, without whom I might still be in my own once-green field, with my own shotgun-of-a-sort, reading books and canning pears and talking to Mrs Robinson but no one else.

She was a kitten when I found her staggering along the high tideline of Marlow Beach, where I'd gone to watch the turtles lay their eggs. Robinson, after Robinson Crusoe and the Swiss family. Mrs, just because she was a she. I wasn't thinking of the song, or of the woman in the film.

It was past midnight, but the moon was full, and I couldn't have missed her. There were no turtles that night, only this shivering mess of matted fur that I scooped up, along with string and seaweed, to wrap tightly in a cardigan I held close to my chest and filled with warm breath every sandy step back to my car.

It took us a long time to get home. The highway was blocked for a stretch by flashing blue lights, and the zippered bag of an accident

I must have missed by minutes as I'd headed north an hour before, and I drove very carefully, keeping her as comfortable as I could in a nest on my lap.

Maybe someone threw her in the water at Milligan, where the Barra River runs into the sea and there's a boat ramp people use for odd things at night. They found a German tourist once trapped in a tangle of rope and rubbish, pale and bloated and half-eaten (the papers didn't say by what). With enough air, and a tight enough knot in a plastic bag, a kitten would have had a better chance.

I wasn't a cat person particularly. They say you either are or you're not, but I wasn't, and then I had this small helpless thing to take care of. Its being a cat made no difference to me. That she was tiny and helpless, that I could help, was what mattered. I kept her in the pocket of my apron like a joey, and I fed her with a dropper. She grew well, and she grew up, and she stayed with me.

It was nice to have some company. I'd never planned to live alone, but there are reasons people do the things they do. There are scars on people's hearts. There are words in people's heads, and pictures in the pink light of closed eyes. Things happen and secrets are kept.

There is a reason I came from a small, wet, green town in New Zealand to live quietly in a place few people knew enough about to try to find. Although Winifred was pretty, and although I helped in the library on Thursdays, and bought tinned food and milk from Woolworths on Flinders, it was not where I chose to live.

Magpie Beach was barely fifteen minutes south of town. There were few magpies and there was no beach. There were no barbecues or picnic tables. There were pitted rocks, silver crusted with oysters and powdery once-were-worms. There were tiered saltwater pools, thick-waisted trees, sandflies and mosquitoes. There had been a battered sign up on the highway, but it leaned and then it fell and then it disappeared and never was replaced.

I was twenty-three when I arrived, and I was not alone. Two ran away and, road-weary and dog-tired of dust and gum trees, two took the road to Magpie Beach. We thought we'd find a quiet place to camp for a few nights, away from *Who are you?* and *Where've you come from?* We stayed those few nights and then we stayed a few more and then we cleared a proper spot and began to think about staying a while. There was no power, no electricity, no sewerage, but we'd found our plan and purpose.

Sonny was a fitter-turner and the factory snapped him up. We put in a septic tank and laid a slab, rigged gutters around the caravan and filled rainwater tanks. There was the odd *How long are you staying?* but no one really cared. We were outsiders, so we stayed outside.

I kept the house and dug around it, planting vegetables and fruit trees. I raised chickens. Sonny fished from the rocks when the sun was still an hour off rising. I'd slip eggs onto his toast as he lay whatever he'd caught in the sink. He'd take his spear when the moon was full and plough through the swell, diving to places I'd not have dared to. He'd climb back up the rocks with a fish still twitching on the end of his spear, his mask pushed up into his hair and shoulders warm to touch no matter how cool the early morning. If there were fishery patrols or licences, they didn't bother us. It was a different world. It was our world. We smoked the fish. We sucked crab legs. We lay on dappled grass and made shapes of the clouds dotted above us. Beneath the chirp and hum of native bees and dragonflies and floury bakers, 'Read to me,' he'd say, because he knew I loved to; and I would turn summer-soft pages until the afternoon drew heavy, and wake at twilight with one hand in the soft fold of his arm, book marked and closed on the blanket between us. Little wings beat the air around my heart, and I thought we'd live like that forever.

But seasons passed. Rain fell, storms came and, too soon after, he was gone.

CHAPTER ONE

Meg

I'd been at Magpie Beach for seventeen years when the Lambs came out from Winifred. Four with Sonny, four all alone, and nine with Mrs Robinson. There was a house on the other side of the headland, but I rarely saw the woman who lived there. Once a month she walked the track and took a taxi into town. It came for her at nine o'clock and had her back by twelve, and away she went through the bush, her shopping trolley bumping along behind her. I didn't always see her, even then. I didn't need or want to. Once a month, it was no task to keep out of her way.

But the Lambs, when they arrived, arrived completely.

It was March. The sandflies were at their worst and the fishing at its best, and the roof leaked in a different place each year. I was laying mackerel fillets in the smoker when they came. The rain was more of a mist than anything else and nothing louder than drips broke the silence. Mrs Robinson was smoothing figure eights around my ankles and we both started at the roar of Eddie's Kingswood as it slid into the clearing at the end of the lane, spattering wet dirt up along its flanks and startling the pigeons.

The car hunkered, growling and steaming, and for a moment—just a moment—I thought it might slip its nose around and slide back up the lane to the highway and back up the coast, back inland to Winifred where it belonged. But the moment passed, and the big car shuddered into silence.

Eddie climbed out first. Red-haired and freckled like a cloth beneath a tree, he was no stranger to me: the Butcher's Son, the one who didn't want his name on the window. I knew he had an older brother and a cousin and a limp. Pulling his shirt down over his pocket tops, he spat into the rain and walked around to open Rosemary's door. Taller, thinner, darker than him, she stepped barefoot out of the car without looking down.

She was quite beautiful. Dark eyes, long lashes, brows swept wide. If she wore make-up, I did not notice. Her hair was so black it was almost blue and ran down her back like oil. He tried to hold her still and they stood locked side by side for a long moment before she stepped away. She curled her arms above her head and opened them deliberately like branches, letting each finger stretch to its reach, as if the rain they channelled did her good, as if the car had kept her too long folded crisp.

She wore a wattle-yellow dress I would have had to hem, but on her it rode high. Straight knees, brown legs it was plain to see could run and climb and hold on tight at the faintest call of *Let's go*, *Come on*, *Bet you can't*. Her calves tensed so I knew her toes were curling in the mud, and I knew then that they would stay.

What did I know of her?

I'd seen looks exchanged and eyebrows raised. I'd watched her grow up between the library stacks. There was no library at Winifred High, so the set books came through us: *New Patches for Old*, *Walkabout*, *Animal Farm*. They sat in the storeroom in big cardboard boxes through the summer holidays waiting for us to beat the silverfish away and tape loose pages back in time for the new school year and the readers who'd come in with their teachers in long chattering lines. Rosemary had come in with them, though not really with them, so that Catherine and I knew her apart. My grandmother would have called her a funny thing, meaning funny peculiar, funny Magpie Beach (where there were few magpies and there was no beach). She was not what was expected. She was not what the town expected her to be.

She was the youngest of Roy Cole's daughters. Everybody called him King. He kept the camera shop on Arthur Street. Arthur after Arthur Cole, his father's father. There'd been Coles in Winifred back when there'd been Carneys, he told anyone who asked, and he steered many a conversation to the asking. There weren't many other families that went back as far. The Lambs came close, the Danzies, perhaps, and the Murrays on Beak Street, who descended from a cousin of the Widow Winifred herself. Cole was a name that meant something in town, but Rosemary did not look the way a Cole was meant to look. Her sisters were shorter by a head. Their hips were wide and their complexions pasty. Their hair grew in honey-pale tangles, and in summer they turned a milky pink, while Rosemary went the colour of a rich beef stock.

There was a lot of talk around the town when Rosemary Cole was born. Winks flew across the mince and mashed potatoes. 'She's not his,' they said, and other things, because there was no doubt at all that she was hers.

Joanna Cole was a woman who wore sunglasses indoors. Years ago, she'd come to the library with three broken fingers all bound up together, and I'd helped her take her library card out of her purse. She hadn't wanted my fingers in her bag, but it couldn't be helped; she couldn't manage by herself, and Catherine wasn't there. She thanked me afterwards, but only because she had to.

'Not the full Aussie made,' Catherine said of Rosemary Cole.

Catherine was the librarian and a policeman's wife. 'You mustn't say anything to anyone,' she was fond of beginning a story, and she knew everybody's secrets, though she didn't tell them all. Some she let lie, let sand and time bury quietly. *The Cole Girl*, Catherine called Rosemary. Though there were four Cole girls, it was Rosemary she gave the capital letters.

I heard her called worse.

I watched her eat a lizard once, coming down the side of Discount Dan's where they flattened the empty boxes and skipped the bread outside its use-by date. Five had Rosemary up against the wall, books fallen around her feet and a margarine tub pushed up under her nose. She was only a girl then, one of half-a-dozen in stone-grey skirts and knee socks.

'Eat it,' they growled. Voices thick with menace.

'Eat it!' Chanting.

And Rosemary took the little lizard by its tail and dropped it in her open mouth like whitebait.

'Freak!' they screamed at her then, and they ran off shrieking with laughter.

She waited more than a minute before she spat the lizard carefully into her hand and set it on the ground, picked up her books and went on her way.

She didn't belong in Winifred any more than I did.

CHAPTER TWO

Rosemary

Eddie promised we could get a dog once we had our own place. It wouldn't have been fair to keep one while we were staying in his parents' caravan, parked down the side of their house, in and out quietly, pretending we weren't actually living in it so the neighbours on the left wouldn't call the council. There are strict rules around camping in suburbia, though I think they mostly concern emptying your black tank, and we never used the shower or the toilet in the caravan; we always used the bathroom in the house. Still, I'm sure we were breaking other rules. Councils make so many of them. It's one of the reasons we wanted our own bit of land.

I didn't mind the caravan. It reminded me of a doll's house we'd had when I was a little girl. With three older sisters, by the time my turn came to rearrange the furniture it was all a bit worn and torn. There were brown scribbles in the toilet. The fridge door was glued shut, and all the tiny bits of food that had once filled it were long lost or swallowed. Only one of the dolls survived (and Batman, whose legs didn't bend, so if I wanted to settle him in front of his television I had to sort of ramp him up against a chair), but I loved playing with that doll's house. There was a spot for everything, and everything had its spot. That's what I liked about the caravan. Eddie was right, though—it wouldn't have been fair on a dog. A tiny little one might have been alright, but I wanted a kelpie or a cattle dog, something with a bit of gloss and bounce.

We saved and saved for a patch of land to build on. It was Eddie's dream, really, but I was happy to hitch my wagon to the back of it. Eddie wanted space for a shed and a workshop, and I just wanted to get out of town. A place where the sky was bigger than any patch we'd get above a yard we could afford; next door's screen door slamming with every load of laundry, kids yelling, heads bouncing up and down behind the fence.

We started off looking up and in from Milligan, but we were better off towards the coast, Eddie said. He fancied himself as more of a fisherman than he turned out to be. Imagined himself casting from the rocks at sunset, a cold beer in one hand and twitch after twitch of his rod in the other, when what he settled on (once we were settled) was the remote control on the arm of his chair and a bellybutton full of crumbs. He always had a cold beer in one hand, though, so that was something of a dream come true.

As it turned out, the land cost us less than we'd expected. It belonged to an old lady Eddie's nanna knew. They lived in the same nursing home, where they ate lunch together and sat side by side in high-backed chairs to watch *The Bold and the Beautiful* on weekday afternoons. We visited one Saturday, and were introduced, talk led to talk, and it turned out she owned this bit of land she was happy for us to have, on condition that we lived there and didn't sell it on. She didn't really care for paperwork, but we had to do it properly, Eddie's mum said, as if we would have done it any other way. We knew there'd come a time we needed proof on paper. Questions always come up, and things come out, though not always the way you worry that they will. So, it was all above board. 'There's nothing but snakes and rocks,' I remember the old lady warning us, and I remember thinking (but not saying) that there were plenty of both of those in town.

I wondered what dreams her husband might have had for the place when they'd bought it. We knew he'd died much younger than either of them expected. Maybe she'd tried to sell it then, or maybe she'd wanted to keep it in her family. I don't think she had any children, but maybe she did. Maybe she sold us the land so they wouldn't get it. People can turn bitter towards the end. They look down on everything around them as if they're in a place to judge. They wield their specially angled knives and forks and cut all that they have left into pieces they dish out as if everyone around them's desperate for a mouthful. My own nanna left everything to my sisters and nothing to me. It was her way of having the last word and letting everyone know that she had not approved.

I didn't care. China dogs and jugs with faces, ugly little paintings and cardigans still in their packets—my sisters were welcome to it all. I might have liked some of the photographs, but I'm sure I wasn't in many (if any) of them.

Anyway, we got five acres for a song. We borrowed money from the bank, of course. We still needed to build the house itself, get a decent generator and a proper septic tank, but we had a chunk of savings between us, and Mum let me have some of the money she'd set aside for me when Dad died. Eddie's parents chipped in. The factory paid well enough, and Eddie still had some workers comp coming, so the repayments were manageable.

My first trip out to Maggie Beach was in the pouring rain. Halfway between nowhere and nowhere else, the road in was thick with mud, wet leaves stickering the windscreen, branches scratching all the doors. Eddie had been out twice already and considered a couple of spots, but the patch at the end of Shank Lane saved us the trouble of bulldozing another track in from the highway.

He parked the Kingswood in the clearing at the road's end and made a fuss of opening my door. He wanted me to love it, but he needn't have worried, as I'd already decided that I would. The mess of trees; roaring surf beyond the bush; big sky—clunky and grey now, but it would be blue in summer, full of stars at night.

'This is it,' Eddie said, as he slung an arm across my shoulders. I felt burdened by the weight of him at that moment, even as it bent him crooked having to reach up and round like that. I thought of Jesus in a picture that his nanna kept above her toaster. Struggling with the cross on his back, on his way up a hill to plant it next to two others already there. But standing in the mud and drizzle, I could see the house we'd build, the space we'd own, and the freedom we might have out there surrounded by possums and parrots and all that sky. Eddie could have his big shed and his workshop.

'What do you think?' he asked me.

'Yes,' I said. The answer every question wants.

'Rain'll stop soon enough.'

'And we can have a dog?'

He laughed at that and let me go. 'You can have anything you want,' he promised.

CHAPTER THREE

Meg

It didn't take Rosemary and Eddie long to build their house. Eighty-one days of hammering and drilling, scraping and grinding. They'd raise an arm in greeting, but they never came to call with a casserole or hands that needed shaking. Eighty-one days, and once they'd finished it looked like it had been there all along.

A cabin with baskets strung along its eaves and wide, wooden steps around a wide, wooden deck might have looked odd in Winifred, where doors were shut and windows matched and roofs were painted, but out where we were, it was only in the way, settled as it was in the clearing at the end of the road.

I had to pass by to get to the highway to catch the bus on Thursdays. I could have cut through the bush, and I often did, but autumn dirt was sticky, and tangles pulled holes in my tights.

'Did you come in on a broom?' Catherine asked, and though I knew she only meant it as a joke, I was embarrassed and ashamed, so I walked past the cabin carefully and quietly to get to our unsealed road.

Sometimes I'd see the Lambs, rubbed up close together on the steps like cats. Her mug was iris blue, and her toenails were always painted. I watched him tuck strands of her hair behind her ears or wrap them back around her ponytail. I watched him lift her feet into his lap, hold her hand and turn the gold band on her finger. She chewed the pen she used to do the crossword and left crusts on her plate.

They never noticed me creeping by, and that suited me just fine.

There'd been few voices but my own since Sonny died. There'd been no man-made sounds but those that came from me: the soft clatter of cutlery in a sink of soapy water, the chop-chop-chop of a knife on a board, the tink-tink-tink of a teaspoon on the lip of a cup, the scratch of dust and daddy-long-legs swept across a floor. My floor. My mug. My board. My sink. One knife, one fork, one spoon.

The Lambs brought a hammer tapping and the whirring of a sander; calls in to lunch, calls out for another beer, a hand for a minute, a time double-checked. They brought a smell of sawdust and coffee, burnt toast and beeswax, and other smells I didn't know, to mingle with the paraffin and possum, eucalyptus, jasmine and the cold-tea smell of coral spawning through the early summer months.

They brought country music.

Some nights I stood in shadows that hugged the trees and watched Eddie whirl Rosemary in circles beneath a swinging blue light that zapped the bugs which must have bothered them. He held her waist as tenderly as you'd cup a broken bird. More than once (twice, fifteen times), I woke up stiff in a crumbled bed of twigs and leaves, lights long snuffed, and Rosemary and Eddie tucked away behind a flutter of curtains and wind chimes.

Some nights when I couldn't sleep, or if the moon was full, I'd walk around the tip of the headland, across the rocks and to the far side, where the Englishwoman lived. It's all I knew her as: the Englishwoman (the Butcher, the Baker). As it turned out, all anyone ever knew about her was her accent.

I stood so far away she'd not have seen me even if she looked, but the house had been empty for many years before she'd come to claim it, and I'd been close enough to press my face against its walls and lie still and flat on the porch that wrapped around it—planks wide and windswept where they faced the ocean, thick with leaves and cobwebs on the side where they did not. Before the Englishwoman came, storm shutters battered up against windows built to slide and let as much of outside in as possible. An artist built it, Catherine said, positioned it for light and isolation, but moved to the city after all to settle for the opposite. One pipe emptied a kitchen sink and another drained the bath, either side of a wall or not, I couldn't tell. Cable ties and shadecloth patches kept snakes from travelling in and rings too loose for fingers from washing away. A water tank stood up on stilts, so gravity filled taps, and solar mats warmed water. I would have liked to wander through, imagining the artist there. I would have liked to look for signs of others who came after—growing children marked on a pantry door. It would have been a small house for a family (one bedroom, I was sure), but you never know; a lot can be going on inside a house you wouldn't know from walking two, three, fifteen times around it.

When the Englishwoman came, she brought a generator. She lay a mat beside the door and planted flowers in pots she placed to catch the rain the gutters missed.

Sonny said it was a waste of space and energy to grow a thing you couldn't eat, or tend to animals you couldn't milk or breed or roast. That's what it was about, he said, living where we did, the way we chose to live: pickling the fruit we picked, and scrambling the eggs we found with gentle fingers, warm and soft and safely lain in hay we'd set in boxes. We didn't bring a lot of money with us; savings—Sonny's mostly—which bought the caravan and a car to tow it. We took things strangers set on verges to be taken—timber, tiles and garden chairs, a tin bath and a table—and we did without the little things that others took for granted: frozen food and air conditioning, television, bright lights and refrigeration. We cooked on gas and lit the night with kerosene and candles. Grey water went on the garden and peelings fed the worms. Showers were short in summer, a wet cloth rinsed and run through cracks and creases. If the tank ran dry, we'd top it up with drums that Sonny filled at work. Winter rains let us draw the tub and six turns of the kettle warmed it. Cold nights were thick with blankets.

If the council came to check on rumours, they did not move us on. We were not the squatters they might have imagined. We'd lain a slab and dug the long drop properly. Sonny's wages went on food and fuel and treats—a slab of beer a fortnight, and a bottle of Jack Daniels now and then.

There was always a light on in the Englishwoman's house. No matter what time of night or early morning. Sonny would have said that was a waste as well, but he was long gone when she got there. I thought she must have trouble sleeping too, and wondered what she worried might creep up on her without it.

It wasn't hard to make a way along the rocks, with the sea falling away to one side while the bush grew thinner on the other. It wasn't a cliff, but it was far enough to fall, steep and slippery enough on an outgoing tide to break an arm or worse.

It was dry but not too bright the night I came across Rosemary Lamb. I watched my feet for most of the way until the ground softened and spread enough to let things grow and be grabbed. I looked up then, and there she was only steps in front of me, moon-blanched, at the point of the headland where we could see down to the light of the Englishwoman's house, and up the coast to the lamp the council lit beside the boat ramp at Milligan, and back into the shelter of Magpie Beach and the lantern that swung on my own front porch.

I might have turned and headed straight back to it and the sanctity of home and all within if she hadn't already seen me, if it hadn't seemed to me that she was waiting.

'Hi,' she said. It hung between us like something that wanted taping back.

We stood for a while side by side in moonlight and silence, staring out at nothing and everything else.

'Sometimes I find it hard to sleep,' she said.

Sometimes I find it hard to sleep. I've known nights I wished for death so hard I cried myself unconscious and woke up disappointed.

'Sometimes I lie awake just wondering where there is apart from this. Do you ever wonder that?' She turned to face me, and I didn't know whether to nod a lie or let my head shake honestly because I hadn't for many years. In the end I only closed my eyes.

After Sonny left, I felt nothing for a long time but a cold vacuum of Doesn't Matter. I sat on the same rocks and let the tide wash in and over me until I was cold enough to need to move, and some nights I simply moved into the water until little waves that shone white in the moonlight broke over my face, but something always kept me from letting go completely. If I'd been a stronger person, I might have put a gun to the roof of my mouth the way Mrs Carney did, or strung a thick rope from a strong limb, but I could not commit to that. Something held me. Hope, perhaps. Faith. It's not that I believed in God so much; I think I simply lacked the faithlessness for suicide.

Sergeant Scanlan saved me in the end. I never knew why it was he came to Magpie Beach that afternoon, but he didn't expect to find me there. 'I thought you'd have gone home long ago,' he said. He thought someone would have come for me. Wrapped me in a blanket and taken me away. Taken me home. Taken me back. But no one did. Had I hoped they would?

When he returned, he brought his wife. 'She's not all there,' he whispered to her, which was true enough, because everything I'd ever been had died with Sonny.

'The first step's always the hardest,' Catherine said. She brought with her bread and books and asked me could I use a little money. Would I like a little job?

'I'm not very good with numbers,' I told her.

'Well,' she said, 'you're a reader, so I'm guessing you're pretty good with words.'

'Catherine's the librarian,' Sergeant Scanlan said. There was pride in the palm of the hand that warmed her shoulder, and she blushed; and I nodded as if I didn't know already, but who else did he think might have stamped the books I borrowed?

He drove me to town the following Thursday, and Catherine met me in the library's great glass doorway with a hug that rubbed in circles like a mother's. 'Time will heal,' she promised, but it never did.

I drove myself to town the following Thursday, and every Thursday after that, until one morning the car wouldn't start, and then I caught the bus.

Rosemary was gone when I opened my eyes. I watched her bend and straighten as she slipped across the furthest rocks, and when the black of gum trees had pulled her in, I picked my own way home to Mrs Robinson, and tried to sleep without dreaming.

I saw her often when I walked after that, so that I began to walk to see her and wonder what it was she missed that made her ponder what there was beyond the darkness. I didn't question why she couldn't sleep. I'd often seen her with her coffee in the morning, tugging at a custard-coloured shirt, so I guessed that she kept odd hours long before Catherine told me.

'I hear the Cole Girl's moved out your way,' she said, and I must have nodded. 'Works out at the factory, I hear. Nights, I believe. Four on, four off. Same shift as old Jan Spencer.'

I knew about the hard hats and the hairnets, and later I would learn that Rosemary cleaned and disinfected, and drove a ride-on sweeper with rolling brushes that soaped and scrubbed the factory floor.

As a figure on the headland, she became as familiar as the light that burned in the house on the other side, and I thought about that often—about the Englishwoman and Rosemary Lamb and me—six eyes wide open in the middle of the night. I thought: Here is a way in which we are the same, the three of us. I thought: Here is a way in which I am the same as other people.

CHAPTER FOUR

Meg

Jessie Else disappeared the summer the Lambs came to Magpie Beach. Not that the two events were connected at all, in reality; only in my own head, in my own world. They marked for me the end of a certain quiet time and the start of a more complicated living.

They didn't find Jessie until long after they'd stopped looking and moved on to other things. Seasons passed and there wasn't much of her left by the time a second winter fell, so what they found, in the end, was not a little girl, only what remained of one. *The body*, the newspapers called her then. *The victim. The missing child*. She stopped being Jessie Else.

When the Lambs arrived, she'd been gone only a fortnight. The police had come to the library with a sheaf of posters they put on every wall and window. *Have You Seen Jessie Else?* There was a colour photograph, a list of clothing she'd had on the day she disappeared, and a twenty-four-hour phone number to call. Catherine said they'd brought extra officers from Townsville to help with their investigation, but they sent a local out to Magpie Beach. I recognised him but wouldn't have known his name without the badge.

'You'll have heard about Jessie Else?' He handed me a photograph tucked into a plastic sleeve, greasy at its edges and soft with well-feeling.

It was the same picture that looked out of every shop window in town: Jessie's smiling year three portrait. Her second set of teeth were just coming through, the front ones, only halfway down, still frilly on their edges. I imagined Mrs Else fumbling blindly through desk drawers and photo albums, or maybe not. Maybe Mr Else only had to slide it from his windowed wallet.

'Do you recognise her?' asked Constable Pike.

I did.

'Not from the news, I mean. Do you recognise her from before all that? Had you seen her before?'

I nodded. She came into the library with her mother, who would never come again. She liked books with a splash of glitter on the cover: ponies with wings, fairies with magic, schoolgirls with secrets.

'Did you know her?'

I shook my head. *Not really.*

'When was the last time you saw her?'

They came in when their books were finished, and I wasn't always there. They'd already had Catherine check the records. He wasn't asking if I'd seen her at the library; he was asking if I'd seen somebody take her.

'She was wagging.'

She'd set off for school on a pink bicycle with a plastic basket and strips of ribbon on the handlebars. It wasn't far for her to go, but they found her bike in the car park of St Anthony's church, opposite the supermarket, in the centre of town, and quite a lot of people had seen her outside Woolworths with a notebook and a pen and a rattling tin of change that turned up months after her little body, in among Who'd-Done-It's things. Key evidence, they called it then, because there weren't very many tins the same. It had come from Scotland long before, full of shortbread, with a pony and a thistle on its lid. She'd been selling cookies. There was a prize on offer for the girl guide who raised the most money and perhaps her mother hadn't taken her door to door. How would that feel now? I wondered.

'Do you remember where you were on February fourteenth?'

St Valentine's Day. I wondered if Mr Else had given his wife a card, kissed her on the cheek or on top of her head as she buttered his toast that morning; made love to her before it was properly light, before the rest of the house woke up. I wondered if they'd had dinner reservations that evening, who had called to cancel, and what they might have said.

I still remember where I was and what I did that Valentine's Day, because of Jessie Else, because Constable Pike came all the way out to Magpie Beach to make me think about it so soon afterwards.

It was a Monday and I cleaned the henhouse. I scraped crusted chicken shit off its wooden floor and rustled fresh straw in the boxes while Jo, Beth, and Amy scratched around the bush. I patched up a split I worried a fox might find, and then it started to rain and I went inside and made myself a cup of tea. I drank it with my feet up on the bed, Mrs Robinson purring beside me, and *Oscar and Lucinda* open in my lap. The sounds around me were too familiar to have meant anything unusual. I would have heard a little girl calling out. I'd have bought a box of cookies if I'd had a chance.

'Did she come out here? Out to Magpie Beach?'

He knew as well as I did that she didn't. I didn't get the pie-drivers or the free-quote pest controllers or even the Jehovah's Witnesses, but he was ticking his way down a list. He'd written my name at the top and got me to sign on a line at the bottom as a formality, so they could catch me out if I lied.

'Thanks for your help,' he said, though we both knew I hadn't been any. He asked me to call the number on a card he gave me if I thought of anything else, 'anything at all,' as if there were different types of anything.

'Is there a road?' he wondered then, pointing his clipboard vaguely towards the point.

There was a road to the Englishwoman's house, unsealed and twenty or more kilometres down the highway, winding up from the south. He set off on foot as everybody did, along the narrow track that cut across the headland, through the bush, to ask her all the same questions he'd just asked me. He pretended to switch papers from his car first, but he was only making sure he'd locked it. Worried I might steal his screwdriver, his extra shirt or one of his Monte Carlos.

CHAPTER FIVE
Meg

March brought wind and rain. April, clear skies and a calm of ordinary, and then it was May, the month of perfect nights. Warm enough for covers to slip off the bed, but cool enough to sleep right through without waking; without needing to turn the pillow or stand naked in the dark against a eucalyptus.

There were a million things whose lives took up after dark at Magpie Beach. Feral cats and rats and possums ran across the roof. Whiskery things stripped bark from trees, sucked fruit and snapped at smaller things which buzzed and hummed. Roosting birds were woken, frogs sang, fruit fell, but it wasn't one of the usual night-time noises that slipped in to me with the moths that night. This was slower and steadier than a scurry. Heavier than anything that lived in the bush, and the laboured breath, the sniff, and stifled cough were unmistakably human.

I wondered if curiosity had got the better of Rosemary Lamb. I thought about Jessie Else, who was still missing, and I lay very still.

The shuffling stopped and I knew he was looking in the window before my eyes adjusted. The breeze was snubbed, and in its place crept the smell of butter menthol. He was thin, as pale as curd, and looking straight at me.

The Englishwoman's taxi driver asked me once if I'd ever seen the Old Man. It wasn't her usual driver. This one was early and caught me with a skirt of mangoes. He'd got out to stretch his legs and pushed his Winfield Blue into the space between us but pocketed the packet before I shook my head.

The Englishwoman's usual driver never got out of the car, even when he brought her home. He never helped her with her shopping, and often stayed for half an hour enjoying his library book and a sandwich, with an elbow out the window and a sweating Coca-Cola on the dashboard. 'He can't possibly have read all of those already,' Catherine would say, but he read a lot of murder mysteries and courtroom dramas and they're not easy to put down once you've picked them up. I walked past him sometimes, waiting in his taxi on the can't-park bit of William Street, reading, always reading. He'd barely look up when a fare climbed in the back, just keep reading till they settled in and told him where to go. His name was Ted Henney. I didn't know this other one, though I remember looking at the badge clipped to the pocket of his shirt and thinking that it didn't look like him. He had a moustache in the photograph and longer hair that curled around his collar.

'Bit of a handful, I think,' he said, meaning the Old Man.

I thought of a handful of something: sand trickling between fingers, splashing a face as fast as you could keep enough water in cupped palms; something alive and trying to get away running hand over hand over hand. And then the taxi was gone. The Englishwoman had arrived and climbed in the back and been driven off to town. She might have said good morning. The taxi driver probably said goodbye.

The old man in the dark wore a tie. That's what made me think of English. His being at my window in the dead of night said he was

The Englishman (capital E), the Englishwoman's husband. A Bit-of-a-Handful, he'd slipped through her fingers, and here he was for me to catch like a mouse down the back of a sofa.

'Please help me.' The words peeled off him like a bandage.

I hurried into my dressing-gown and outside.

'I don't know where I am,' he said, looking at his slippers. They were tartan with the toes worn through. When I went to take his arm, he pulled away, but there was no strength in it, and he slumped against the window.

It wasn't easy for him to talk. His face twitched and his mouth watered. 'No,' he told me. 'Don't!' And I felt sorry for the Englishwoman, this woman I'd glimpsed but never met, hidden away with this shell of a man. 'Don't take me back.' Who was she to him now?

My grandfather lost his memory. At the start, we talked of it as something that might be found at any minute. There was no fancy word for it back then, or if there was, it wasn't a word you heard on the radio. I wonder if that was better for him—never knowing how bad he was likely to get. When the first of his memories slipped out of reach, when he drummed his fingers against his forehead and squeezed his eyes shut trying to catch the thread of them, he wouldn't have known that it would go so far beyond not knowing what he had for breakfast, that in time he wouldn't know his own name, and beyond that (if he lived that long) he wouldn't know why his mouth was watering and even if he did he wouldn't know how to swallow. I don't think that he ever completely lost his wife. He didn't always know her name or recognise her face, but her voice anchored him like nothing else. When his mind began to trick him and his fight-or-flight responses kicked in violently, it was her voice that reeled him back. 'It's me, Vernon. It's Nancy.' He'd put down the shoe, the plate or book and give her his hand. Mum would sweep us out like a broom, away down the street and onto the bus back home.

'What's wrong with Pops?' my brother often asked, but I never did, even though I was younger. I knew he'd gone, melted away like snow.

When he died, Granny set him up on a cloud with Jesus and King George. 'God will take care of him now,' she said. She never gave Him any of the blame.

It was three o'clock in the morning by the time I got the Englishman home. It was easy to follow the track that crossed the headland, but the Englishman walked slowly and stopped when his slippers filled with leaves and stones. 'Please, no,' he said when I slipped them off one at a time to tip them out, and, over and over again: 'I'm sorry.'

A light wind caught and rained a slight saltwater shower against us as we climbed the three stone steps to their front door. There was a can of insect repellent and a mat (*Please wipe your feet*), a pair of shoes beside it, each shoe wrapped in plastic like a hunk of cheddar.

I knocked twice—a force of habit from another life—and after a moment there was movement and light.

'Who's there?'

She didn't open the door completely but peered out from a strip of white, her face milky and drawn. She was so much shorter than me it was like looking down at a child. Chin high, sinews stretching like the strings of an instrument, a nightgown gathered at her neck like a PE bag, and there was sleep in her eyes and grey hollows beneath them. How long had she slept peacefully before the rap of knuckles?

'We don't keep any money in the house,' she told me, a hint of tobacco on her breath.

'I have your husband,' I said. I didn't tell her that I knew he'd run away.

The door opened a little wider. 'He's ill,' she said. She knew I knew. 'He's not the man I married.'

When he saw her, the Englishman began to cry. He put his hands up to his face. The backs of them were loose and spotted like the belly of an old dog.

'I'm sorry,' he mumbled one last time, and added, so quietly I could barely hear him: 'I won't do it again.'

I looked away while she took his elbow and drew him gently back inside their home. 'Where were you off to then?' She sounded like my mother (*Where do you think you're going? What do you think you're doing?*) 'Now, let's let this lady get back to bed.' And to me: 'We're sorry to have put you to such trouble, dear.'

'No trouble.' But we both knew that it had been. What I meant was that I didn't mind. It didn't matter.

She didn't say goodnight. She just pushed the door shut and double-locked it.

If there's anything I can do, people say, but there's nothing ever can be done by those who need to ask.

CHAPTER SIX

Meg

Sonny and I planted fruit trees, but others had grown from picnic scraps or wild seeds dropped by birds. There was a tall, thick mango tree which gave so much in summer that I'd spend whole days at a time making chutney, and avocados whose higher branches sagged with promise come June. I left boxes by the front steps of the library and people took what they wanted and left coins in exchange.

The best of all the trees grew in the drier soil, closer to the Lambs' house than my own, and once they moved in, I took care to pick while they were sleeping or when the Kingswood was away.

I was heading home with an early bag of still-brown avocados when I realised Eddie hadn't left with Rosemary an hour before. They'd been at Magpie Beach for months and I'd come to think I knew their habits. Catherine had told me Rosemary worked nights, and I knew everyone at the factory worked twelve-hour shifts—four on, four off, days or nights, depending on what you did. I was always quiet and careful on the first day because I thought it would be the hardest one to sleep through, and I knew she'd need to get ahead of herself or be nodding off come two or three the next morning. It had taken me a little while to work out where she was on her roster, but I had those first days ringed in red on my calendar.

Eddie was working in the shed they'd gone on to build. It was open on the side spared wind and weather, and I'd looked inside but never seen him in it, only lumps of green tarpaulin, tools on a workbench, drifts of wood and sawdust, and a dusty generator.

I meant to steal quietly around the back before he saw me, but I stood for a minute, maybe more than a minute, in a thick shade of lemon gums, and watched him work.

He was making a rocking horse, carved from wood the red of a proper peanut. Its neck arched like a quarter moon. Its legs leaped in full stride and its ankles flared. I supposed he cut those back and shaped them last of all, turned them somehow into hooves that would make a sound like coconuts halved and clapped together if the little horse could ever climb down from its rockers and canter around on concrete.

He was sanding the bridge of its back, where he'd buckle on a proper leather saddle made especially by a man in Biloela, but I didn't know that yet. I didn't know he'd use real horsehair for its mane and tail. I didn't know its eyes would be glass marbles—emerald or chocolate brown or marmalade. Every one of Eddie's horses was different, but I didn't know that yet either. Or that he carved his own name into the bowed wood they rocked upon.

I didn't know Eddie Lamb at all, only things about him.

I knew he was older than his wife because it was written on their faces. It was clear to see one of his legs did not bend easily. I'd heard there'd been a milling accident years before, when he'd tried a life beyond where he'd grown up, but it was never spoken of. I knew his father had a glass eye which didn't move or water, and I remembered Eddie working for him, for a time, stuffing sausages and pushing little chef's hats on the racks of lamb, but deep down he didn't want to be a butcher. Everyone knew that.

I don't know how long I stood there watching Eddie sand his wooden horse. It could have been three minutes or an hour before he spoke.

'And then there's pine,' he said. 'She's a different thing altogether than red cedar here.'

I can see you, is what he meant.

'A damn sight cheaper, too, though it won't last you as long. Won't be around for your children's children, and their children, like this one will. Full of knots, too. They grow them too bloody fast.'

He stopped sanding and looked across at me then, wiping his forehead with the back of his hand and leaving a smudge of red cedar dust on himself.

'There's a bigger one, you know,' he said. Nodding towards the tree he must have seen me coming from, and flicking fingers towards the bush beyond. 'You've just got to get up and in a bit.'

I thought he was going to give better directions, but he changed the subject.

'You're looking for Rosemary.'

I wasn't, but it hadn't been a question.

'She's at the movies. Goes every Tuesday when she can. They have a film club.' He made inverted commas with his fingers and stressed the usually silent 'l', and then he went back to sanding his horse. It was a thriller this week, he told me, and that Rosemary liked thrillers; romances best, but she'd watch anything. 'If the wallpaper moved, she'd watch that!'

They didn't have wallpaper; I knew because I'd looked through their windows.

'They send me to sleep half of them,' Eddie carried on, 'but you can't beat a good comedy. That Steve Martin . . .' and he began to laugh, remembering something funny Steve Martin must have said or done.

He made a final sweep with the sandpaper and stood up slowly, straightening his bad leg carefully and keeping one hand on the horse's head for balance. His t-shirt was torn and there was a stain down the front of it. Maybe not a stain, it could have been his breakfast—not yet stained but needing washing. He wasn't fat, but his belly was round like a pudding. His freckled arms were covered in fine red dust, his white-blond eyebrows raised as if to say, *Now it's your turn.*

It had been a long time since I'd been expected to join a conversation. Catherine chattered and I listened. A wave, a nod, a shake of head (good morning, goodbye, yes please, no thank you).

'And a decent action flick's alright, isn't it?' he prompted.

'I like old stories,' I said after a while. I meant books that swept me to a time and place I never could have been: Camelot, the Colosseum, Aztec empires.

I could tell I was too quiet by the tilt of Eddie's chin.

'*The Last of the Mohicans*, now that was a damn good movie,' he went on. 'And *Platoon*. I liked that.'

'I like old stories,' I said again, a little louder.

'*Breakfast at Tiffany's*,' he said. 'That's an old one isn't it?'

I nodded.

'Have you seen it?'

'I read the book.'

'I haven't read a book since I was at school.' He laughed, and I wondered what it was—the last book he ever read—and I wondered if he'd known at the time that there would be no others after that.

'I have books,' I told him. What I meant was: *If you'd like to read another, I can bring you one.*

'I know.' *I know who you are and where you work and what they say you did.* 'So, have you seen it? *Breakfast at Tiffany's*?'

I shook my head. I hadn't been to the cinema since Sonny died. We went sometimes on a Saturday night. There was a cinema in Christchurch we used to go to, too. We saw Robert Redford in *Jeremiah Johnson*, shared pāua fritters and hot chips from Tasty Tuckers afterwards and joked about running away together on the way home. It was drizzling and we sheltered close beneath a tree. I was damp and shivering and just turned eighteen.

Eddie was still talking about the film. He told me I should see it and I must have promised that I would, but I'm sure he knew I wouldn't.

He looked at his watch then at his horse then back at me, squinting. 'Best get on with it, I suppose,' he said. *You can go now.* 'Nice talking to you.'

'You too,' I said, but I don't know that either of us meant it.

CHAPTER SEVEN

Rosemary

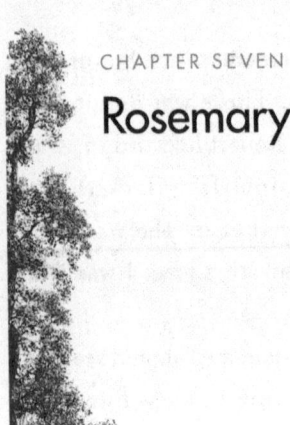

Mad Meg we called her. It's what everyone called her when they thought to call her anything at all. She'd been who she was for such a long time that I doubt many people talked about her anymore. She'd been up the avocado tree again, thinking she was hidden in the leaves, her arms and legs wrapped around its trunk like a clip-on koala. It's a wonder she never fell with that massive bag on her back. We saw her much more than she thought we did—picking things, burying, planting, digging things up. She leaped off like a deer if she heard us coming, but if she thought there was a chance we wouldn't see her she just froze.

Sometimes she came to watch us, creeping closer in spurts until she was tucked up against the trunk of a tree or leaning awkwardly into the shadow of a broom or shovel. You'd think of waving or calling out just to let her know she wasn't invisible, but that would only have embarrassed her and, really, I never wanted to do that. There was nothing *Single White Female* about her sneaking around. She didn't spy on us showering or going to bed. Nothing went missing off the washing line. She watched us pour tea and puzzle over crosswords. She watched us brush cobwebs off the water tank and leaves off the porch.

She watched me paint my toenails on the step. It was easy enough to guess her motives. There was no need to yank them out into the open.

'You should ask her to go with you next time,' Eddie said. But I didn't think I would.

I'd thought about introducing myself when we first moved out, but I hadn't wanted to intrude. We knew that it was our land now that she was squatting on, but neither of us minded her being there. There was enough sky for us all. We'd moved away from town for peace and space and privacy and, mad or not, we felt Meg had a right to keep whatever it was she'd come to Maggie Beach to find, though I knew that wasn't loneliness.

She hadn't always been alone. (She hadn't always been mad.) There'd been a husband. Years ago, she'd been one half of a regular couple, shopping for groceries, ordering counter meals at Carney's, laughing all the way down William Street with no one giving them a second glance. I don't remember him, but I do remember the rumours that ran around once he was gone.

Eddie's dad remembers them coming in together for their meat, just like everybody else did back then. People were more community-minded, his mum reckons, but if you ask me, there's something to be said for people not minding the business of everyone in the community quite so much. Meg's husband was good-looking, Tom said. He had tattoos, and a nice smile, and he liked to chat. Women stared.

He disappeared when I was still in primary school. The rumour was she'd killed him, but I don't think anyone really believed it. Some people thought he'd run off with a backpacker, but I don't know if anyone honestly believed that either. The sad part I think now, looking back, is that we really didn't care. *Tattoos, and a nice smile*: he didn't mean anything more than that to anyone but Meg, and Meg didn't mean anything much to anyone other than him. I mean, she didn't have family, she didn't have a job—workmates to offer cups of tea and shoulders to cry on—and she didn't even have a neighbour to keep an eye out. Who knows when she got the cat?

It is terrible but fascinating how Meg changed when she lost her husband. However it was that she lost him, whether he was dead from natural causes, or murdered and chopped up into little pieces, or run away with another woman (or man). People started seeing her out on the highway in her nightie at three o'clock in the morning, or on her knees outside St Anthony's. She covered one grave in stripped twigs pushed into sand-filled jars and little stones she built up into piles, and that might have been understood and forgiven if it had been her husband's grave, but he didn't have one—which of course added to the mystery of what had become of him.

Kids at school said she was a witch. And then one day she began working in the library. People didn't know what to make of that and whether to be worried, outraged or embarrassed. Dad had a word with Sergeant Scanlan and put a petition together to keep her away from children, but it never came to anything, and when he could see that it wasn't going to come to anything, he pretended it wasn't him who'd started it. I never understood what all the fuss was about. She wasn't there very often, and when she was, all she did was push a trolley up and down the aisles and slot books back where they belonged. She didn't talk. She didn't bother anyone.

A couple of weeks after she'd spoken to Eddie, I was going to see *Breakfast at Tiffany's*, and Eddie knew it because I'd stuck the flyer on the fridge. I doubted Meg had honestly told him she wanted to see it, but I must admit, I was curious to meet her properly, so when Eddie told me for the umpteenth time I should invite her, I said I would.

'You can't ask her,' he said. 'She won't go unless you tell her she has to.'

'What, with a gun?'

'If you ask her, she'll say no.'

I couldn't imagine her saying anything at all.

She'd lived at Maggie Beach as long as I remembered. There'd been a time when teenagers drove out on midnight dares to find her, but the novelty had worn away over the years. They still came occasionally but looking for other things now, buried in the folds of girls and boys on blankets and back seats.

There was no sign on the highway, but people knew Shank Lane would bring them out to Maggie's. It was marked on some maps as a track, but it was wide enough for two cars to pass if neither driver minded a few scratches, and there were only a couple of dips deep enough to need a run-up and a Hail Mary in the rain. We just called it Shank. Its end frayed into the sandy soil where Eddie built our house, a fair stretch from the pancake flat where Meg kept her old, broken-down car, and she lived a couple of minutes' walk past that, along a track worn through the bush. I don't know how they got their caravan in there. Bush grows, I suppose. They could have burned it back.

I knew it was there, I'd glimpsed its roof, smoke through the trees, a yellowy light at night, but that morning was the first time I'd seen it properly. It wasn't much longer than a garden shed, standing on blocks and surrounded by vines and creepers which ran up and along complicated stick-and-string scaffolds Meg had pegged into the ground. Gutters were held in place by cable ties and rigged to run into an old grey water tank which stood up on fat timber sleepers. There was a lean-to at either end (a smokehouse and a washhouse, I learned later), a wide window to the right of the door and, although she wasn't up against it, I could see her face as clear as day behind a busy sill of jars and bottles and sprouts in plastic tubs.

I half-expected to hear the clatter of a back door and the dry crunch of leaves as she leaped off into the bush, but instead the blue door opened slowly and there she was, dragging to the side one of those fly-strip curtains and slipping off her glasses.

She was stick-thin. The scoop of her t-shirt hung lower than it should have, and her chest was bony and tanned. Tanned like leather, not in the Elle Macpherson way. No bra (no boobs). She had on board shorts that looked like they belonged to a man. She'd pinned them, I think, at one side, and it gave her the look of someone with a dicky hip. Come to think of it, everything I ever saw her in looked like it was too big—like she'd been bigger once, or else the clothes she wore belonged to someone else.

'Hello,' I said.

She gave me a very small nod of the head, but that was all. It was up to me to speak again.

'I like your flowers.'

She looked at the plant nearest her feet and I thought I saw a slight colour light her face. Was she embarrassed by my attempt at conversation or flushed with pride that someone had noticed her garden?

'They're chillies,' she mumbled. She had a soft voice, a little bit deeper than I'd imagined it. Her hair was long and thick and brown-streaked white, and when the plait of it swung around I saw that it was tied up top and bottom with purple bobbles.

'I'm Rosemary.'

Another nod. Did she know that already? Until that point it hadn't occurred to me that Meg might have heard some of the things they said about me. What did they say? I didn't really care anymore.

I took a few steps forward. Close to, I could see she'd made the curtain out of plastic bags and sticky tape.

'Eddie said you wanted to see *Breakfast at Tiffany's*?'

A look of fright came over her and I remembered what Eddie had said about telling, not asking. I'd made it a question and I could see she was about to shut me down and send me on my way.

'Eddie said you wanted to see *Breakfast at Tiffany's*,' I said again quickly, a statement this time, and then I babbled: 'The one with Audrey Hepburn? It's black and white—old—I think it's from the fifties. Anyway, the ticket'll be six dollars because it's Tuesday and there's a special on. It's called Film Club, but it's not a club, not really. I mean, you don't have to join anything, but it's a special price . . .' Racking my brain for anything else I could scatter at her. 'I'll be leaving at ten. Please don't be late. I don't want to miss the start.' And I fled before she could say *No, thank you* or *Get off my front step* or whatever else she might have been thinking to say. 'Bring a cardigan—it can get a bit cold!' I shouted over my shoulder, but I'm not sure she heard it, I was practically running by that point.

CHAPTER EIGHT

Rosemary

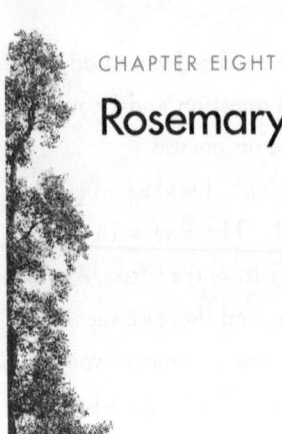

I honestly didn't think Meg would come, so I was as shocked as she looked to see her standing by the Kingswood at ten to ten on Tuesday. Her hair was wet; I could tell even from a distance because of the damp patch darkening the back of the dress she'd changed into. She had her glasses on a ribbon around her neck and her purse in a plastic bag, and of course she was wearing her woolly hat. You never saw her in town without it, hand-knitted in random stripes of pink, green, and brown. It looked like a tea-cosy. (It might have been a tea-cosy.)

'You've got to feel sorry for her,' Eddie said, standing beside me at the window, and I did, a bit. Sorry for her sadness and her loneliness, but sorry too that I hadn't thought to think of her before.

The Galaxy was only a small cinema. They might have one of those big multiplexes in Winifred now, but they didn't back then. There weren't enough people to have kept it open.

I'd seen pictures of Audrey Hepburn, but I'd never actually seen her move and talk, so I'd been looking forward to *Breakfast at Tiffany's*. Not that it really mattered. I'd have gone on a Tuesday morning whatever was showing. Mr Breadsell could have stood up on a chair and called out his shopping list and I'd still have gone.

Mr Breadsell had owned and run the Galaxy since time began. Mum and Dad went when they were courting. They went to see *A Fistful of Dollars* and somehow fell in love over a couple of choc tops and a tub of popcorn, and Mr Breadsell was there then, like he was there every Tuesday morning in a spotty bow tie with his half-moon glasses perched on the end of his nose like a Disney grandpa. He sold us our tickets, and then he tore them in half, and he stood by the bins as the credits rolled and thanked everyone for coming, addressing most of us by name, as we filed past on our way out.

He knew his cheapskate Tuesday die-hards, and he knew that if he showed the same film two weeks in a row he'd be screening to an empty auditorium, so he gave us Film Club. Sometimes it was a new release and sometimes it was a 'modern classic'. It was rarely anything very old, though *The Wizard of Oz* and *The Sound of Music* were dragged out from time to time. *Breakfast at Tiffany's* was a proper treat.

'Welcome . . .' he said to Meg that morning. The end of his sentence hung like Barney's in *Pretty Woman*. '*And you are his . . . ?*' I knew it would be like pulling teeth if he waited for her to offer him more than the corner of a smile, so I just went ahead and introduced her as well as I could without actually knowing her name.

'This is Meg.'

'Of course it is,' Mr Breadsell said. 'It's so nice to see you, Mrs Cooper.'

I heard her gasp ever so slightly, as if he'd shown her something she hadn't seen for a long time. So she must have been to the cinema before she went mad. Before she *became* mad.

It was a nice movie, and it funnelled me far away, so when the lights came up it was almost a shock to see her sitting in the next seat, blinking at the credits and then at me.

'What did you think?' I asked her, but all she did was nod a couple of times and fiddle with her plastic bag.

She only said one thing to me all morning, but she said it twice. We were back at Maggie Beach and she'd just climbed out of the car.

'Thank you,' she said. 'Thank you.'

I took her with me again the following Tuesday. She was kneeling on a muddy sack, patting the soil flat around the stalk of something when I found her in the morning. 'It's a comedy,' I said. 'It's supposed to be pretty funny.' And there she was by the car at ten to ten.

If she laughed it was on the inside, but her smile was a little wider when the lights came up.

I took her again the next week.

I didn't mind her company. To be honest, being with her was a lot like being by myself, but I'd never minded that either. She didn't fidget or give dramatic sighs to question a twist in a plot. She didn't chatter through the movie like the old couple I took great care to sit away from. The husband was hard of hearing, so I suppose he needed his wife to repeat certain things, but he struggled to understand the simplest storylines.

'What did she say?'

'You're a liar.'

'What?'

'SHE SAID: *YOU'RE A LIAR!*'

'Why?'

There were two sisters who gossiped through the previews, and I tried to sit as far away from them as I could too, because I liked to see what was Coming Soon, even if it never did come all that soon to Winifred.

By the fourth week, I didn't think I had to call for Meg, but I waited five minutes and she didn't come.

'I said you'd have to go and get her,' Eddie called out from his shed.

She was sitting in her kitchen with the door wide open. She had her hat on, and her plastic bag on the table in front of her, so I knew she was ready to go even before the smile burst on her face.

'I'll expect you every week unless I've something else on,' I told her as we jogged towards the car. I never did have anything else on, and after that she was there every Tuesday morning without fail, with her cardigan or without it, but always in her woolly hat with her purse in that same plastic bag. If it was raining, she'd stand under the tiniest bit of Eddie's shed. Just enough of the roof for her to stay dry, but not so much of it that you could say she was actually inside. She never had to wait for long. As soon as I saw her, we were off.

As the weeks passed, I came to genuinely enjoy Meg's company. She began to loosen up and show some measure of emotion in the dark. She laughed quietly but with delight at any slapstick gags, and everyone jumps when a killer sits up in the back seat.

It was nice to catch someone's eye now and then, share a packet of tissues or a box of popcorn. It was nice to be able to pick apart a story on the way home in the car, to say *I couldn't believe he died* or *Wasn't she brilliant* or *That was the most ridiculous thing I've ever seen*, even if Meg didn't really give much back (well, not to start with, anyway).

Eddie wasn't someone worth bringing your opinions home to. He just didn't care whether it was a good movie, or a plot was predictable, or an actor deserved his Oscar. He'd say, 'Hmm,' or, 'Wow,' but he didn't mean it. He couldn't mean it without having seen the film. Sometimes he'd say, 'Well, don't spoil the ending!' as if he was going to see it himself before it came out on TV, heavily edited and with holes torn by commercial breaks. Eddie hadn't been to the cinema since we were dating, and what did we see then? Comedies, mostly. Even in the beginning, Eddie only did what Eddie wanted to do, and by extension that's what we did together. That's all we ever did together.

CHAPTER NINE

Meg

'I'm going to have a party,' Rosemary said. She'd come for a lemon. She popped around sometimes for something I might have growing, or just to talk, though she knew by then I wasn't much of a talker. There was a shiver in the air when I heard her coming along the path. I liked that she arrived to find me at whatever I was doing without fuss or comment. She'd just come along and be there, leaning on a shovel or sitting on the ground not too far away, picking and scratching at whatever was close and loose.

My grandmother had a neighbour who popped around whenever she liked for chats and cups of tea. We called her Aunty Molly, though she wasn't anyone's aunty, and she wasn't always welcome. Often when Granny heard the clop of Molly's heels on the front path or a yodelled *yoohoo* as the gate swung open, she would pull the ugliest of faces and push my brother and me behind the blunt end of the sofa so Molly wouldn't see us if she cupped her face up against the dimpled glass panel in the front door. My brother often gave us away. He didn't mind if she made it inside. Aunty Molly had ruddy cheeks and the laugh of a cheerful smoker. She kept lollies in her pockets and tissues up her sleeves, and she told funny stories and asked us about things other people rarely bothered to.

Other than Aunty Molly, I hadn't a lot of experience in people popping around.

'Nothing big,' Rosemary went on. 'Just a few of the girls from work, and Eddie's parents and his nan—you'll like her.'

I was a little hurt by that, but I couldn't have said why.

She twisted a ripe tomato off the vine and rubbed it on the hem of her shirt before biting into it like an apple. It felt reckless to have someone so familiar.

'Will you come?'

Would I?

'I'd really like you to come.'

She handed me a slip of paper, creased now from holding the tomato stalk while she'd pulled the fruit off with her other hand. *YOU'RE INVITED*, stars, balloons and a cocktail glass and strands of information, all in a curly font that fluttered a memory of string coming out of a can.

I hadn't been to a party for a very long time, and the thought of going to this one softened my stomach.

'It won't be a massive thing.' She'd already said that. 'Nothing dress-up fancy. Just a few beers and a barbie. Eddie says it'd be a shame not to do anything. It's my twenty-first,' she added shyly. (I'd seen the number on my invitation.) 'I'm going to invite the woman who lives over that way, too.' She waved the tomato loosely towards the headland. 'I don't know if she'll come, but I'll ask her anyway.' She tossed the stalk end of her tomato into the bush. 'D'you wanna come with me? To ask?'

She didn't know about the Englishman. I hadn't told anyone. Who else would I have told?

I shook my head.

Rosemary shrugged. 'Alright. I'll see you. Thanks for the lemon.'

She didn't thank me for the tomato, but I didn't mind.

CHAPTER TEN

Meg

It had been crackle-dry for weeks, not a drop of rain, but there was a low-pressure system building up and rolling in. The black cockatoos felt it and had been in the treetops all day. Every now and then a warm gust of wind brought a stickiness and, as the evening drew in, lightning sparked over the water.

Rosemary hadn't given me a chance to say no. 'I'll send Eddie to walk you over,' she'd said, as if I was seventy years old.

I remember my own twenty-first. My parents and my brother and a steak supper at the Worm and Monkey. Sonny brought a single yellow rose to the restaurant and touched it to my cheek before he held it out for me to take. 'Happy Birthday, little one,' he said. It hung in the kitchen for weeks until it dried, and my mother threatened to throw it out with the potato peelings and the pumpkin seeds. It was standing in a wine bottle when I left it (and most of everything else) in the blue-black darkness of my bedroom, too brittle to be pressed. If I'd known what the next few years had in store, it might have found its way into the bags I carried quietly down the stairs, tissued flat between the pages of a book. It might have made the secret journey out onto the cold, quiet street and around the corner into the back of the taxi that waited to take us to the airport. It might have heard Sonny say, 'We'll be okay, you'll see. I'll look after you, little one.'

Rosemary had set chairs up on the verandah and laced strings of Christmas lights along its eaves and around the baskets of geraniums and petunias that hung on nails she'd bent up with a hammer. A silver Happy Birthday banner taped above the screen door lifted with every swing of it as a trickle of women carried covered dishes in and out.

'Do you want to . . .' Eddie dipped his head towards the bowl in my hands and indicated the general direction of the house. 'Do you want me to . . . ?'

I shook my head, and he limped away to join the other men around the yawning barbecue. I hadn't meant for him to go. It was only the weight of the salad I wanted to keep, and I stood for a little while wondering whether I should really be there at all, or back in my own home with a cup of peppermint tea and the book that was waiting for me, with the soft comfort of Mrs Robinson, on the end of my bed.

It was Eddie's mother who helped me decide. I knew her face and learned her name.

'You must be Meg,' she said. 'I'm Leonie. Let's take your salad in to Rosemary. She'll be so pleased to see you.'

That warmed me very much.

I'd never been inside Rosemary's kitchen, with its parsley green walls and patterned linoleum. Her fridge was painted like a cow, with large black puddles and a pink udder at knee-height. I'd seen it, but only through the window. There was a cluster of women in front of it now, taking things out and putting things back in. 'Did you paint it yourself?' one of them asked. There was laughter, and most of it was kind.

Their backs were to me. Six women: pretty summer dresses, loose shorts, tanned calves, cracked heels, strappy sandals, rubber thongs. 'Look who's here!' Leonie sang, and they all turned at once.

How must I have looked, standing in the doorway with my best bowl? I'd taken a long time to make the salad. Potatoes from my garden, shallots and chives; eggs pulled from warm feathery beds that morning; juice from a lemon that fell from my tree; mustard powder from long ago.

Rosemary clapped her hands. 'Everyone!' she said. 'This is my friend and neighbour, Meg.'

It had been a long time since I'd felt as if I were either of those, and I know I couldn't have helped but smile.

There were hellos, urgent hands that I shook, two looks exchanged, and one pocket of silence, but it was done, and once it was done it was over, the bowl was taken from me and replaced with a glass of wine, their chatter reignited, and I was amid the froth of it, bobbing around like a cuttlebone.

Back outside, I was introduced to Eddie's grandmother and offered the chair beside her. It was one of those folding director's chairs you can only sit on; there is no curling up or settling in. 'Nola,' Eddie's grandmother said. Her hand was soft and powdered like a bread roll that comes in a bag of six, covered in grey flour. She had a kitchen chair of sticky brown vinyl, one of a set of four dotted around a chain of tables, along with half-a-dozen stackable party chairs and at least three milk crates. I was not comfortable and so I counted. At the furthest end was Rosemary's wide, wicker armchair, the only piece of furniture that truly belonged out there on the porch. One of its legs was unravelling, and the elephant cushion that lived on it was worn pale and puppy-soft. I'd watched her sink into it and read for hours on rainy afternoons.

'It's lovely out here,' Nola said.

I didn't know whether she meant here outside, where we were sitting, or out at Magpie Beach, away from the busyness of town, but I nodded. It didn't matter.

Though he set platters on the table for others to help themselves, Eddie brought Nola and me a plate each with a chunk of steak, a lamb chop and a rissole.

'How's this for service?' Nola laughed, and people looked over and I wished they hadn't.

Salads were passed, servings helped, and sauce bottles slid along the table like shots of whisky in a saloon. Glasses were filled, jokes were told, and candles flickered in jam jars.

I helped to clear away the dishes.

'You stay put,' Leonie told Rosemary, patting her shoulder and nodding at Eddie to top up her wine. 'We'll be done in a jiffy! You won't want to be getting up to this lot in the morning.'

I wouldn't have minded getting up to it. Sonny and I used to sleep in on Sunday mornings but now I woke with the birds and had trouble getting back to sleep.

Most of the plates were paper, so the bag in the bin was filled almost immediately, and Leonie tied its top and called Eddie in to swap it for another.

One of Rosemary's factory friends followed him inside. 'Wash or dry?' she asked me.

I didn't mind, so took a tea towel from a drawer I'd seen Rosemary open. I thought the other woman would prefer to wash. Most people do.

There was a short hall leading off the kitchen, and jigsawed on its walls were photographs in frames someone had painted. I waited for the sink to fill, bubbles to build, things to assemble on the draining board. The photos were of Eddie's family mostly: his brother, bare legs straddling a motorbike on a hill too high to have been local; Tom and Leonie, faces pressed through stand-up cut-outs of Batman and Robin; his grandmother, Nola, in younger years, holding one child on her hip and another by the hand, a small dog by her feet; Eddie's parents and both boys positioned on a fence beside a tractor. I must have touched the frame because Leonie, standing at my shoulder, said, 'That was when we had the farm. Look how little they were! God, they used to run amok. Into all sorts of trouble—especially Eddie!'

'Talking about me again?' he asked, passing us on his way out with the rubbish.

There were pictures of Rosemary and Eddie's wedding. A close-up of the two of them together; a sweeping group shot taken by the lake. Faces I recognised but many more I didn't. There was one picture of Rosemary as a child—a baby—propped up and held tight by her sisters' pasty legs like a puppy. Rosemary and Eddie either side of a tree with a ribbon, in the rain; smiling across an empty-plated table in a restaurant, Eddie in a collared shirt, Rosemary's shoulders all but bare. There was a framed cinema ticket, faded too far to read whatever movie it remembered, and I would never ask in case its ruin had been overlooked. There was a cartoon of a cat in a canoe, cut from a magazine, a large, pencil portrait of a beautiful young woman with a high chin, a thick curl of hair wound around two fingers, and a sense of something interrupted. It looked unfinished, only the irises of her eyes were coloured, feathered green and brown, like the underside of a mushroom cup.

'Did you know Rosemary's mum?' Leonie asked.

I shook my head. I'd known so few people, really, and Joanna Cole was not one of them. I had seen her. Heard things about her. Helped her with her purse the time her fingers had been broken. Checked her library books back in when she moved away. But I never would have guessed the portrait was of her. She was harsher in real life, with points and edges. The sketch there in the frame was dusty-soft and biscuit-sweet and crumbly.

'She was quite the looker,' Leonie said, and there was something like a sting to it.

Eddie had come back inside 'She wasn't that much of a looker!' he scoffed, pausing on his way through long enough to leave a greasy thumbprint on the glass. 'I've always said whoever did that must have been half-pissed.' He made no secret of the way he felt towards Rosemary's family, and it seemed to upset him more than it bothered Rosemary that none of them was there that night.

I'd been standing by the car when she'd told him, 'They can't make it. They've got stuff on.'

'What stuff? What the fuck!'

Rosemary had only shrugged, but I'd watched Eddie pace the length of the deck. 'They've not been out to visit once, you know,' he told me when she went inside to fetch her bag. 'Not even her mother. Snobby fucks, the lot of them.'

'Time takes a chunk from all of us,' Leonie called after him now, but he was out of earshot. She smoothed her dress over her hips when she said it and pulled her stomach in a little bit. 'Although, in all seriousness,' she added just for me, 'she really did have a much bigger nose.'

Perhaps I laughed out loud. Perhaps it was the wine. The factory friend was drawn across and scratched my shoulder lightly. 'Having a nice time?' She had a beautiful smile—apple-cheeked and Colgate-white.

I'm sure I nodded.

'It's been a while,' Leonie said. It was no secret.

There were other chairs around the table, but I was relieved to see my place beside Nola was still empty when we went back outside. While I was gone, someone had lifted her feet onto a stool. Her ankles were swollen like sausages about to burst their casings, but I imagined they were as perfectly grilled as those of all these younger women when she'd been young herself. Leonie was right: time took a chunk from all of us.

'All finished and packed away?' Nola asked.

It was.

She'd been talking to Eddie's aunt, she told me, the mother of the cousin who worked with Tom. They'd been talking about baking bread and whether you should use a lot of milk or none at all. What did I use? she wanted to know.

I hadn't baked for years. You don't bake yourself a cake, and how much bread can a person eat before it's only good for breadcrumbs? I didn't have a freezer. I turned the glass in my hands—one, two, three times—and was grateful when Rosemary slipped in between our chair backs and the deck's edge, lit a cigarette, and blew the smoke behind her, over the railing and into the night. She'd been inside my house and knew I didn't have an oven either.

'Meg makes an amazing chilli sauce,' she said, and the subject was fended off.

'Are you having a nice time, love?' Nola asked her.

'I am actually!' As if she hadn't expected to. She was standing stork-like, one knee high and bent, and she swept the hand with the cigarette in a wide circle that included everyone at the table, the Happy Birthday banner flapping above the door, and the patch of ground lit by fairy lights where people were starting to dance. 'This is really nice.' It was the same word her friend had used, in the kitchen.

I've heard it said 'nice' isn't good enough, but when every little thing about a time or place is just right, then there is no better word.

Leftovers were covered and stacked in the fridge, the music grew louder, shoes were kicked off. I wasn't going to stay much longer, but between Nola's legs and a string of strangers there was no melting away. Leaving would be loud and clear with goodbyes and thank yous and Eddie insisting on walking me home. I thought about sliding under the table and slipping out between the railings, but I didn't want it to be like that. Not tonight. And then Eddie brought me a small glass of Baileys. 'I think you'll like this,' he said, not knowing I'd had it before. I knew its name. My life had not all been what he knew it to be now.

Rosemary was talking with the woman who'd helped with the dishes when Eddie tried to pull her up to dance. He descended on them like a cloud, expecting a shower of smiles and a gust of joining-in, but Rosemary didn't want to dance, she wanted to listen to whatever it was her friend was saying, and Eddie was disappointed, everyone could see, so one of the factory women stood quickly and pulled him by the hand into the pool of candy-light.

Girls often asked Sonny to dance in high school. 'Ladies' choice,' DJs announced through shower-hose microphones, headphones cupped over one ear. Sonny danced with all the girls who asked him, no matter who they were or what they looked like. Beyond everything, he was kind. Generous with his smile, and careful with his words, he was a beautiful boy who grew to be a beautiful man.

Eddie was singing along to 'Islands in the Stream', one hand resting on his partner's hip while the other held a fistful of her lacquered nails tight against his shoulder, and the wine and the Baileys conjured more memories: cold nights when my brother kept me safe from the People Downstairs, who woke us when the pub closed, and wore their wide, wet boots indoors, and pissed in bright, beery arcs from the back steps. Our father loved Dolly Parton. 'She writes all her own stuff,' he'd shout proudly, as if he had something to do with it, and as if he hadn't told them all before.

More people were dancing now, singing and laughing and throwing shadows into the bush that twittered and trilled around them. Moths and midges swarmed in a lip of light, but beyond that in the felt of dark between tree trunks, a thicker shape was moving slowly. Something was in there, taller than a turkey but straighter than a kangaroo, on two legs but dropping to all fours and freezing when it thought I might have seen it.

I waited for it to move again. The couples in the light kept dancing, blind to the darkness. Eddie knew every word but others joined in as the chorus came around again, and whatever I'd begun to doubt I'd seen there in the bush moved ever so slightly. Its head turned just as shadows parted, its eyes caught the light, and for the briefest moment I saw it clearly. It. She. Her: the Englishwoman.

It wasn't how I'd imagined her when I'd seen mud on the shoes outside her door and realised she mustn't always stay on paths and pavements. In my head, she strode through the bush in thick, peppery socks, reaching with a stout stick and looking sharp for snakes and spiders and centipedes. I hadn't imagined her like this: on her hands and knees in the dark, frozen like a possum in the swing of a torch beam.

I glanced down the table, wondering if anyone else had seen her, but they were busy with each other, with beer and cake and sweet tobacco. Nola was laughing with the women on her other side, and when I looked back into the bush, the Englishwoman had gone, and I wondered if perhaps I hadn't seen her after all.

CHAPTER ELEVEN

Lily

I never wanted to come here. I was happier in England. I had a garden full of roses and squirrels at the bird table; I knew what things were called and where to get them. 'More opportunities,' Norman said. What did I want with those? He promised me better weather, but what did I want with that? I had a coat and good leather boots and more than one pair of gloves. I liked a wind with some bite and a crust of frost on a puddle. I liked the spring that sprang from cold dark winters and pushed up sugary pink crocuses. I liked gardens that grew when they were watered properly by nature; delicate blooms that wouldn't fry like eggs as soon as the sun came out; soil that didn't stain your trousers; earth you could shove your hands straight into with nothing to think of but slugs and worms. I liked my birds twittering and flittering, not squawking and smashing trees to pieces, and you didn't have to worry an English spider might rot your foot off.

'A change is as good as a rest,' the travel agent said, but I didn't need a change or a rest. I liked the business of my life. I had my own little car and a library card. I had family we saw at Christmas; I had a drinks cabinet with mirrors in its door. That seems so frivolous now but there it was. Sherry on a Sunday, wine with dinner, and gin with women who made me laugh—women I'd thought were the closest of friends till I left and all that boiled down to was barely-in-time-for-Christmas cards with shorter and shorter notes enclosed.

They say Adelaide's a lot like England, but it isn't. Not really. Church spires and chocolatiers, cricket pitches and antique shops, but there's nothing in them older than eighty or ninety years. Their botanical garden is lovely, but the valleys aren't really. It didn't hold a candle to Yorkshire, but nonetheless, there we were.

The garden came along—all agapanthus and hydrangea, but we made a go of it. Norman did well at work, we went to functions, he got his bonuses. I learned what was what and where to get it. We had people over for dinner. We played golf. You could say we were settled. But then Norman got sick, and we had to move. Again.

I lived with Norman a long time not knowing he was ill. It's only looking back that I can see now, there were signs. Could I call them symptoms? He knew a long time before I did, he's admitted as much, but he couldn't hide it forever, and after that, well, everything had to change.

Doctors used to prescribe warmer weather for vertigo, menopause, anaemia—if it couldn't be cured with Epsom salts, a hot bath or a cold compress, they'd recommend Spain. Take the air, take the water. I don't know that it ever did anyone any good, but we had nothing else to lose.

Perth was warmer than Adelaide and drier, and it was home enough for a couple of years, but it didn't make Norman any better. And by then I knew he was only ever going to get worse.

So then we just wanted a place we could put down the last of our roots. Somewhere we could be together without being bothered. I didn't want them taking him away, and I knew they would if they found out how sick he was; they'd have him off me by teatime, and what good would that do? He'd never get any better. The best they'd do was stretch the time he had left, but they'd have him in a place where they could keep an eye on him while they did it. I wanted to be the one to take care of him. We'd always been together. What would he want with strangers? For better, for worse; richer or poorer; in sickness and in health: these promises were all tested over the years, but they were promises we'd made and it was up to us to keep them—up to me to keep them.

We just needed a place to be. A kettle, a radio, a blanket on the bed, a shelf of books, not too many steps and shops close enough. We didn't mind the warmer weather and I'd heard that humidity loosens the joints. The ocean was a bonus; they say the salt air opens up the lungs (curses your garden, but that couldn't be helped). More than anything else, we just wanted to be left alone.

It took us a long time to get to Magpie Beach and we stayed in a lot of grotty motels on the way. Once or twice, we slept in the car—seats wound as far back as they could go and I buttered a lot of sandwiches at picnic tables. It's not a glamorous story. But we were lucky to find the house. 'It's a dear little place,' the woman had said, and little was right. In Adelaide we'd started off with four bedrooms, two bathrooms, a study and plenty of room for the children neither of us ever actually believed we'd have, as it turned out. At Magpie Beach we had a bedroom, a bathroom, and what they'd call a kitchenette. There was no proper electricity, but the generator was new and easy to run, and the water tank was rarely low enough to worry us. We burned what waste we could and buried what we couldn't. It was an easy trip to town, where they had everything we needed, and a pleasant enough walk along the rocks north and south with nowhere else to go but out to sea.

It's funny, when it comes down to it, everything you think you can't live without—those essential bits and pieces, favourites and habits—well, you can. You whittle what you've got down to as much as you can pack into the back of a car and you cobble together the bits you're missing out of what you find when you get to where you're going, and you make do and get on with it.

We kept ourselves to ourselves and we pottered along. I kept Norman safe, and we kept each other company, and then the gypsy woman came to call in the middle of the night, hammering at the door in her dressing-gown.

'He's alright,' she told me. But we both knew that he wasn't. It was years since he'd been alright.

It was such a shock to see her there. What must she have thought when she found him wandering around in the dark? I was embarrassed that I hadn't missed him, and that she knew I hadn't missed him. She knew I'd been tucked up in bed, dead to the world until she'd knocked on the door and woken me up. He'd climbed out of the window, I realised later, and I hadn't heard a thing. Fast asleep—what sort of carer was I? I didn't even thank her. I should have thanked her for bringing him home.

I went to find her the next day, because of the pickles. I'm not a fan of cucumber and it touched on snooping, I thought, sneaking back the way she must have in the dark to leave a jar by the mat, but it was a nice gesture, and I did want to thank her for it, and for bringing Norman home—but mostly I wanted to make sure she understood I could take care of him. I didn't know whether she was the type who'd make a phone call, express concern, request a visit, let Them know there was a man here who needed the sort of care his wife was not providing. We didn't want to be found, you see. We'd hidden ourselves quite deliberately. Left no breadcrumbs and swept away all footprints.

She was burying something when I got there, some sort of bulb or bean, and we talked about gardening for a while. She didn't have a lot to say, but I'll admit that I enjoyed the conversation, and I shouldn't have worried; I could see from the way and where she lived that she didn't want to be bothered any more than we did. She wasn't about to call anyone in to come and check on anything.

How do you keep a secret?

You tell no one.

CHAPTER TWELVE
Rosemary

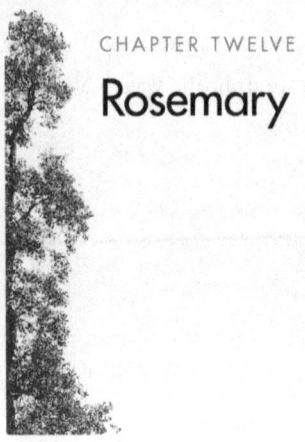

They say a snail can stay in its shell for three years. It just crisps up its opening and hibernates, and then the rain comes, and the snail slowly loosens its foot, or whatever it is that's stoppering the hole, and out it comes. Well, that was Meg. The rain began to wet her toes and, slowly, out she came.

It was only a week after my birthday, so it shouldn't have been that wet, but it was. The whole month's rain fell in two days. Clouds were bundled up in the sky and everywhere was silky grey and slippery.

Meg and I were standing in the lobby waiting for Mr Breadsell to finish serving and come across to open up the curtain, but we weren't in any hurry. The movie wasn't going to start without him. It was a monster thriller we'd seen previewed a few weeks before and I was jogging Meg's memory of that when I recognised the Englishwoman, standing over at the ticket counter, checking her watch and glaring at Mr Breadsell, who was busy shovelling popcorn.

She was shorter than anyone else in the lobby, with that stocky sort of stance that shorter people sometimes have, as if they think everyone around them's set on knocking them over. She wore a heavy brown coat, thick tan tights and the same ginger shoes I'd seen wrapped up in plastic outside her front door. I'd only knocked on it once and I wouldn't be going again. She hadn't been friendly. She'd crossed her arms deliberately once she'd opened the door and barely glanced at the invitation I'd handed her.

'I'm sure you've heard my husband isn't in the best of health,' she'd said.

Who would I have heard that from?

'I thought you lived alone,' I'd told her, and she snorted.

'Did you now?'

I did. I had. But then I only wanted to turn around and walk away.

'Well anyway,' I said, 'you're both welcome to come. Meg will be there too.' I'd thought she might have been encouraged by the promise of a familiar face, but she only screwed up her own and said, 'Meg?'

Everyone knew who Meg was. 'The woman in the caravan.'

She shook her head then, with a face that said I might as well be talking Klingon, but she must have known. I'd seen her take her taxi. I didn't know where it took her, but it picked her up from close enough to Meg's place that she couldn't have not seen it.

So, I didn't really like her. You don't have to tell everyone your business, but unless they're asking for something you don't want to give them, I don't think there's any need to lie.

I'd have been surprised if she'd come to my birthday party, but I was even more surprised to see her at the Galaxy, on the rainiest day we'd had for months, waiting to watch a movie about a werewolf.

I nudged Meg, and we watched the Englishwoman check her change and push her purse deep down into her bag before she left the counter.

She reminded me a lot of my dead Nanna Cole, though there wasn't so much of the Englishwoman. More walk and work than Nanna'd ever done, less sitting around and eating pies and chocolate, but they had the same hair, home-rinsed a frosty lilac and set in prickly curlers.

Nanna Cole didn't believe in make-up, where the Englishwoman's nose was powdered and her lips waxed peachy pink, though only in the middle, as if she'd pursed them to apply her lipstick. Her eyebrows were sketched in high surprise.

I could have guessed that she'd pretend she hadn't seen us. It was in line with her pretending not to have seen the sprawl of Meg's home when she must have walked past it a hundred times. She busied herself with the clip on her handbag as she came across and stood right in front of us (which was a bit rude, because there was a loose sort of line). She put her back towards us to begin with, but then she turned around, avoiding our faces to look behind us, up and over our heads, as if she'd let go of a balloon.

I had to say hello. It would have been too weird if I hadn't. Even Meg had to trap a giggle.

She looked at us right away then with pretend surprise. 'Oh!' she cried, and predictably: 'Fancy seeing you here.' (For God's sake!)

I introduced Meg, but they'd met before. I could tell by the look on Meg's face, when the Englishwoman took her hand in a limp one of her own. It was somewhere between surprise and amusement.

'Pleased to meet you,' the Englishwoman said. 'You can call me Lily.' As if it wasn't her name.

'I've never seen you here before,' I said.

'Well, I'm surprised we haven't bumped into each other!'

I wasn't. If she'd ever been before it wasn't on a Tuesday morning, but what's the point in challenging a lie? What would you ever learn that you didn't know already?

'Is it one you've been waiting for?' I nodded towards the curtain, which Mr Breadsell was about to pull aside.

'It is,' Lily said, but the dart of her eyes made me wonder if she knew what it was she'd just bought a ticket to see.

We filed into the theatre behind her, and it would have seemed rude if we hadn't followed her into the row she chose and taken seats beside her. I didn't mind, but I think Meg did a bit. She kept her bag on her lap instead of tucking it down between her feet, and her neck seemed shorter somehow. I sat between the two of them, and it was a relief that Lily didn't talk, and a bonus that she shared a packet of biscuits she pulled out of her pocket once the lights went down.

I studied her as best I could through the adverts, without turning my head. Her earrings were fancier than I would have pegged her for: a cluster of canary-yellow stones and crystals wired together like braces and screwed onto, not through, the wattles of her lobes. Three gold chains were sticky in the creases of her neck. A gold ring, a cross and a curly name too small for me to read without leaning in and giving myself away.

Lily did not enjoy the movie. She bit her lip and swore under her breath at every jump, and towards the climax she avoided scares by tidying her handbag quietly. I snuck a look inside it and was surprised to see a pack of Longbeach Menthol. She didn't have the smell of a smoker.

When Mr Breadsell asked her how she'd liked the movie, as we all filed out, she told him it was 'different'.

'It's certainly that!' Mr Breadsell laughed, and it was a tight smile she gave him back. She wouldn't have been sure whether he was laughing with or at her.

'It wasn't as good as I expected,' she told us, in the lobby, when I pressed her for better than 'different', but she couldn't say anything too terrible since it was a movie she'd wanted to see.

'Well, I'm away to sort a few things,' she said, taking a plastic rain hood out of her bag and tying it carefully over her head. It was still pouring, and I knew she didn't have a car so I offered her a lift home.

She looked torn between the prospect of a dry ride back and whatever errand it was she had to run.

'When are you going?' she asked.

Now. Of course now. Or soon? 'Maybe twenty minutes?' I said, and Meg looked surprised. What were we going to do for twenty minutes?

'Aye, alright then,' Lily said. 'Where will you be?'

I had no idea. We'd made it outside and were standing under the awning, out of the rain. Across the street was the Pink Fig Café, a fluorescent sign flashing *Open* in its window beside a *Have You Seen* poster of little Jessie Else and a chalkboard mostly undercover, on the footpath, advertising coffee and cake. 'There.' I pointed. 'We'll be in the cafe.'

'Right,' said Lily and marched off down William Street.

Meg was fiddling with her plastic bag, unrolling the neck of it then rolling it back up again, her woolly hat pulled low and a worried look on her face.

'My treat,' I told her. I would have linked my arm through hers to buck her up and reassure her, but I thought it would be too close and confronting, so I was surprised to feel her tug on the back of my jacket as I stepped off the kerb. It wasn't a busy road. It didn't need clever timing or a break-out into a run. It was only William Street, but she held on all the way across, like a child. For all Meg's independence and self-sufficiency, there was something stunned and unsure about her, like a little bird that had flown into a window.

The following week, Meg was standing in sunshine beside the car as usual at ten to ten, and away to the side stood Lily, in a skirt and matching cardigan. She was shifting from one chunky shoe to the other, twisting her watch then looking at it and up and around like she'd lost another balloon.

I knew the part I was supposed to play. She'd pretend a taxi hadn't come, and I'd say, 'Do you want to come with us?' She'd apologise and offer petrol money and I'd say, 'Don't be silly.' She was irritating with her *What caravan?* and *Pleased to meet you (even though we've met)* and *Fancy seeing you here (though I've never been before)*, but what did I want her to say? *I'm lonely. Can I please spend a couple of hours with the two of you?* It would have been cruel to push her all the way to honesty, so I waved and called across, 'Are you going in to town?' and she came with us to *Muriel's Wedding*.

She was ballsy, I'll give her that. She didn't wait for me to ask her if she wanted to come with us the next week; she just turned up. I made sure she took the back seat, so Meg would know she hadn't lost her place beside me. Lily took the third ticket and was the last one into the row and first one out at the end of the movie, but she was welcome.

The movie we saw that week is still one of my favourites: *Only You*. It was *A Love Story Written in the Stars*, according to the poster, and we all floated out with tissues in our fists and smiles on our faces. When Mr Breadsell asked the women in front of us how they'd liked it, one said it was an absolute delight and the other one told him she'd liked it almost as much as *Sleepless in Seattle*, but when he asked Lily, she actually snorted, 'If only life were like that!'

'Well, I suppose, deep down, we all believe in a little magic, don't we?' Mr Breadsell smiled, but Lily pursed her lips and shook her head as if the whole idea disgusted her. She'd have been the one to rip back the curtain on the wizard in Oz.

I wanted to talk about it. Ask her what was wrong with a little magic. Why couldn't life be like that? And even if it never was or would be, what was wrong with dreams-come-true endings?

'Are either of you in a rush to get back?' I asked, and they looked at each other before shaking their heads in unison. There was still a bit of *Do you want to? Shall we? Why don't we?*, but I hooked Meg's arm through mine, and we crossed William Street and took the table by the window in the Pink Fig.

We went every week after that. We sat at the same table and took the same chairs around it, Meg facing the door and jumping ever so slightly when the little bell above it jingled; Lily with her back to it, not caring who or what came in; and me between them with a clear view out of the window. The waitress came to know our order—two cappuccinos and one black coffee with cold milk in a jug on the side ('I'd rather add it myself, please'). We had whatever cake came with the special, though every week Meg waited to find out what it was before she nodded her order, and Lily would say, 'In for a penny, in for a pound,' though I never really knew what that meant.

I'd come to enjoy Meg's quiet company, but I enjoyed Lily's conversation too. It was clear she'd been a long time without much of it. She made us laugh. Not that she was trying to be funny; she just grumbled all the time and rarely had a nice word to say about anyone or anything. Tom Hanks looked a simple sort, Mr Breadsell ought to tidy himself up a bit, and Jessie Else shouldn't have been wagging school in the first place. Service was scrappy, cups were filthy, cakes were a bit dry, but she knew when to keep quiet. She never questioned which movie was screening, she pretended not to see the junk strewn on the back seat of the car, and she never, ever spoke even the mildest of harsh words to Meg.

CHAPTER THIRTEEN

Meg

When Sonny was alive, Sunday breakfast was something special: sausages or bacon, scrambled eggs and mushrooms, toast and jam and a pot of coffee. If the juice in the jug wasn't thick with pulp it had no place on the table, and we read the papers until noon. I'd had nothing like a Sunday since Sonny died, until the promise of those Tuesday mornings.

For Lily, too, it was something special. Acting as if it was barely worth the bother was the coat she wore, but there was a bounce in her step that wasn't there when her trolley dragged behind her. She set her hair early in the morning so that it rose around her scalp like fairy floss, tied a coloured scarf across it when the wind was blowing and a plastic hood if there was a spit of rain. She was rigid in her belief that early was on time, on time was late and late was unacceptable, but we nodded our hellos and shared the shade of the lemon gums. We waited separately for Rosemary, but we stepped into the car together like hens coming home at sunset.

Rosemary was a finch, chattering all the way to town and on until we'd settled into the velvety fold-down seats and the lights began to dim.

There was quiet as the heavy curtains swung aside and the pearly screen flickered into life, and then something special happened to us all.

Cars raced and chased through cities we'd never seen but knew. Meteors struck, rivers of lava separated families and walls of water carried towns away; creatures mutated, babies were taken, lovers met and then were torn apart. Lessons were learned. We sat in wide-eyed witness to acts of uncommon valour and unfathomable cruelty. And as far-fetched and incredible as most of the stories were, as implausible were the survivals and impossibly happy many of the endings, we believed them all in the moment, sitting there in the dark.

Or I did. Rosemary did.

Lily was old enough to remember the sort of war that challenged faith and changed a generation. She painted her nails but the skin on her hands was loose and the jewels of the rings on her fingers often spun into her palms. Her teeth shared one straight edge and her gums were milky pink and plastic. She understood what men were capable of with enough encouragement and the confidence steel gave them. But despite all that she didn't trust, and hadn't time for, the fools she wouldn't suffer, and the holes she poked in scenes and storylines, she found the magic of escape. For an hour and a half, we shut our own lives out in the cool of the foyer, and the bindings of them fell away from us like salt from the popcorn that gathered in the corners of the bucket that occasionally passed between us.

In the Pink Fig afterwards, Rosemary critiqued the plots, rated the actors' performances, and gossiped about the lives they led between the pages of the supermarket checkout magazines. 'You'll never guess,' she'd say, and neither Lily nor I ever did. We had nothing much to contribute to a storyline's dissection, no earlier performances to compare, no celebrity couplings or un-couplings to reveal.

I wondered why she took us with her, but even in my own quiet I didn't handle the question too much and only held it carefully from time to time in open hands, like a moth.

'You mustn't look a gift horse in the mouth,' my grandmother used to say.

We were eight movies in to our new routine when the Englishman escaped again. Coming home from *The River Wild* and a peppermint slice at the Pink Fig, Rosemary swung the Kingswood into the clearing by the cabin and there he was sitting next to Eddie on the steps. He was wearing his pyjamas, a blue cardigan, and the same tartan slippers he'd had on the night I'd found him.

Lily took a sharp and sudden breath, held it while she tamed it, then blew out carefully.

'That's that then,' she said. That was the end of Tuesday mornings for her. No more trips to the cinema. No more time for herself. *Goodbye and thank you, Mr Breadsell, you shan't see me again!*

'No,' Rosemary said. 'It doesn't change anything.'

'Of course it bloody does,' Lily growled.

Rosemary stretched an arm and patted the back of my seat. She couldn't reach Lily's knee, but, 'He's fine,' she reassured her. 'Look—you can see he's fine.'

'He's not been fine for years.'

'Alright, but he's safe. He's safe with Eddie.'

There was space between Eddie and the Englishman. A roll of sandpaper and the wooden seashell of a horse's ear lay beside two mugs and an open packet of biscuits.

We climbed out of the car and Lily strode across, all angles and purpose, but, 'Now then, what are you doing here?' is all she said, and she spoke calmly and kindly as if to a cat found under a bed in a thunderstorm.

I wondered if inside she was screaming, *What the hell do you think you're doing? You're going to ruin everything! Can't I have one bloody morning?*

'Sorry for the bother,' she told Eddie, and she set her handbag down in the dust and bent to slide a hand under each of her husband's armpits to lift him to his feet. 'Come on now,' she said to him. 'Let's get you home and I'll make you a nice hot drink.'

'It's fine.' Eddie laughed. 'Leave him. Really, leave him.'

He's not been fine for years.

Lily stood up straight and put her hands on her hips, wrestling with what-to-do in her head, and in the end she sat down next to her husband and took his hand as if she'd decided, now the skeleton was out of the closet, she'd own up to everything that fell out with it. Perhaps she expected an avalanche of questions, but Eddie went back to whittling the wooden ear in his lap and the Englishman went back to scuffing a pebble in the dirt with the toe of his slipper.

What was there to ask that we didn't know already? He was unwell, old and weary. His memory was gone. His brain didn't function the way it used to. He needed looking after, and Lily didn't want any help, but she needed a couple of hours away from her reality every now and then.

'He's been no bother at all,' Eddie told her. 'Have you, Norman?'

His name. We hadn't known his name.

Norman shook his head shyly, keeping his focus on the pebble and his slipper.

Rosemary walked over and kissed Eddie deep in his ginger hair.

'You know what?' he said, talking to all of us. 'I quite enjoyed the company.' And something kind and unspoken was understood.

CHAPTER FOURTEEN

Rosemary

Dad died when I was twelve. I slept through all the fuss of the police coming, and if Mum cried at all she did it quietly, because I slept through that as well. When I got up for school in the morning, she was sitting at the kitchen table in the same clothes she'd had on the day before. The ashtray was full.

'He's dead,' was all she said, and here's the truth: I felt like it was Christmas morning and I was about to open something I really, really wanted, and that's not even the awful bit. A second later I had this incredible wash of worry—what if she meant someone else?—and I think my voice shook a little bit when I asked her, 'Who?' to be sure, to be absolutely certain.

'Your father,' she said then, but I knew she meant King, and I was Christmas-morning happy all over again.

Everyone knew he wasn't my father, though no one seemed to know who my father actually was or, if they did, they were never going to tell me. Nanna got drunk once and said she doubted Mum even knew herself, but that was the only time anyone even acknowledged it wasn't the man we were all supposed to pretend it was.

King was short and fat and everyone thought he was a merry old soul, hence the nickname. They didn't know him like we did. He liked to be in control. He wanted receipts from his housekeeping and change down to the last cent, and if he didn't get it then he liked the way Mum's feet struggled to reach the floor, and the way white dimples spread beneath thick fingers at her neck when he pushed her hard against the wall. He liked the sounds we made when he threw a glass across a room. He liked the look on your face when he snapped a thing you loved across his knee. He liked the way you pushed against him when he twisted your arm around and up your back.

It was a hit-and-run, the police told Mum. He was left flattened like a crow on the side of the highway in the middle of the night. No one knew for sure what he was doing out of his car (or out of his bed, for that matter), but they didn't dwell on that. He often went out late, came home late, stayed out all night. Mum didn't mind. They were the nights he went straight to bed or fell asleep where he fell on the couch or in a heap at the bottom of the stairs. They were the better nights.

The Carney Courier called him a Pillar of the Community. He was hit by a white van or truck, they wrote. They could tell from the angle and the force that hit him. They must have picked the colour from paint chips in among the blood and bits of bone.

The hit was buried and the run ran. They never found him. 'We're optimistic,' Sergeant Scanlan told the *Courier*, but they wouldn't have been. There's seventeen hundred kilometres of Bruce Highway between Brisbane and Cairns; the driver could have been travelling either way, and every other car in Queensland's white.

'A truckie, probably,' Mum said. 'They'll never find him, and what does it matter? There's no bringing him back.'

Thank God.

It was quiet for a couple of years then Mum met Graham, who was really nice. He was happy to sit through movies he'd seen and didn't spoil the endings. He looked at you properly when you spoke, and his face actually responded to the tone of the story you were telling, so you knew he was listening. He kissed Mum on the lips when he came over. He bought me a Bon Jovi t-shirt for my birthday and wrote more than *to* and *from* in the card (not much more, but enough for it to mean something better than *here you go*).

Graham had a good position in the Commonwealth Bank, and there was talk of moving to Melbourne and having a fresh start. He organised his transfer and they went for a week to get the lay of the land, Mum said; to have a look and see what they thought. 'It's quite cold there,' she warned me. 'It rains a lot.' I didn't care about the weather. I was fourteen years old; Melbourne for me meant the latest movies, the latest fashions, *Hey Hey It's Saturday* and Luna Park. I was desperate to ride the Great Scenic Railway roller-coaster. Daryl Somers had done it with a cameraman beside him in the front seat, and I couldn't wait. I told the girls at school I was moving to Melbourne and enjoyed the sort of fuss I'd never had before. 'You're so lucky!' they said. They all wished they were moving to Melbourne!

As it turned out, Mum and Graham just didn't come back from that week away. It was all organised with a flood of phone calls, but instead of going to live in Melbourne, I went to live with my oldest sister and her husband on the new estate.

Looking back now, I think Mum had done all the mothering she wanted to do. She had three teenagers slamming doors and fighting over eyeliner already when I came along to give her years more sticky floors and shitty nappies. With me there in Melbourne, it would have been a move but nothing more. A carrying on of the life she was living. You don't get many chances to begin again, and when the tram stops you only have a moment to decide. I don't blame her now for getting on, but I did for a long time. She grew to be someone else in cold, rainy Melbourne. She built herself a career in real estate, bought herself expensive shoes and drank from long-stemmed glasses. She reinvented herself completely, like Melanie Griffith in *Working Girl*.

Michele and Dan gave me their spare room reluctantly. They had a toddler and a new baby and didn't pretend to be taking me in for any reason other than the money Mum gave them in exchange.

'I've enough on my plate without you playing up,' Michele said. Short years before, she'd played netball, run most mornings and raced out to a party every Saturday night, but babies left her with barely enough time to wash her hair. 'You're going to need to pull your weight.'

'One step out of line and you're out,' her husband warned me.

'Once she's finished year ten, she'll look for a job,' Mum promised them, and made me promise her, and that's exactly what I did.

I was interviewed at the chocolate factory the week after my exams. The woman in the big chair had very short hair and a little dove tattooed on her wrist. She said there was no need to wait for my results, as if she knew already that I'd failed, and she didn't make me wait to find out if I had the job. She said, 'I don't think there's any need to drag this on, do you?' with a light little laugh, and I started on the Monday.

Full training provided, she'd said, but to be honest there wasn't much of it. How much training do you need to drive a sweeper and fling a mop about? It's not brain surgery. There were two days of induction, with fire training, which was the most exciting thing I'd ever done. We got to put out a blazing fire, and learned which things would burn low and smoulder, which chemicals gave off toxic fumes, and not to park the sweepers anywhere they were likely to ignite. But mostly the training was Health and Safety: keeping your hair in a net, your nails short, and walkways clear.

The money was good. The girls I worked with were okay, and the company was generous. They threw a Christmas party every year in the function room at Carney's, with a sit-down dinner and dancing, candles on every table, a huge tree in the corner and all the wine and beer you could drink—and that was on top of your pay-packet bonus and the frozen turkey everyone took home on Christmas Eve.

'You really fell on your feet there,' Mum said, and I let myself believe the pride in her voice, and neither of us mentioned that the woman with the little dove tattoo was Graham's sister.

I was a good worker, and I stuck to most of the rules because that's what they paid me to do and there was sense to them. If I forgot to sign out when I nipped to the Coke machine in the middle of the night, I was back on the floor before anyone noticed I'd been gone, but I could see how a cigarette butt or a finger cut off in the twist of a diamond ring would lose us all our turkey bonuses.

Eddie and I met at the Christmas party. He didn't work at the factory, but he was going out with a girl who did, and she danced a lot with the factory manager that night. There was nothing in it. Mr Shale had a pretty wife and a little girl he brought with him to work sometimes (I'd know she'd been in because his desk would be covered in pictures of potato people holding hands). 'Stuck up little shit,' I'd heard Margy Clarke call him through gritted teeth, but he wasn't. He was richer and smarter, but he had a smile and a greeting for us all on his way in every morning, as we were on our way out.

Anyway, what with Eddie's date dancing so much with the boss, I got to dance with Eddie, and the rest, as they say, is history.

We got married in the Baptist church on Lakeview, though neither of us were Baptists. It wasn't a big wedding, but there were enough of us to half-fill the function room at Carney's, and book a DJ and a strobe light. Mum and Graham came up from Melbourne, Michele and Dan came with their kids. My other sisters and Eddie's brother, Shane, were too far away by then, but Eddie's cousins were there and his parents and Nola. He had a few school friends and some of them had partners and children.

It was a nice wedding with plenty of laughter. Feet were tired from dancing, and shoes were carried out. The bar was busy, and the food was good (Michele threw up in the car park and blamed the chicken, but everyone knew it was the chardonnay).

We took a tent to Eungella for our honeymoon. I would have preferred Fiji, but we didn't have that sort of money, and Eddie wouldn't have wanted to go there even if we had.

'I've absolutely no desire to go abroad,' he said.

The *Courier* stopped him in the street once for a thing they used to do called 'Local Profile'. They took a photo of him, side on, and asked him ten questions. I can still remember most of his answers:

Favourite food? 'Reef and beef.'

Favourite drink? 'Bundy and Coke.'

Movie? *'Three Amigos.'*

Singer? 'Johnny Cash.'

Dream holiday? 'To go the length of the Bruce Highway in a campervan,' he gave them. I don't know what I would have said, put on the spot coming out of Discount Dan's, but not that.

I asked him, 'Wouldn't you like to see the pyramids? Wouldn't you like to go on a safari?'

'Why?' he said. 'What's wrong with Queensland?'

Not long after the wedding, Michele and Dan moved to country New South Wales. My other sisters were long gone. Liz taught photography in Sydney, and Fran was a motorcycle courier in London. I never saw any of them again. They say blood's thicker than water, but what does that mean? Soup's thicker than water. If you think about it, there's not much thinner than water, actually.

Mum stopped by once on her way to or from Mackay, visiting someone on Graham's side. Eddie and I were living in his parents' caravan at the time, but I told her we were planning to build at Maggie Beach.

'Why?' she asked, as if there was a deeper reason than cost and space. 'What the hell would make you want to live out there?'

'If it's money,' she said, in a moment when the two of us were by ourselves, 'you know there's some put aside for you for later, for a rainy day.'

'We're fine, thanks.' I didn't want her fingers in my pockets, but she wrote a cheque before she left.

'I don't know what I did so differently with that one,' she told Graham as they drove away and he wasn't quick enough to wind up the window.

Of course, she did know. Everyone knew: the man I'd called my father, Liz and Fran, Michele and Dan, the Lambs and the Coulters—they all knew. Little Lucy would learn, and baby George would be told when he was older. The girls at the factory knew. The whole town knew Joanna Cole had cheated on her husband. But Eddie was the only one who let on he'd ever wondered who it was she'd cheated with. The only one who ever let me wonder too.

I think that's what drew me to him.

'I don't think it was anyone special,' I said. But I'd always hoped he might turn out to be.

'You'd think someone would remember,' Eddie mused, because the features blunted by my mother's were not Carney County's.

'Just someone passing through.' I shrugged, as if it were a cardigan I did not want on my shoulders, when what I wanted more than anything was to pull it close around me. Close enough to learn its thread and weave and smell, to feel its warmth, know its pulls and buttons, cross my arms and tuck my hands back up into its sleeves.

CHAPTER FIFTEEN
Lily

It was childish, all of her not-talking. Rosemary gave her too much attention for it, if you ask me. It was like watching an overprotective parent by a seesaw. She'd start her sentences, finish her sentences. I couldn't be doing with it. Meg could talk if she wanted to, but she could shut herself up like a clam if she wanted to do that. As if she were the only one who'd ever lost a thing they cared about. As if she were the only one who'd ever had a love that spoiled, or a life they'd loved that turned to shit.

Don't get me wrong; I didn't dislike her. She was nice enough, just so caught up in herself all the time. But they came as a package, I could see that. Rosemary felt sorry for us both. Meg had lost herself out there, hadn't she? Me—I knew exactly where I was, but by God I was lonely.

It might have been different if I'd had children, though by the time we moved to that house any child we'd had would've been all grown up and minding their own business. They'd not have stuck around—even a daughter—not with Norman being the way he was. I'd have been lucky to get a card on Mother's Day, and no flowers. There wouldn't have been a florist who delivered so far out of town.

No, it was better, I think, that we stayed on our own, but I did miss being around people. I missed the gossip and the news, even hearing what people's kids were getting up to, once they got to an age where they did more than cut another tooth and fill their pants.

I missed Norman—the way we'd been in the beginning, in the years before he got sick, and the years before that, back in England, side by side in our recliners in front of the television on a Saturday night, two glasses and a bottle of wine on the nest of tables between us, Bruce Forsyth and the Two Ronnies. God, we used to laugh! I'd give anything to have just one of those simple Saturday nights at home again. That home. The one I thought we'd live in forever. Just one night.

It's incredible how completely your life can change when you haven't made any steps to change it yourself. They say time passes and things change, and of course it does, of course they do, but you're not always responsible for those changes. You can call it fate or consequence, but sometimes it's just other people knocking a bloody domino.

All Norman did these days was stumble through jigsaws and stare into space. I didn't love him anymore. I didn't even like him very much. But he was my husband, and that meant something when I took it on. Was I a good wife? Yes, I was, and I was loyal. I kept every promise I made. As God is my witness, they can't say I didn't do that.

Do you know, he asked me to kill him a few times. In his more lucid moments, he'd held both my hands in his and pleaded with me. 'I can't take it anymore,' he whispered, and I could have done it, held a pillow over his face and pushed hard. I don't suppose it would have been that difficult; he had about the strength of a plastic fork. And I don't suppose there'd have been any suspicion—a sick old man dead in his sleep—but for all that I disliked the man he'd become, I didn't want him dead.

I didn't want to be on my own.

And then I met Rosemary and Meg.

CHAPTER SIXTEEN
Meg

Lily brought Norman every Tuesday after that.

'Now you behave for Mr Lamb,' she told him, as if he were six years old and being left with an uncle. There was no need for her to say anything at all, because one look at Norman would tell you he wasn't going anywhere. Once he'd shuffled into the care of Eddie's shadow, he settled like snow.

There'd been three horses finished since the one I'd first watched Eddie sand smooth from the shade of the lemon gums. They all had manes and plaited tails and leather bridles and rocked side by side under plastic, waiting for the market at Calliope.

Norman browned in the sun as he watched the fourth's own nutty hide take shape. He sat on the steps, or in an armchair which had only recently appeared in the shed, and he watched Eddie chisel out its nostrils, the scoop of its pricked ears, and the contours of its brow. Perhaps it reminded him of a toy he'd had himself, stabled in the corner of a nursery filled with Enid Blyton toys that came to life at midnight. Lead soldiers that marched with muskets, and tops you pumped to spin. The rocking horse, named Dobbin or Ned or Silver, ridden wildly by wilful children in billowing blue-white nightgowns.

As under Eddie's tools and touch the cedar curled like butter from the horse that hid beneath, so Norman's skin seemed to tighten and his back slowly straighten as weeks and Tuesday mornings passed, and after a time it was someone else entirely counting brass tacks into a tin when Rosemary, Lily, and I came home.

We took to staying a little longer in the Pink Fig.

'I've got stuff I need to get on with,' Lily often said, but I don't know if she ever actually did. 'We should get going.' But still we sat, and after a little while she'd lean back in her chair and stop looking at the clock behind the counter—and she'd talk.

She was a lot like my grandmother with grass so green back home, but my grandmother had left only cuttings—a plate on a table you could never hope to reach, with its better cakes and biscuits, manners and newsreaders—nothing very much compared to the land and life she'd chosen. God's own country, she called New Zealand, while the greener grass of Lily's England rolled over everything Back Home.

The first story she told us was of a viaduct stretched across a cold black river that froze solid in the wintertime, where a little girl was lost through ice that wasn't thick enough to skate on before February. 'Not that we had skates,' Lily said, 'but boots worked well enough,' and they were lucky to each have a pair of those.

She started life in London, where her brother's school was bombed to bits. All that was left was a pile of rubble, broken glass and chairs and chalk. 'We thought it was grand,' Lily said, but it wasn't, because it meant the Germans were on their way with guns, and who knew what they'd do if they arrived?

So, the children were packed onto puffing trains that blackened hands and faces, and sent away with their names pinned to their coats on cardboard circles. Sent to a place of rolling fields and dry-stone walls, where blackberries grew wild for the picking, and there was little need for the masks that hung in boxes around their necks. They wore their mittens on lengths of wool that ran up one sleeve and down the other. They wore belted gabardines and shoes with buckles they were taught to shine.

For Lily, Yorkshire was God's own country. She never went back to London. Or perhaps she did and only let us think she didn't. She wound the stories onto our splayed fingers but hers was the yarn, the mass of it turned with care, and the peeling thread held tight between forefinger and thumb, careful not to give us too much, though what might we have done if she had? Who would we have told and what would it have mattered?

Most of what she told us was a whorl of young years in the country. Did she still have her brother? I wondered because she never mentioned him beyond stunts and treats and injuries, so I don't know that he ever grew to be a man.

I didn't ask, and Rosemary (who'd never had a brother) didn't think to.

'How did you and Norman meet?' Rosemary asked. 'How did you end up in Australia?'

But these were questions Lily moulded with warm fingers and pressed into the shape of other things, and every story headed back to Calcutt, until we knew so much about the place, we felt we'd lived there for a time ourselves. I could walk you through the village even now. Tell you where the river bent so oars got stuck in tree roots. I could tell you how the foxes played in dew-wet clearings, and all about the butcher who came in a van. I could walk you around the ruins of a castle thick with flaming gorse and tell you about the gypsies who threw a curse on anyone who wouldn't buy a sprig of heather.

Once Lily began, only half of her was with us pouring milk, spooning sugar, pressing crumbs into the cream that stuck to the back of her fork; the rest of her was years away and happy. Happier in a place where butter was a luxury, nights blanket-dark, and envelopes trapped terrible news, and Lily's stories took us away just like Mr Breadsell's darkened theatre did, so that when we went our separate ways it was with her memories as our own.

Rosemary told her she should write a book and Lily laughed, but people would have read it. I've seen the sorts of things that people like to read.

That Lily had been happiest as a child was so obvious that I wondered what her life with Norman had been like in the beginning. I wondered if her stomach had ever trembled with butterflies, her chest filled with a sudden sweet breath, as he stepped up behind to draw his arms around her waist. Had he ever brushed her hair? Had he held her in the rain and told her that he loved her more than sun and moon and stars, and always would? Because if he had, how was Calcutt better than that?

She kept a photo in her purse of a smart young man in black and white, a flower in his buttonhole and a shiny new ring on his finger. The smile on his face could have skinned a peach, and a whole lifetime stretched ahead of them both in that moment. She never showed us the photo; we only saw it when she swung her handbag on the counter, opened up her purse, and counted out her coins. She never talked about the man she married, but I wondered did she thumb through curling photographs in the stillest hours of three, four, five o'clock, and I wondered if it would be easier once he was gone for her to look back, faraway-safe, and remember him as openly as she remembered Calcutt.

When we met.

Our first kiss.

The things we used to do that no one else did.

Would those be the happiest of her memories then?

The old man she left on the steps with Eddie had nothing left for her, and she had little to say about him. Some things he needed. Some things he forgot. Sometimes he thought he could do a thing he couldn't, but with only the fog of a memory to tell him he might have been able to do it before. There were trips and tumbles, and his shins were often bruised.

'You don't always see the step, do you?' Lily said.

I remembered my grandfather's knees and elbows, scuffed as an eight-year-old's.

'I hate you,' I heard Norman tell her once. It was tucked under a breath, but I saw the way it stung her, and I pretended not to have heard.

Which is worse? I wonder still. To have love snatched away in one tight, violent second, or to have it dragged off slowly like a heavy carpet ruined in a storm?

And for the love that leaves, which would be better? A sickness that thins the fabric of your life until there's barely a thread worth clinging to, or something that comes hurtling out of nowhere? No inkling of something wrong, no tinkling bell of warning, no count of ten, and no best-case scenarios whittled back in stages. Just one almighty all-of-a-sudden that lets you live carelessly right up until the moment of impact. No goodbyes. No wounds to stitch or flapping ends to tie. No promises to elicit.

'It's best not to know some things,' my grandmother used to say. (What goes into a sausage roll, who said the thing you heard about your father.) She would have said it about Jessie Else, I think, whose parents were still pleading with the man who might have taken her.

At what point had she understood she wasn't going home?

'She's a good girl,' Mr Else told the television cameras. 'Always helping, always lending a hand. Please don't hurt her.' Hoping that whoever took her might still have her, though on other days he may have hoped whoever that was might have killed her quickly.

'It's the not knowing that would finish you,' Catherine said.

Six of one and half-a-dozen of the other.

CHAPTER SEVENTEEN
Rosemary

They taught us about the two world wars in school, but what I knew about them came mostly from the screen. Men were drafted, food was rationed, bombs fell from the sky. I'd known who Hitler was, of course, but *Schindler's List* had come as a shock.

Lily was the first person I knew who'd really been or come from anywhere else, and was prepared to share it.

The odd times I saw Mum, she wouldn't tell me anything I didn't know already about Melbourne: it rained a lot, and the wind blew icy cold straight up from the Antarctic; sometimes you might recognise a face you knew from television. I wanted to know more. I wanted to know what it was like to live there. Did people travel everywhere by tram and bring their groceries home on their knees? Did people chat or pass each other by? Were the gardens at the front or tucked behind the houses?

I'd been to a few markets with Eddie, but they were all in the same small towns: a flat patch rented out in squares; a pub with the same counter specials and beers; and black-and-white photographs of men with long saws clearing the bush to plant the place, in the beginning.

I went to Yeppoon for year six camp, but that hadn't given me much more to draw on. No one wanted to sit next to me on the bus or take the bunk below. We made damper in a campfire and learned how to snorkel, but the seals on all the masks were leaky.

I wished Fran back from London for a day. The questions I had for her. Was it as busy as it looked in movies? What was it like riding her bike between fat black cabs and double-decker buses? What did people do on Sundays? What did she miss, if she missed anything at all?

Even Liz, who was the oldest and the sister I'd known the least growing up: I would have had some questions for her about Sydney.

I wished Eddie's brother would visit from wherever it was he'd settled in the end. Belgium, I think. I didn't know anything at all about Belgium. I thought it was quite rainy, but it's not all about the weather.

Meg spoke sometimes, but not often, and she never gave us much. It snowed where she grew up, and she told us once about its cold and quiet. I'd imagined the patter of rain and the wind that pushes ahead of a cyclone, but it didn't make a sound, Meg said. 'It's quieter than silent.' Lily snorted at that, but I suppose what Meg meant was that it muffled everything else like a pillow. It fell in the night when everyone was asleep, she said, and when you opened the curtains in the morning there it was, like a surprise, all over everything—bikes and buckets and washing lines—and it sparkled. I'd never have imagined that either.

To know properly about something is second best to knowing it properly yourself.

My real father wasn't Australian. What I mean is that if he was Australian, he wasn't the type who lived in Carney County. Mum used to tell people I looked like her side of the family, where there was a swarthy Uncle Joe. Both her parents were dead, so no one could add to that (or take from it). A handful of photographs curled in an old brown case under her bed, along with our birth certificates and other papers. They were baby pictures, mostly, and strangers grouped around tables. No one looked like me. They gave nothing away. I don't know whether she took them with her to Melbourne or threw them out, but when I packed to move in with Michele, all that was left in the case was a drawing she'd had done at a fair that stopped in Winifred when my sisters were little. They remembered camel rides and toffee apples. I'm sure Mum only kept the picture because it made her look prettier than she'd ever actually been. In real life she had a pointy chin. I had Joe's chin. I don't think there even was an Uncle Joe, but it made me think that might have been His name. It was my first clue.

I asked her about him twice. The first time I was seven or eight, and Dad had been shouting in the night. He'd called her names and threatened to kick us both out on our own. I'd told her in the morning we should go and find my other dad. I reckoned he couldn't be much worse, and of course expected him to actually be much nicer and sorry that he'd left us. I thought we could pack our cases in a hurry and be on the train before King got home from work, but Mum slapped me hard across the face and growled ugly, 'Don't you ever suggest anything like that again.'

My cheek stung, and my ear rang, and tears rolled down my face. I was embarrassed and ashamed and I was angry, but she was angrier.

The only other time I mentioned him was not long after King died. I worked myself up to simmering-excited, expecting her to put the kettle on and tell me everything she remembered, and that in no time, we'd be off like the Goonies on the trail of One-Eyed Willy.

'I don't know what you're talking about,' she said then, and when I tried to reason that it didn't matter now, and anyway I wouldn't tell anyone else, she just shook her head. 'You are Roy Cole's daughter,' she told me.

'But I don't want to be!' (I might have wailed.)

'Well, you are. And whether you like it or not, that counts for a lot in this town.'

I didn't like it. I'd never liked it, and I was never going to like it, but 'The subject is closed,' Mum said, and it never opened up again.

I could have asked other people, when I was older and had free access to them, without my mother by my side and in the way. I could have asked Leonie, who might have remembered something. Eddie always insisted she and Mum had been best friends, but I have no memories of them ever standing close enough to share a secret, or even a bottle of wine—and anyway, if Leonie had known anything, she would have told Eddie, and Eddie would have told me.

If the town had heard a whisper, they would not have kept it secret. I would have heard it. In among the names called and the notes passed and the compass scratches on the toilet doors, I would have heard it. I would have picked it out.

I used to fantasise that my real father would come back for me, cast somewhere between Daddy Warbucks and the King of Siam, stinking rich, hands up and hopeful. Sorry he'd lost me, and desperate to make up for the time we'd spent apart.

As I got older, the fantasy shifted and it wasn't a father I imagined coming for me, but a soulmate. A handsome stranger who arrived as unexpectedly as one of Meg's snowfalls and whisked me off into a better life.

In that quiet half-hour before sleep, I'd pull my pillow close and lose myself in wide-awake dreams rich with detail. Even more so after a night at work, when I had the whole day to lose if I chose, and the bed all to myself.

Sometimes he wore sneakers with a suit and a smile, and he bought the factory and worked late and ordered takeaway and we laughed and shared sesame chicken and eventually moved together to Hong Kong, where I wore heels and took his notes at long-tabled, high-rise meetings.

Sometimes he was a famous actor whose yacht ran aground at Maggie Beach, who didn't want Hollywood rags to find the story, so stayed with us. I mediated boat repairs while we fell in love, and when he sailed away into the sunset, it was with me beside him at the helm.

He was a wealthy widower whose young twins took a shine to me while riding Eddie's horses at a market, and could I come away with them and be their nanny in a rambling Queenslander on the banks of a river at the base of a mountain far away from Carney County? You bet.

If Eddie had a part in any fantasy, it was purely platonic. A strong supporting role, a caring older brother or best friend, not the lead, as I'd actually cast him in real life. Not the one I'd given all my promises.

I can't tell you how many nights and afternoons I fell asleep dreaming of Richard Gere. He was your ideal whisker-awayer, back then.

Mary Mudd worked at the factory. The others didn't like her because she didn't make much of an effort to fit in, which only meant she didn't laugh at every joke and didn't pack sandwiches like the rest of us. They called her China, and pretended it was because she was small with creamy skin and a perfect little mouth painted on. 'You just look like a little doll, don't you!' Shirley told her with a smile, but she didn't really. She looked like me.

The first time we met, she spoke to me in a language I didn't recognise, and she was embarrassed when I answered her in English. 'I'm so sorry,' she said then. 'I thought you were Filipina.' She wouldn't have been sure I wasn't going to take that as an insult. (She knew why they called her China.)

'That's okay,' I told her, and smiled wide as a tawny frogmouth so she'd know I wasn't like the rest of them.

'I was born in the Philippines,' she explained, and we talked for a while about her family who were still there. Her parents and brothers, aunts, uncles and cousins, and the grave of a younger sister who died of pneumonia when she was only small.

I packed rice to take with me for dinner the next night. 'Flied lice—that's nice!' Margy Clarke said, and she hummed 'The Siamese Cat Song' from *Lady and the Tramp* whenever she came across Mary and me sitting together after that. It was like being back at school, but I really didn't care.

There were questions I wanted to ask Mary Mudd, that's why I sat next to her in the crib room. (She didn't need a reason to sit next to me; she was happy to have the company.) I wanted to ask her if she thought my father could have been a Filipino, but that would have left me wide open, so instead I said, 'My father came from the Philippines,' to see if she'd accept it.

She looked pleased. 'Where's he from?'

'I don't know. I never met him.' I didn't want to lie about it all. I wanted her to tell me things, but I didn't want to ask too much.

She came from an island called Masbate, which was beautiful, she said.

'Do you miss it?' I asked her, and she shrugged.

'I love it, of course,' she said carefully. 'I miss my family, but my husband and I visit. We're going next year.' She smiled at the thought of that. 'He loves it, too. Maybe when we retire, we'll move there.'

'What does your husband do?' I asked.

'Well, actually, he's retired,' she said, and we both laughed.

Mary's husband picked her up from work at the end of every shift. I'd only seen him from a distance. He met her at the gate on an orange moped, kissed her on the lips and buckled a helmet up under her chin.

But one morning he wasn't there. I waited with her for ten minutes, and then it started to rain, so I offered to take her home.

'I should wait,' she kept saying. 'He will come.' Like Shoeless Joe Jackson in *Field of Dreams*. But in the end, she let me take her. I told her if we passed her husband on the road, we'd honk and flash the lights, do a U-turn and catch him up, but we didn't see him.

They lived on a sailboat. 'We were living in Gladstone for a while,' Mary explained, 'but the marina was expensive.' Muddy had been to Winifred before. 'It's nice,' Mary said. 'No one bothers us.'

Mary had been living her life on Masbate when her Prince Charming had sailed in, and when he left, she was on board. A real-life whisking-away. She told me all this as we drove through the rain and along a road I'd never taken that ran beside the Barra, where their boat was anchored. *Muddy Duck* was its name, but I wouldn't have known it had one if Mary hadn't told me. You couldn't read it from the riverbank. It looked old and sinkable, with rusty brown streaks down its sides and green slime in a strip that touched the water. It was a far cry from the yacht that sailed in to rescue me in my dreams. Mary whistled and shouted for her husband, and eventually he appeared up on deck looking flustered (and nothing like Richard Gere).

'Before I met Muddy, I'd been nowhere,' she told me, as we waited for him to row over in a little wooden dinghy (*Ugly Duck*, that was called. You couldn't have read that either from a distance, but up close it was clear enough), and now they'd travelled all over the place. 'I am very grateful,' she said.

He was older than I'd pictured him. He wore tight denim shorts and a yellow raincoat open wide with no shirt underneath. The skin on his chest was baggy and his grey hair was pulled back into a ponytail.

'Oh God, I'm so sorry, Mary!' was the first thing he said when he got to us. It had stopped raining, but the dinghy was half full of water.

'Thanks for bringing her, love,' he said to me. 'Very good of you. She doesn't like being left alone.'

It was a strange thing to say, I thought, but Mary only nodded.

Muddy reached up awkwardly to shake my hand. 'Rosemary, isn't it?' So she'd mentioned me. I liked that. 'You'll have to come out for a sundowner some time—you and your husband—when it's not, well . . .' He indicated the weather and I nodded.

It was starting to rain again, and Mary clambered into the dinghy. 'See you tomorrow, Roz!' she called above the splash of paddles.

Roz. I liked that too.

CHAPTER EIGHTEEN

Meg

The market in Calliope was the last Sunday of every month, but the biggest of the year was in November, and with Christmas galloping in behind it, that was the one Eddie took his horses to.

Rosemary left with him early on the Saturday, and they were back with more space in their trailer mid-Monday afternoon. Eddie was pegging up Christmas lights when I arrived that Tuesday morning, singing those of the Twelve Days he remembered, and wearing a singlet which read: *I'm not Santa but you can sit on my lap.* He invited Lily, Norman and me all at once, and there and then, to join them for Christmas Day.

'Unless you've got other plans?' Knowing we hadn't.

'It doesn't feel like Christmas,' Lily grumbled in the weeks leading up to it. It was too hot, it was too bright, and without an open fire, a turkey in the oven or a frozen river to skate on, it was clear she'd rather Christmas didn't come at all.

But it did.

Stencilled snowflakes gathered in drifts at the corners of store windows, and blinking angels lit the length of William Street. Catherine set up the Nativity scene in the lobby of the library: a child-sized Mary flanked by Joseph and three kings, Tiny Tears Baby Jesus asleep between them in a manger filled with hay she bought fresh every year from the pet shop. We put a tree up by the front desk, and hopeful little hands dropped lists and letters in the box we stood beside it.

When we were children, my brother and I used to go with Dad to choose one of the stocky pines that grew in the forest. We ran behind him, really, his long legs covered so much more ground than our small legs could manage, and we stood where he told us while he swung his axe and brought the little thing down. All that effort taken to grow, all that rain and sunshine and push through a crust of forest floor, for what? I remember thinking. Only to be chopped down and propped up in a corner of our cramped little house and left to shake and shush a needle-shedding death. I preferred the un-trees of Queensland, in all their glorious colours, with trunks that snapped into pieces and legs that slotted together. Sonny and I bought a pink one barely the length of his arm. It came with its own coloured lights and decorations—plastic bells with velvet bows, and glittery golden baubles—and had spent thirteen years in the dark of its cardboard box, but even I was swept up in the spirit of the season.

December was dry and everyone blamed El Niño. Picnickers were photographed up to their necks in the soup of Lake Carney, holding beer bottles high. 'I've lived here all my life and this is the hottest I've known it!' they told the *Courier*, and FEELING HOT, HOT, HOT! was a front-page story. On another day they had the manager of Elliott's Electrical lying in an empty chest freezer, underneath the headline CAN'T COOL DOWN! He was wearing a sombrero. The council voted to begin Carols by Candlelight an hour later than usual, and both supermarkets ran out of Rainbow Rockets.

There was no real news, nothing but the weather and Christmas fast approaching.

I passed Mr Else crossing the street, late one Thursday afternoon. Plastic bags full of groceries, he looked lost-in-the-middle-of-the-night. There was still no sign of his daughter, who seemed to have vanished into thin air. 'It's the not-knowing that would finish you,' Catherine had said, and as I watched Mr Else half-trip up the kerb, I wondered if it would.

Mrs Else didn't come to the library anymore, and I overheard she'd stopped going to church. I read somewhere that more suicides are recorded over the Christmas period than at any other time of year, and who wouldn't believe it? It is the loneliest of holidays. I knew a boy who shot himself on Boxing Day, just after we moved to Christchurch. My brother was with them when they found Kerry Presland, floating down the Waimakariri with the left-hand side of his face blown off. He must have fallen on his gun, they said. Everyone knew he hadn't, but he was buried on the right side of the cemetery's wrought-iron fence.

A selfish little boy, my mother called him, though he'd turned eighteen and was no more a boy than my brother, who'd been out of school and working for two years, and who saw Kerry Presland in nightmares for a long while afterwards, but it was Christmas and *He should have given more thought to his poor mother*. I wondered, even then, if things might have turned out better for Kerry Presland if his mother had given more thought to him.

Stupid little bastard, my father said. It's what he called all of us at one time or another, and especially around the holidays.

Eddie's parents arrived only minutes before the rest of us on Christmas Day. They'd brought their caravan and were busy transferring bags and bins from its open door into the kitchen. Nola had already been settled into one of the chairs Rosemary had pushed around the tables pressed together on the deck.

'Merry Christmas, Meggy!' she called out, raising a hand and wiggling ringed fingers, in case I hadn't seen her.

'Merry Christmas.' I was still trying it out, and it didn't fit well, but she didn't seem to notice.

'Slow *down*, Norman,' Lily grumbled behind me.

He was going to bruise the peaches that swung in the bag at his knees, and Rosemary skipped down the steps to take them from him, singing her own greetings.

Tom offered Norman his right hand for shaking and squeezed his shoulder warmly with his left. 'Happy Christmas, mate,' he said.

Norman nodded jerkily.

'You look tired, Rosemary,' Leonie said, and we all turned to see how tired Rosemary looked.

She rubbed a finger under each eye in a gesture that I remembered smudged eyeliner back into the beds of lashes. 'Do I?'

I shook my head, but she was asking Leonie, who'd already decided for all of us that she did.

It was Lily who dusted that away. 'Well, we made it!' As if they'd come much further. She'd cut Norman's hair and set her own, and she carried the shell of a pavlova carefully in a Tupperware container. I wondered if she might pretend she'd made it, and perhaps forget she'd told us that she didn't have an oven.

'Do you want to bring it inside?' Rosemary asked her, and she snaked the hand that hadn't taken Norman's bag of peaches around my waist and drew me up the steps and back into the kitchen with them, fingering the ribbon I'd tied around my waist to keep my skirt from dropping. 'I'm really glad you came!' she told us together. There was coffee on her breath but mostly she smelled of apple shampoo.

Lily gave a deep nod that hid the chains around her neck for a long moment.

Eight swelled to ten when Rosemary's friends Mary and Muddy arrived. They buzzed in on a scooter with lollipop helmets and sunglasses, like something that had broken from a swarm. I recognised Mary's pretty face from Rosemary's twenty-first, but I felt that I knew his from further afield.

'I think I've seen you at the library,' he said, shaking my hand. But that wasn't it.

We functioned as a whole that day. There was no *Can I help? What can I do?* It was there to be done and we did it together: the chopping and whisking, spooning and carving and topping up and taking out. And although the day was hosted by Eddie and Rosemary, Christmas was shared, and cheer spread between us all like butter on cold toast.

'Have another drink,' Tom kept telling Lily, filling her wine from the box that Rosemary had to remind him, over and over, to put back in the fridge.

'Chateau la Boîte,' Lily called it.

'What la what?' Rosemary laughed, but she liked the sound of it, I could tell.

Plates were passed. I put enough on mine for no one to insist that I took more but not so much that anyone could think me greedy. Thick pink slabs of Tom's ham with its cloved and honeyed rind; a salad like I'd never seen, with toasted nuts and noodles and crisp green shoots. There were other things: other meats and salads; corn I'd cut before breakfast and soft bread torn still steaming from the oven. Hats made their way from tight rubber-banded wads onto our heads, glasses were raised, thank yous exchanged, and praise heaped as high as Rosemary's golden roast potatoes. Music played all afternoon, chestnuts roasting and snowstorms raging, but ours was the song of crickets and frogs, laughter heard on high, and the solstice bells of bottles tossed into an empty carton by the bin.

Still, it hadn't rained.

'Do you want me to bring the fan out?' Rosemary asked Lily, who was dabbing her neck with the clean side of a napkin.

'I'll be right, love,' she said, but still complained about the heat, the flies, and the ants. I wondered how long it had been since she'd sung a carol or bitten on a sixpence.

I gave her a rose-scented candle I'd been so pleased to see in the window of the Anglican shop beside the chemist. I knew she loved her roses; if she didn't, she would have given up on them long before. Eddie was the only one who ever asked her why she grew the kinds of flowers that were bound never to grow in a place where the ground was hard as biscuit and all the rain fell in one go. She told him they reminded her of home, and Rosemary might have given him the crumbs of tales she told us about Calcutt, with its primroses and badgers, because I'd heard him wonder out loud more than once why Lily stayed; why she didn't take Norman back to the England she so loved, where Christmases were white and gardens grew; but there was more to it than that.

I gave Norman a jigsaw puzzle. *Complete* the sticker on the box promised, and I hoped it was. In the picture, a castle held fast on a hill high above a harbour with bitter grey walls. 'I've been there,' Norman said quietly, and he pressed the flat of his hand on the box as if it were a window.

'We didn't get you anything,' Lily said, as if to get was why a person gave a gift.

I sent a parcel home the first year we were gone, a brown-papered box with gifts carefully chosen but I don't know if it was unwrapped, or if it was binned with the turkey's carcass, or thrown onto a fire in a drum. I might have sent one again the following year, but Sonny stopped me. 'Save your money,' he said, meaning his money. 'She'll think what she wants to think, no matter what you do.' Better to forget her, he meant. Better to forget them all. So, I bought for him, and he bought for me; and after him, and after a while, I bought for Catherine and for Mrs Robinson. Little things.

It was nice to give a little more.

Books to the Lambs. Emily Brontë, John Grisham, Sara Henderson, Di Morrissey and Wilbur Smith—I found them all in the Anglican shop.

'I haven't read a book in years,' Eddie said (again). *I don't read*, was what he meant. *You shouldn't have.*

'I know,' I told him. *But you should.* I'd found something he'd like, if he'd only give it twenty pages.

Nola told him he ought to be ashamed of himself, turning her own book over as Eddie began to open something else.

They gave me a wide-brimmed hat that cast my whole face in the shade.

'You can throw that other thing out now,' Leonie said, laughing, but Rosemary was quick to shush her. I put a hand up to my head and felt the familiar thread and weave I wore beneath crepe paper.

'Yes, I will,' I said, but I was fairly sure I wouldn't.

We played charades. Rosemary had filled a sock with movie titles handwritten on pieces of paper triple-folded into rectangles. She guessed right more than anyone else, but everyone took a turn, and she held her suggestions back so they were never first or loudest.

Nola fell asleep and Eddie woke her for the cake, which was hers to cut. Leonie carried it outside. Lily followed carrying her pavlova, and Rosemary came behind her with the trifle her mother used to make.

In their creased crowns, they were like the three kings offering gold, frankincense and myrrh, and there was a quiet competition between them, so I had a little of everything, even though I would have been more comfortable squeezing in nothing more at all.

Norman reached for the trifle, but Lily pushed the big bowl out of reach and instead passed him a sliver of Jean's frosted cake. 'He's not a fan of custard,' she explained. 'You're not a fan of custard, are you?' she reminded him, and he looked surprised, as if he hadn't known.

'I like a chocolate custard,' Eddie said. 'They should add it to the stuff they make here at the factory. It'd sell well at Christmas, chocolate custard. Your fella thought it was a good idea.'

'Whose fella?' asked Leonie.

Eddie flicked a hand at Rosemary and Mary, who were covering what was left of the pavlova. 'Their boss, what's-his-name—we were talking at the Christmas party.'

Rosemary's shock was crystal clear. 'This year? Last week?' And we all laughed at her surprise.

The conversation wandered towards the factory, and which of what they produced were people's favourites, and that's when Lily touched my hand and whispered: 'You can leave, you know.'

For a moment I thought she meant the party and, wondering why I'd thought to come, I half-raised myself up out of the chair I'd been comfortable in, before she pushed me back down with a firm hand on my knee and more than a hint of frustration.

'This place,' she hissed. 'Magpie Beach. You're free to go whenever you want. Just you remember that.' She spoke quietly but her words were firm and formed carefully, one at a time, like bubbles. 'You could go somewhere else and start again. There are other ways. There are other places. You're not tied up here like she is.'

We both looked at Rosemary, who was still questioning Eddie, wondering what else he might have said to her boss at their Christmas party.

'I'm too old,' Lily said, 'but you could do it, you know. All you have to do is drag that car out of the weeds and pull yourself together. There's a big world out there, you know.'

I knew. I'd seen glimpses of it. Heard talk. Imagined myself once upon a time exploring its here and there. Re-reading *The Count of Monte Cristo* in the spring shade of the Eiffel Tower, Dickens with a cup of tea from a flask and my feet in the Thames.

'Have a little faith in it,' Lily said.

A little faith, like cream in an otherwise ordinary cup of coffee.

Lily left soon after that, which was time enough before the evening ended for it to seem too soon, the sweet mess of dessert not yet cleared and Norman knee to knee with Tom, laughing with his mouth wide open. Leonie was sitting back in her chair with her feet up on another, Nola had dropped back to sleep and was snoring softly. Muddy was telling a story, arms flailing, and face pulled into a look of shock or terror, Mary's eyes wide as she nodded validity to the tale, which involved a spear gun and a triggerfish which charged with force enough to crack the tempered glass of Muddy's mask. Lily stood up, quite suddenly, as if a whistle called her in a pitch too high for anyone else to hear.

'We must be going,' she said. 'Time for cocoa and bed, I think.' She thanked everyone, took Norman by the hand and led him away.

'Hang on and I'll walk you, love,' Tom called out, pushing his feet into his thongs, but they were well on their way, 'We're right, thanks,' thrown over Lily's shoulder like salt.

'There's more to them than meets the eye.' Nola was awake again.

'You're not wrong there,' Leonie said. 'Those shoes.' She chuckled, but there was fondness in it.

'She doesn't like spiders,' Rosemary tried to explain. That was why. That was why you never saw her in thongs or sandals. That was why she took them off at her own front door and banged them on the decking and sprayed them—so there'd be no nasty surprises for her next time.

'She wraps them up,' I said, and at once wished that I hadn't.

'She what?' All eyes were on me, and Leonie, who'd sat up tall to straighten a kink in her back, leaned forward, all attention.

'Nothing,' I tried, but she put her hand in the hole I'd opened.

'Not nothing,' she said. 'You might as well tell us now. She wraps her shoes?' Fingers scrambling for purchase, she was laughing, and I looked to Rosemary for help.

'She doesn't like spiders,' Rosemary repeated.

'So, she wraps her shoes?' Leonie gave a little snort of delight. 'In paper?'

'Maybe,' I tried again.

'In plastic,' Rosemary cut in, and she gave me a tight little smile. In for a penny in for a pound, but it was gossipy and disloyal, and we both knew I had started it.

Tom just laughed, happy to stay barefoot and where he was. Muddy cleared his throat and Rosemary jumped in, prompting him to go on with his story, and the light of Lily's torch dotted its way out of sight.

Tom and Leonie were spending the night in their caravan. Nola was sleeping with Rosemary, and Eddie was taking the couch.

No one wanted to drive after all the beer and wine and Baileys, and with Tom having one glass eye.

I never learned how he'd lost the real one. It was one of those rare secrets swallowed like a ring on a beach. If Catherine knew, she never told. I never asked, and for everything she shared there was plenty she kept in her pockets.

'He shouldn't really drive at all,' Leonie said.

'Bullshit,' Tom began to argue. 'Six-twelve vision, in one eye or two. There's nothing that says I can't.'

'Well, there's that bit about peripheral vision, Dad,' Eddie reminded him.

'There's too many fucking rules is what there is!' Muddy grumbled, and he raised his bottle towards Tom in quiet solidarity, though sitting where he was, on Tom's left, I don't know that Tom could see it.

'There are too many kangaroos,' Rosemary said.

'Twice as many after what he's drunk,' Muddy joked, and Tom was lost to a fit of coughing that hadn't been his first.

'You need to get that checked, Dad,' Eddie said, but Tom wiped the comment away with a tissue he dug out of his pocket, and Leonie changed the subject.

'I hit a cow once.'

Tom was still clearing his throat but, 'We don't want to hear about that now,' he managed. Something you say when you don't want to hear it again yourself.

'He was a big bastard. Made a helluva mess.'

'We really don't need to hear this story, Mum,' Eddie said, and he and Tom shouted her down with jolly jeers and sweet distractions. I remember thinking that if it was a cow she'd hit, it would have been a she.

I slept in my clothes that night—beneath the bottlebrush, not even on a blanket. It was the first Christmas in twelve years that I had not spent alone. Company came on the breeze. Laughter exploding as Muddy shouted the punchline of a joke. I don't know how late he and Mary stayed, or which of them drove the little yellow scooter home. Perhaps they spent the night on chairs pressed together, or cushions patched together on the floor, and left with Tom, Leonie and Nola in the morning.

Right before I fell into the treacle of sleep, there came a high and rasping scream. I heard Mary's and Rosemary's fright, and laughter reassuring them. Others knew the barn owl's call, the sweetheart markings on his face, his ghostlike spread of wing.

Twice he called.

I knew the rhyme—*One only maybe, two brings a baby, three for no bread, four someone's dead*—and I smiled at the thought of a baby among us.

There was a distant, over-ocean rumbling. Black cockatoos were roosting low. Leaves had rolled. The barn owl shrieked again.

And again.

Something of a storm was coming.

CHAPTER NINETEEN
Meg

A new year melted in, and the brown mud flooding started.

Once the rain began, it barely stopped. It rained morning, noon, and night. Great fat drops that fell straight down and warmed and softened everything they landed on like wax; gorging the bush until even the most sheltered trees were dark and dank, and the ground beneath a mush that spat like porridge underfoot.

Sometimes I woke and in the purple of night wondered what had woken me. I'd lie still and listen hard before realising it was the no-noise-at-all. The rain had stopped, its gush replaced by a timpani of drips, and I'd drift off back to sleep relieved that maybe the lettuce would recover and the tomatoes fruit after all, only to wake in the morning to the too-familiar hiss and a suspicion in myself that, like the arms that crept around me when I slept, I had been dreaming and it hadn't stopped at all, not even for a second.

Winifred flooded as it always did, year after dripping, drowning year, only this time it was later and this time it was worse. This time Carney's had to close for a week because of all the water. The carpet was ruined and the paper in the lounge bar puckered and peeled off the wall in strips.

The rain poured on and on. It flowed through the streets and the lake turned red and crept up around its edges. Homes were evacuated as roofs collapsed, gardens slid and sank, and the river mouths at Milligan and Guilder were thick with bark and branch and bits of garden furniture.

And still it rained.

Mr Breadsell stood buckets in the damper corners of the theatre, and ticket takings dwindled as people found more pressing things to do with their wet Tuesday mornings.

By February, they were calling it The Flood, the Biggest and the Best, the most there'd ever been. Comparing every figure with years past, and with what had fallen elsewhere, the *Courier* took an honest pride in printing that what we were getting was the very worst there was. Front-page after front-page after front-page story: WORST FLOODING IN THIRTY YEARS. WORST FLOODING IN FORTY YEARS! LAKE CARNEY AT AN ALL-TIME HIGH. PLANS FOR PREMIER TO VISIT. By the end of it, more rain had fallen than had caused the flood of 1936, the one with all the capitals.

Flooding had never really bothered us at Magpie Beach. The water from the higher land wore a path down through the bush in places, but we'd all been careful not to plant our homes in the way. I was the only one who felt the brown mud flooding that year, because it was The Flood and not just a flood; because more rain was falling on the headland than had ever done before.

For the first time, I had to barricade my home with bags of sand. They lay like corpses in a pile two, three, four deep, after a while, absorbing water from the sticky skirt of mush that gathered around the caravan until I had to pile logs up beneath my bedroom window and come and go through that.

'It'll pass,' Eddie said, but it didn't.

'There can't be much more, surely?' Lily said, but still there seemed to be.

It was a Thursday morning when the big slide came. The bus was late, the rain coming down so hard on the highway that with wipers and headlights on full the driver still couldn't see his way to make good time. No one cared. It had been that way for weeks. The bus was almost empty, and as I felt the cool of condensation on my cheek, I closed my eyes and remembered Lily's story of the train that took her away from the wreckage of London as a little girl, north, to the hills and heather and fresh air.

Someone had to shout my eyes open when we got to the stop outside the library.

'You've not missed much,' Catherine said, as I hung my coat and backed the trolley out of its bay behind the counter. It was as scantily filled as the bus, but Catherine liked it empty, and I liked putting the books back, and the look of them in order on the shelves: Doyle next to Dove next to Dostoyevsky. (*The Brothers Karamazov*. No one ever read it.)

I never put a book back on a shelf without first fanning through its pages. People forgot their bookmarks, their ticket stubs and shopping lists, receipts and strips of paper. Through the years I'd found a couple of photos which I'd pinned up on the noticeboard with the Lost, For Sale and Babysitter flyers. I once found five dollars trapped inside a Stephen King, but my favourite was a picture postcard of a bronze lion. A Brisbane landmark, as it turned out, modelled on four in London I'd once dreamed of visiting. The lion in the postcard had his sculpted paws together and his head bowed just enough to hint at humble. He reminded me of Aslan. The postcard had been stamped and sent and I could have returned it to its owner, but I didn't really get the chance or think they'd care that it was lost. It was very old, and there was only the scribble of an appointment as a message. A meeting long passed. *March 2, 10 am, don't forget!* The curl of an initial in the corner: a *P* so exaggerated that it could have been an *A*. I used it as a bookmark myself for years, and it was tight and dry between the pages of *A Prayer for Owen Meany*, in the bag that swung on a peg beneath my coat, when Catherine led Rosemary around the corner.

'Here she is!' As if the other wouldn't have seen me if one hadn't pointed me out. Then, 'Just leave that, darl.' It's a word they use in Queensland. It sounds like doll, is short for darling, and I knew then that something terrible had happened.

My caravan was gone. Swept away, Eddie said. Like a dog on a pier, or a woman in a bonnet and in love. There were fallen trees and the rubble of a hillside in its place, and under and on top of everything a thick brown frosting of mud.

The chicken coop had travelled but its roof was visible, and I lost my shoes in the clag, running to dig for Jo, Beth, and Amy. There were other things beyond it, slabs of wall and window cracked like peanut brittle, my front door torn from its hinges, the legs of a chair—its seat upside down and deeper, the water tank still upright, and Eddie, up to his waist in it all and wrestling with a rope he'd tied around my chest of drawers, which as it turned out was the heaviest of everything I'd ever owned.

'Stop!' Rosemary shouted above the weather. It was still raining. It didn't stop to see the damage it had done. Broken glass and bare feet. 'Meg, stop!'

Eddie turned, words lost in hiss and spatter but shouting too, shaking his head.

And I stopped, and Rosemary came to cradle me in her arms, and we sat together in the filth that had been my home.

It was the only thing saved: that chest of drawers that we heaved out on the end of a rope like a cow, Eddie, Rosemary, and me, steaming in the rain. We carried it up and onto their porch, which is where Mrs Robinson found us days later, and where Rosemary and Lily and I went through its drawers together. There wasn't much in them: jerseys and socks, underwear and a thick winter blanket. Useful enough, but not what I'd have filled them with if I'd known I was to lose everything else I owned. There'd been books (so many books); letters and cards and ticket stubs in a box I'd pulled from under the bed on my loneliest nights. There'd been a teddy Sonny had cuddled in his crib and grown to give me, and a lock of his hair trapped in a pillowslip. All gone, out on the tide like a message in a bottle.

'At least you've got some clothes,' Lily said.

And, incredibly, some photos. The last ones taken—in the bottom drawer, kept dry between the pages of *Grant's Guide to Fishes*, which had never made it to a shelf. A gift I'd bought before the sickness came, so that the birthday didn't really. At least there had been some small recognition of a day, with cake and song, but by then a gift like *Grant's Guide* would have been too cruel. By that last birthday, we both knew he'd never fish or dive again.

Inside it, in a still-crisp paper sleeve, twenty-four photographs and four strips of negatives.

We'd been at Magpie Beach three and a half years. The Christmas tree had been out of its box four times, and Sonny would be dead in eight months, though we didn't know it then. There were no dizzy spells or headaches.

Five days we spent in a cabin on a beach, where we swam all morning, drank all afternoon, and whispered half the night. Twenty-four photographs: pinky purple skies, and plates of food, a bat hanging under a bathroom sink, a towel twisted into a swan—and Sonny.

Sonny dressed for dinner, in the shirt I'd bought him, only half a joke with its pineapples and parrots, soft on strong brown shoulders.

Sonny caught by surprise and freshly woken, between morning-bright sheets.

Sonny standing in shallow water, waves lapping at his ankles.

Sonny sitting on a towel, his face hidden in the shadow of a pine tree, but the tilt of his head and the slope of his back telling everything, saying, *Enough now, Megs. Put it down.*

'What was he like?' Rosemary asked. Sonny and I, shoulder to shoulder. Both of us squinting at a stranger. He would have handed her the camera; did she mind? It was always him: *Can I go first? Is that seat taken?* 'You don't know if you don't ask,' he used to say.

The same beach then, but without us. The blur of a monitor lizard, another shade of sunrise, and then Sonny and I together again for the last time. The picture taken by a waitress whose outline was reflected in my glasses. A half-carafe of red wine and a half-eaten fisherman's basket on the table between us, we were halfway through our supper, and our lives were almost over, but who would know a thing like that outside Mr Breadsell's enchanted darkness? If she'd known, would the waitress have framed the picture better? Held the camera in steadier hands? Would we have ordered the champagne?

No one lives for today. For some days, perhaps, but not every day, and rarely the days that matter.

Who knows how tenderly King Cole might have made love the night he was smashed and smeared across the Bruce Highway? And what about Jessie Else? Did she have a proper breakfast the day she skipped school? When she left the table, did her parents tell her that she'd never grow up big and strong with just a sparrow's appetite?

They might have, because they wouldn't have suspected for a moment that she'd done all the growing she was ever going to do. That what mattered in that instant—in those few, precious moments they had left with her—was that she really felt the arms they wrapped around her and the kisses that they buried in her hair.

The holiday I held there in my hands should have been the first of many, pasted in an album on the far left of a shelf. But we were living our last—that wordless sequence in a movie, the winding-down of a farewell, though in the movie they would have ordered the champagne because they would have known.

If only life were like that. It's what Lily said to Mr Breadsell, and he'd questioned it, when he should have known better.

The screen door rattled as Rosemary backed her way out through it. Her fingers were hot and damp from the mugs she set in front of us, and when she took a biscuit from the packet Lily handed her, her thumb melted its print into the chocolate.

'What was he like?' she asked again.

What was he like?

How many beans in the jar?

Describe blue.

He was kind and funny and warm to touch. The first thing that mattered every morning and the last at night; he was my sunrise and my sunset. He climbed first and waited with strong arms.

'He was everything,' I said. And that was more than I'd ever said to anyone about him. He was a secret that might not exist out loud, something that could fly away on a breeze or be swept away on a tide of mud and rain like an old caravan.

The last drawer was almost empty when Rosemary spoke again. The clothes lay in piles on the floor: lights and darks, waiting to be washed. There was plenty of water. The tanks had been overflowing for a month.

'Do you miss him?'

Do I breathe?

'Every day.'

Rosemary was quiet for a long moment before she asked, 'What if he wasn't dead? Do you think missing him would have felt the same?'

'What's that supposed to mean?' Lily scoffed, but I thought I knew what Rosemary was asking.

If he'd chosen to leave, would that have hurt me more?

'I don't know,' I told them honestly, but it was a question that burrowed in, because he would have left eventually. I had always known it. What we'd had would not have been enough for him forever, and when he'd gone then, would missing him have felt the same?

Rosemary was watching me, palms pink around her steaming mug. 'Worse?' she wondered.

Could anything have possibly been worse?

'I think so,' I said.

He was my best friend and my turkey carver. He held my hands and helped me up and stood in front and waited while I drew deep breaths. 'Let me worry about that,' he used to say. 'Leave it to me.' And I left so much that in the end all I had was what he'd shown me, and it was not enough, I was not ready. I don't think I would have survived his leaving me. If he'd chosen to go, dropped his arms and stepped over my pieces, left me wondering what he might be doing, every day, and whether he was happier without me; wondering whether he might be missing something of me; wondering if he might come back. The not-knowing would have finished me.

CHAPTER TWENTY

Meg

Eddie brought the paper back from town and slid it across his cluttered kitchen table. 'Don't get upset,' he warned me. 'It's actually really nice.'

They hadn't got much of a picture: a grey wash of mud with a couple of books, semi-submerged, that hadn't been mine. 'I expect the reporter threw them in there,' Eddie said when I wondered where they'd come from, and I wondered then whether she'd fished them out again afterwards.

LOCAL CHARACTER LOSES HOME.

Meg of Magpie Beach, they called me. I didn't need a surname. I was like Stig of the Dump, or the Bunyip of Berkeley's Creek.

There was a man in Christchurch whom everyone knew as the Director. He planted himself in the middle of random intersections from time to time and directed traffic. He wore a white helmet and rubber gloves, and he waved his arms extravagantly and might be seen in any type of weather. He wasn't a nuisance. He didn't jump in front of cars or spit-swear or expose himself. It was almost a treat to see him, like a rainbow. 'There's the Director!' people on one side of the bus would cry, and everyone would turn their heads and chuckle fondly. When he died, *The Star* called him a Local Character, and in the course of one morning we discovered he'd been a pilot and fought in a terrible war, lost a wife and a daughter in a fire, and died alone wrapped in newspaper.

'It makes you think, doesn't it?' my mother said, but no one thought for more than a minute about it. There were other Local Characters: Gregor Monk who stood in his robes on a box outside the bus station, and the man with the elephant foot who lived in Hagley Park. No one thought any more about them than they ever had about the Director.

The Carney Courier printed what they found of my own story. No family, they wrote. It's what Sonny and I had told the few people we'd told anything at all. It's what I'd told Sergeant Scanlan, all those years ago. A close friend told them I was 'devastated' and 'left with nothing'.

'It wasn't me,' Rosemary was quick to say.

'It wasn't anyone,' Lily scoffed. 'You won't believe the lengths they'll go to for a bit of dirt.' And I imagined men in raincoats burrowing through my rubbish, winding car seats all the way back in waiting, camera snipers hidden in the bushes. But I wasn't a celebrity, and it wasn't that sort of story, and Eddie was right—the things they wrote were not unkind.

Things began to arrive quietly in the night and early morning. Plastic bags and boxes, skirts and cardigans, a warm yellow nightdress (brand-new with its tag still on), tinned food, blankets and three sleeping bags, dropped at the turn-off on the highway. Some came with short notes tucked inside: *Thought you might be able to use this. Hope this helps. Thinking of you.* There was never a name, or a return address, and I was as grateful to them all for that as I was for the gifts themselves, because I wouldn't easily have managed in the face-to-face of so much kindness.

Pots and pans and plates and books. Someone brought a sofa chair all the way out. Too big for any bag, and I suppose they might have worried it would spoil in the rain. It had a torn arm that was nothing to mend. I heard them dragging it off the back of their ute, but it was Eddie who went outside. 'Good on you, mate,' I heard him say.

The sky turned violet then pink then blue, and white whispery clouds sat thinner and higher until Lake Carney backed down William Street, and within a fortnight all the towels were dry. It was as if there'd never been a flood. Except that my home was gone, and many other people's homes were spoiled, and another woman who lived alone had somehow drowned in her own kitchen. She'd been there nine days before anyone thought to check on her, though that wasn't in the newspaper. Sergeant Scanlan told Catherine everything, I think, as he'd taken my story home to her the morning, long ago, when he'd thought to check on me. And I knew, somewhere deeper than the things I said out loud, that it was Catherine who'd called the *Courier*. She'd given them my story in exchange for the help she'd known would come.

CHAPTER TWENTY-ONE

Rosemary

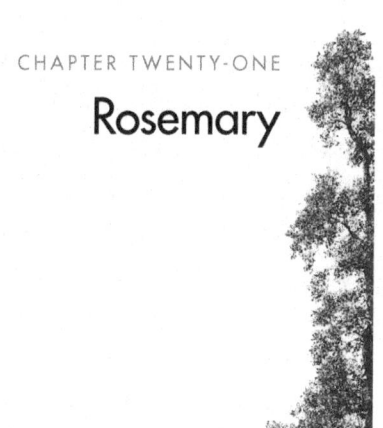

I'd never had particularly green thumbs. My garden was only ever pots and baskets and the types of plants they had in bulk buys on pallets outside the supermarket. I grew cress once on the kitchen windowsill, but I don't know why I bought the packet; it wasn't something I liked, and when it grew I didn't eat it (it looked too much like pubic hair). So, I've no idea how I came to be the one helping Meg put her garden back together after the mudslide.

Lily would have been much better at it. Some days she came around and sat on a big stone to watch us, happy telling us what to do (or, more specifically, what was wrong with the way we were doing it), but not about to work beside us on her knees, even though we offered her a square of carpet to save her pants.

'I'm not stopping,' she'd say. 'I just came over to drop this off,' or check about that or borrow a bit of sugar. But we knew it was the company she came for. Once Lily started leaving her little house, she seemed less and less enthusiastic about going back to it.

Outside her own front door, Lily grew stand-up, straight-stemmed flowers that reminded her of England, though she must have known she'd do better with the sort of plants that like to grow over and down the sides of pots and don't need rods and ribbons to hold them all together. I think she needed those little bits of faraway: roses and hankies and tea in a pot. Eddie, Leonie and Tom and Nola, all shook their heads and rolled their eyes and wondered why she didn't go back if it was so much nicer in England, but Meg and I heard all of Lily's stories, even the bits she skipped on purpose. We knew Lily's little corner co-op had grown up into a great big supermarket where you could buy as much sugar as you wanted. The fields she ran through as a little girl were covered now in houses, and a bypass ran through the woods. Foxes froze in the path of oncoming cars, and the few badgers which had survived all that were baited into torchlight and torn apart by square-faced dogs. There was nothing left of the England Lily missed.

Meg moved into Tom and Leonie's caravan. 'For the time being,' they told her, but I don't think they were all that bothered about getting it back. They were fond of Meg. We all were, but Tom and Leonie had a better memory of who she'd been before.

Carter Young came out with his bobcat and helped us level the ground. We barrowed soil to the water's edge and Tom backed the caravan onto the slab that Meg and Sonny had thrown down eighteen years before.

'We won't be going anywhere for a while,' Leonie said, as we stood out of the way and Eddie and Carter chocked the caravan.

Tom wasn't well. 'It's just a cough,' he'd told us all at Christmas, but it hadn't been. There'd been blood tests and fluids drained since then. Next thing, they'd send a needle in under his arm.

Their caravan was nicer than Meg's had been. It was newer, for a start, with a pop-top and an awning. She wouldn't use the toilet (her long drop was still good), but there was a shower Eddie said he'd work a way to hook up to her water tank. There was a full gas oven, grill and cooktop where all she'd had before was a single burner, and it came with plates and cups and cutlery, and pots and pans. I don't think it was quite as long as Meg's own caravan had been, but it had been plenty big enough for Eddie and me when we'd lived in it, and Meg was much smaller than either of us. I missed the doll's house of it. The two-of-everything and the place for everything and everything in its place. I liked the space of Maggie Beach, the big sky and the tall trees that we'd come for, and I loved our little house, but I worried sometimes at the roots that we were putting down. The ties I knew would bind us. (The ties that would bind me.)

If it had been up to me, Eddie and I would have hitched that caravan onto the car and driven off long ago. Eddie laughed when I'd suggested it once. 'Where would we go?' There was no point answering that. It's not that I wanted to go somewhere and come back, which was what he was asking: where did I want to go *to*. But I didn't want to go *to* anywhere in particular. I just wanted to *go*.

Eddie didn't want to go anywhere. It wasn't just abroad that put him off. Long before we got together, he'd worked a while in a sawmill on the edge of Crediton State Forest, but that was the longest he was ever out of Carney County.

'What was it like?' I asked him once.

'Well, there were a lot of trees,' he said. It was where he'd had the accident that left him with his limp, so he didn't really like to talk about it, and I didn't push.

Two of Meg's chickens came home, and we built a short maze of low walls with the rocks the mud brought down, and a sheet of corrugated iron turned it into a henhouse. It was Eddie's design, with boxes and ramps he cut to measure in his shed. He was a clever thinker. When we started going out, he was always full of ideas, tucking napkin sketches into his pockets, stripping the side off a beer mat so he could jot down a thought that had come to him mid-pint. He planned the house for months while we saved up the money to actually buy the wood and board and tools to build it, and he did most of the building himself even with his bung leg. And after that—well, he had all sorts of plans. There was going to be an ocean ladder, an outside shower and a boat ramp. We were going to save for a boat eventually—that was the Lotto Dream—but when we moved out to Maggie Beach, everything slowed down. I thought it was normal to begin with, after all the work he'd done on the house: the planning, and the actual up-to-the-elbows building and plastering and painting. I thought it was understandable he'd want a break from that sort of thing, and he went to work on his horses. But it ran deeper than that. It was like he'd come to the end of a road. There were no more napkin sketches; plans for the ocean ladder and the shower were lost in a box. It was all 'sun's past the yardarm', and 'I wonder what the rich folk are doing!' So it was nice to see him get excited about Meg's henhouse. It was nice to see that light go on again, even if it didn't stay on very long.

If I'm honest, it was the same for me. Around Eddie, at least, I hadn't much of a spark. We'd just sort of wound down. It was like we needed picking up and revving a few times, pushed hard down on a tabletop, like a couple of toys from a Happy Meal.

Those kisses you see in the movies, where the girl stands on one leg and bends the other up behind her, and the man cradles her face in his hands as he loses himself completely in the dewiness of her eyes—that wasn't us.

I wondered if that was just what happened when you'd been with someone for a while: you slowed down and settled. I watched other people going about their married lives and I compared Eddie and me, secretly, but I didn't know many other couples, and people don't act the same in public as they do behind closed doors, so I could never properly see what they were like together anyway. When I saw Catherine and Mike Scanlan in the street, they were always holding hands, but I didn't know if that meant they were as happy with each other as they had been in the beginning. I didn't know if that meant she'd never cringed inwardly at something he'd said, or pretended to be asleep when he pushed his sweaty belly up against her back in the middle of the night. I didn't know if Leonie laughing at all Tom's jokes meant that she'd never said she had a headache when she didn't, or 'I love you' when she wasn't ten-out-of-ten, swear-on-her-mother's-life sure about it anymore. I'd never seen Meg with Sonny, but I'd heard about them, and anyone with half a heart could imagine the way they must have been for her to have become the way she was without him.

When Mary and Muddy came at Christmas, I watched the way they were together. She didn't just hand him a beer, she took its top off and wiped the condensation with the hem of her dress, and she took his empty bottle even though he was standing closer to the bin. She watched his face for needs and wants while we ate. The wrinkle of his nose and an eyebrow raised: pass the salt. A finger tapping towards the ham, once, twice: two slices. She scurried around him, rubbed his back, took his hand, moved his chair when he stood up. 'I am very grateful,' she'd told me when we first met, standing in the rain waiting for him to row across and get her the morning he slept in and forgot to pick her up from work. She told everyone on Christmas Day, when Muddy told us how they'd met, what he'd found when he sailed in to Pabo Bay in Masbate, and I understood, I really did. Mary was grateful for the life she led now having led the life she'd led before, in a place where everything was the same as it had always been, where there was no ham to pass, no condensation, no electricity, and little chance of any other future. Grateful to God, but mostly to the man who'd swept her away from all of that and into a new life, like Richard Gere.

I suppose I was thankful to Eddie: for marrying me and giving me a name I had a right to call my own; for taking me out of Winifred and away to Maggie Beach, even though it wasn't very far. But it wasn't out loud the way Mary's grateful was. And it wasn't enough for me, the way anyone could see it was more than enough for Mary.

Not anymore.

The dream began to shift. I stopped wishing for Richard Gere and I started thinking bigger, thinking smarter. Dreaming things that had a chance of actually coming true. Considering my options. Making plans.

There's a lot of time for thinking when you're gardening.

Within a few weeks bright shoots began to spring up. Leaves unfurled, and creepers pushed across the soil and up the canes we'd shoved into the dirt. I looked forward to the fluff of baby potatoes, the sweet pop of cherry tomatoes and corn on the cob, crispy lettuce and snapping celery, pumpkin seeds and soup—but as it turned out, most of what we planted never made it into our mouths.

CHAPTER TWENTY-TWO

Meg

After all the rain that had fallen, the trees that fruited first were heavy, and the early evening sky was thick with bats. There was a hum of bees, so we knew the trees and vines that fruited later would be laden too. Green vegetables needed saving from cabbage moths and caterpillars, and Rosemary and I spent much time peppering outer leaves and souring soil with onion water.

Mrs Robinson grew fatter and fatter in the sun and disappeared for five days towards the end of May, returning proud and hungry with a sagging soft-fur belly and an appetite for fish.

I thought Rosemary might like a kitten. Maybe Lily too, though spiders seemed to worry her more than mice or rats. I would put another sign up on the library noticeboard: *Free to a good home*, though I wondered how anyone could ever tell at a glance if a person had one. I don't know that I'd have been given a kitten that was only to go to a *good* home, but Mrs Robinson was happy. *Free to a good person*, I thought I might write on the card this time. Free to a *loving* home.

She led me to her babies. Tiptoeing ahead, she took me up the steep, green strip the mudslide had made way for. Spindly trees and shrubs and grasses grew, gorging on sunlight which hadn't touched the ground in who knew how long. I was surprised how far she'd wandered. Straight up we went and into bush that had hung on tighter. The ocean spread out behind us, still as treacle, lapis blue; you couldn't see the oysters or the mud or the no-beach.

There were four kittens, bundled in a mossy nest my clever girl had built between the roots of a tree. Small and helpless, their eyes glued tight, and when I bent to lift them into the sweatered box I'd brought to take them home, I saw that one of them was dead. His matchstick ribs not moving, and his open mouth already filled with ants, he was his mother's scribbly brown, and I carried him off a little way to where candy orchids grew in longer grass.

I saw it as I threw him. Half dug up at the foot of a strangler fig. A lump of garden-grade plastic bag and fabric.

I wouldn't have seen it if I'd turned the other way.

I wouldn't have known what it was, if it hadn't been worried by paws and claws, if its wrapping had not been torn apart. I might have thought it was only rubbish dumped.

If it hadn't been so close, if the bush that led there hadn't been so thinned by summer storms, I might not have seen the stump of what was left.

'If ifs and ands were pots and pans there'd be no need for tinkers,' my grandmother used to say, but if Mrs Robinson hadn't had her kittens where she did, if the littlest of them had survived, if the rain hadn't fallen all at once and scraped a path down through the bush, they might never have found Jessie Else at all.

CHAPTER TWENTY-THREE

Meg

We didn't eat the vegetables. Rosemary and I pulled them all up out of the soil, forked and raked the roots and bulbs, and fed them to the fish. Then we turned the earth all over on itself and left the rain to rinse it through. Not that there'd be rain for a while, but we would wait. It was the least we could do.

'There's a lot of water's come down that hill,' Eddie said. Meaning maybe only a capful came through the dead girl. You've had tomatoes on your plates already, and what you didn't know then didn't hurt you. But even Nathan Carney dammed his river higher than he set the cemetery, and we'd planted right beside Tom and Leonie's caravan, which stood on the rectangle of cement that marked the spot my own had been. The one that was pushed by land that left the track I'd followed all the way to what was left of Jessie Else.

It didn't seem right for us to eat the vegetables.

Eddie watched us wheel the shoots and tangled roots away and shook his head, but he didn't make a fuss. More seeds, more shovelling and tending, nothing he would have to do, and nothing at all really anyway compared to the body itself, and the fact that it had been there with us all along.

They must have driven down Shank Lane and pulled into our clearing and dragged her little body up into the dark. Had it been dark? I hadn't heard them (hadn't stopped them). Who knew when they'd come? They might have had her for weeks or months. They might have brought her with them still alive, bound and gagged and unimaginably afraid.

'She'll have been dead already,' Eddie said. But she might not have been. They might have killed her right there where I found her, in among the sweet grasses and moss, though there would have been more brush than bed back then; the year had yet to tear it open. I wondered would they have walked her up, or carried her slung over one shoulder like a sack of coal?

'No,' Rosemary said. Just no.

More likely they'd killed her somewhere else, somewhere they knew better, stuffed her into that sack by handfuls like a sleeping bag, brought her out to dump her and then driven home to a wife, perhaps—to a life, anyway.

The police came—great hordes of them, in fluorescent vests, and with dogs, and they walked a slow line up the hill looking for any tiny thing that didn't belong.

Then came the journalists and officers in plain clothes and in pairs this time, like Starsky and Hutch, and they came inside our houses and asked a lot more questions than they had the year before.

Did I put my cat out at night?

At about what time did I do that (if I did it) and what time did I go to bed, as a rule?

Was I a churchgoer?

Did I have a boyfriend (had I ever had a boyfriend)?

Did I have a drink ever at all (one, two or three)?

They were more experienced, Catherine said, and they needed to be because after more than a year of nothing, suddenly here was something. Here was everything.

The journalists parked their vans as close as they were able and drank tea from plastic cups while they waited for something to happen, but the body was long gone, taken carefully and quietly before too many people knew it had been found.

The story was all over the radio and in the papers, and Catherine said it was all over the television too. Helicopter vision and 'just a lot of dust flying', she said, but there was more than dust in the air.

I was the Local who'd 'discovered the remains'. The *Courier* used a photograph they'd taken in the library after the flood to print beside a letter I'd sent to the editor, thanking everyone for all the help and kind notes they'd sent me. This time they printed Lily's picture too (an angry face too slow to pull a curtain), and Eddie and Rosemary's wedding portrait. But the words they chose began to change the flavour until it was something bitter and too-sticky that was being stirred in the pot.

The police took Eddie away for further questioning, wanting answers too big for a kitchen table. They'd bring him back when they were finished with him, they told Rosemary. Not 'when he's answered all our questions'. Not 'when he's helped us with our inquiries'. *When we've finished with him*, as if he was yesterday's paper. But they called him Mr Lamb and Sir and held the car door open while he climbed in like a family friend, so we were not alarmed.

I was relieved when they dropped him home later that same afternoon, but I knew they hadn't finished with him, because for all its Secret Santas, Winifred was still a meat-and-potatoes town, and Eddie living in Magpie Beach (where there were few magpies and there was no beach) with a wife not the full Aussie made, neighbours not all there, or a bit-of-a-handful; people were going to talk, and two and two can make a lot more than four given enough pointing fingers.

CHAPTER TWENTY-FOUR

Rosemary

I knew I was pregnant before I did the test, but I didn't tell Eddie. I didn't tell anyone. I didn't even go to Dr Shaw. I knew what he'd say, and it would start with: 'Congratulations!'

I'd been pregnant once before, not long after we were married, and everyone got so excited and started buying things, and then I miscarried and let them all down.

Dr Shaw would want to see me in six weeks. 'Eat properly, stop drinking, don't smoke.'

I hadn't smoked since I'd given up the last time, and not drinking is as easy as filling an empty can with water.

I think at the start I kept it a secret because of what had happened before, when everybody knew too soon, so when I lost the baby everybody had to know that too. The nurses said it was a common thing, but I still felt like it was my fault. Something I'd done unintentionally, or something that was wrong with me that would come to light after two or three more messed-up goes. 'You mustn't blame yourself,' they said, but that just made me think that under the surface they were blaming me a bit as well.

'It just wasn't meant to be,' Eddie said, but he was gutted, and he made no secret of that. He wanted children more than I did—sooner than I did. I imagined them a way off in the future with the boat ramp and the outside shower, but Now was the time for Eddie. Now was the time for everyone.

'Have them young,' Leonie said. 'So you can enjoy them.'

'No good waiting till you're too old to kick the footy about with your son,' Tom said.

And it would be a son. They'd decided that. And they'd decide it again if I gave them the chance.

I reckoned I had at least twelve weeks. Three months, before I'd start to show. Before I'd have to tell. A lot can happen in twelve weeks, I thought.

And a lot did.

Mary left. She didn't give much notice. She just came in one night and handed an envelope to Shirley. There was no leaving party. They didn't even do a whip-round to buy her a card. 'That's the problem with that type,' Shirley said. 'Transients. They never stay long. You just get them trained up properly and they bugger off.'

I thought it would be nice to be a transient. To sail into town and work a while, then move on whenever I felt like it—when the town grew boring or if the people weren't so nice.

It was time to go, Muddy had said. The cyclone season was over, so they could come out of the river now and push up north. They had a plan and it slotted in with the seasons.

'I couldn't live like that,' Eddie said.

I could.

Mary and I said goodbye at the factory gate where Muddy waited on the yellow scooter which came apart and folded into pieces they stored somewhere on the boat, so they could take it everywhere they went.

Mary and I hugged for a long time and promised each other we'd write. 'You've been like a sister,' is the last thing she said to me before they zipped away, and I cried all the way home.

'It's not like you knew her that well,' Eddie said, and he was right, I hadn't known her that well, we hadn't really been like sisters, and I'd always known she'd leave, but I hadn't expected it to be so soon, and I hadn't thought that it would feel so much like curtains closing.

Mary was a small bird on the windowsill. In catching your eye, she showed you the view, let in the fresh air and the what-could-be. Not that I wanted what she had, but I envied her wings.

I cried on and off all morning, and most of that afternoon. I didn't want Eddie's baby. A Carney County baby that would keep me in Winifred for the rest of my life. A little Lamb who'd go to the same school Eddie and I went to, to be taught by the same teachers. Running home to ask me what one of them might have meant when they said, 'I remember *your* mum very well!' School runs would drag us back into the heart of town, the yellow of the egg, claggy with not-belonging.

The bar was coming down on the roller-coaster of what-would-be. I felt like I had till the count of ten, and then there'd be no getting off.

CHAPTER TWENTY-FIVE

Meg

Five horses stood patiently side by side on still rockers in Eddie's workshop, their plaited tails gathering daddy-long-legs. Two hadn't sold at Calliope, and three more had grown since Christmas, but the winter market was coming up in Theodore. Two markets were enough, Eddie said. It took such a long time to make them, and he couldn't transport more than half-a-dozen without damage. Not everyone who looked would buy. Not everyone had space enough in their car, or money enough in their pockets.

Theodore was seven hours south-west of Carney County, so Eddie would spend the night before the market in a motel. Rosemary wasn't going with him this time. 'I have to work,' she said, but she said it carefully, and I wondered.

'Take a couple of days off,' Lily told her. 'Let the gossip die down.' As if forty-eight hours would make a difference. A mountain out of a molehill, Lily called it. 'It'll blow over as fast as they've blown it up.' And we all swept the dust that floured our steps and chairs in the silence that the newspeople's helicopters had left.

People had begun to talk.

Eddie wasn't sleeping well, Rosemary told us. 'It'll do him good to get away,' she said, and we nodded, but he didn't get away.

Word travels. Maybe someone at the factory had a brother with the police, or perhaps the man who made the saddles for Eddie's horses was a cousin of the Elses. Maybe Catherine asked after Rosemary, and I mentioned the market in Theodore. However it came to happen, three days before Eddie was due to leave, Sergeant Scanlan drove out to Magpie Beach and told him they'd rather he not go so far from town. 'Not just now.'

'He said it wouldn't look so good—my "running off",' Eddie told Rosemary.

'He said, under the circumstances, it might look suspicious,' Rosemary told Lily and me the next morning as we stood in the short line for our tickets at the Galaxy. Her fingers were bitten down to bleeding and she looked tired. Lost-in-the-middle-of-the-night tired.

Lily sucked her teeth, pinched her crucifix and ran it backwards and forwards on its chain, the way she did when things weren't going fast enough or quite the way she wanted them to go. It was the only necklace she was never without, while other pendants came and went. She was wearing the name: *Helen* in fine golden curls. 'Who's Helen?' Rosemary had asked her once, but Lily had shaken her head. 'Never you mind,' she'd said, and that was that. Another life, another time.

'That's ridiculous,' Lily grumbled now, but Rosemary just shrugged.

She didn't mention it again until we were settled in the Pink Fig.

'You were right,' she said then. 'About me taking a couple of days off.'

Our cheesecakes had come with a bowl of berries on the side, and Lily was distributing them fairly with a cake fork and a teaspoon she'd wiped clean with a tissue. There were five blueberries now on each plate and one left over. I expected Lily to eat it, but instead she rolled it up and out of its little bowl and all the way to the edge of the table, where she flicked it away.

I watched it land, against all odds, in the open bag of a mother too distracted by her toddler to have noticed. She'd find the mess of it much later and perhaps not even wonder how it got there. Lily wasn't wondering where it went.

'Out of sight, out of mind,' my father used to say. Laundry kicked under a bed. Bills stuffed in drawers. A wife left home alone.

'Where are you thinking of going?' Lily was asking Rosemary, as if there were a slew of choices.

'I'm going to take the horses to the winter market,' she told us. 'And I thought the two of you might like to come with me.'

CHAPTER TWENTY-SIX

Meg

'You know Norman could have stayed here,' Eddie said.

'There's a nurse who comes,' Lily told him. She'd told us all, but if Eddie believed her, I'm sure he was the only one.

I suppose she left Norman home alone with his radio. We knew he liked to listen to the BBC World Service. It was one of the few things she ever told us about him, and I suppose she left him food set on plates with plastic wrap and post-it notes. It was only for two days, but I worried at the ocean being where it was, a stumble away from a sliding door, a trip from a step. 'He's a clumsy thing,' she'd told us many times. Bruises bloomed like ink in water beneath the flare of his shirtsleeves and trouser legs. He might not have been the man she married, but he could turn a key, lie for days unnoticed.

'He could've stayed here,' Eddie said again.

Lily nodded. 'Maybe next time.' But it was plain as crackers she didn't want the two of them together anymore.

Eddie would not take the track to check on Norman. He would spend the weekend in his shed and eat alone. 'I'll be fine,' he assured Rosemary, when she wondered, but it was clear he wasn't feeling it.

He was disappointed and embarrassed and worried at the why-he-wasn't-going, which was heating up like soup.

We left just before light on the Saturday morning. Eddie stood in his open dressing-gown. Not shy to show his underpants and the high whites of his legs. The trailer had been packed, lashed and hitched the night before, and it was a Sunday market so there was no need for us to set off so soon, but Rosemary wanted to miss the traffic.

Eddie had laughed. 'What traffic?'

'We want to get a good start,' she'd told him, but that wasn't it. Rosemary wasn't one to chase to get somewhere. 'We'll stop and have a proper breakfast on the way,' she'd told Lily and me, but that wasn't it either. There was more to Rosemary's having volunteered to take the horses, and she would tell us when she was ready.

We left in that short time just before the birds wake, when the trill of night dulls, and the day will come and water will boil but not just yet. The streetlight at the end of the lane snapped off as we turned out onto the highway, and Rosemary slid Crowded House into the slit mouth of the CD player. It wasn't the first time she'd played it, and she wasn't the first person I'd heard sing along.

I remembered the day that Sonny and I drove up from Brisbane. I remembered the tapes we played and the things we talked about. Sonny sang while he drove, and I slept while he sang, and we pulled off the road every now and then to stretch our legs and eat peanut butter bread rolls and make tea.

'This is our fresh start,' he told me, and I believed him, and it was. 'You don't have to worry about anything,' he said. 'Leave it all to me.'

In thirteen years, I'd not been further south than the river mouth of Guilder, and when we passed the turn-off something twisted in the highest part of my stomach. I thought of Mrs Robinson and of night falling without me, darkening the windows and the lip around the caravan's flapping door. I imagined a stranger whispering a way through my things—fingers sticky on my kitchen counter—and I broke out in a sweat. I wound the window down a crack and rested my head on the cool cold of the glass.

Rosemary woke me after two hours, and I expected then to take the wheel and the seat she'd left warm, but we were parked along three kerbside bays on a city street. Lily was sitting rod-straight with her handbag on her lap and her lips pursed tight, straining to read the small print on the window that reflected the length of the Kingswood, and the tarp-strapped trailer that stretched behind us.

'It doesn't look much like a cafe,' she said, knowing full well it wasn't. Beneath the tick of the engine cooling down there was a rattle to her chest I hadn't heard before.

Rosemary measured her breath. 'I'm pregnant,' she said, and two raindrops plopped on the windscreen and startled us all. We should have congratulated her but we didn't, because there was more coming. There was thunder in the distance, the light rumble that comes before a deeper crack and yawn. Purple clouds were rolling in.

Lily began nodding like a dog on a dashboard. She undid her seatbelt and shuffled across the back seat and I heard her nails tapping the window behind me, pointing to the place that was not, and had never been, a cafe. The wide venetian blinds were closed, but strands of pot plant poked between the slats and their inside edges were yellow-lit. Names and letters were embossed in gold beside the door, where days and times were printed clearly.

'It says they're closed Saturdays,' Lily said.

'They open specially. Once a month. There's a doctor comes from Brisbane.'

'Because the ones up here won't do it, will they?' Lily was blunt. 'Why don't you want it? Do you think he did it?'

'Did what?'

'The girl.' Lily never said her name.

'Jessie Else?' Rosemary's eyes were saucer-wide but then they softened. 'It's not that,' she said (which wasn't no). 'It's just, I don't think I want to stay.' She looked at me when she said it. Telling Nanna you don't like her meatballs. She was leaving Magpie Beach, leaving Eddie, leaving us all.

Rain had begun to patter on the roof, louder on the tarp covering the trailer.

Lily slid back to her original spot behind Rosemary, and set her handbag on the seat beside her. She took out a crossword and a pen. 'Probably for the best then,' she said. 'But I'll wait here in the car, if you don't mind.'

CHAPTER TWENTY-SEVEN

Meg

Beneath the blinds, we could see the heels and calves of women picketing the door. Five of them had gathered as we'd waited in the Kingswood. They'd appeared like pigeons, pecked each other's cheeks, smoothed car-crumples from their seats and laps, and unrolled ugly posters that didn't match the sweetness of their voices.

A nurse had pulled us in and locked the door behind us with apologies, and Rosemary had been sent to change into socks she'd somehow known to bring along, and a gown which I supposed they'd boil-wash when the morning's work was done.

The waiting room was almost full but quiet as a church. Nervous fingers burrowed deep in handbags or flicked through magazines with minds not really focused. Knees and knuckles were studied. There were no men among us. What happened here was women's work. The girls would wash, the mothers dry, and later on, when everyone was presentable, perhaps some boys would help put things away. But perhaps they wouldn't.

Names were called and nurses in squeaky shoes led mother–daughter pairs around a corner. The heels of the mothers clacked on tile while the girls, who were not so far beyond little, tried not to skate on fluffy socks.

Chairs emptied gradually.

A clock ticked above an empty desk.

'Rosemary.'

She didn't seem to hear it.

'Rosemary?'

They said it twice, and then she stood so quickly that her chair rattled, and the few still in the waiting room looked across before remembering not to. She looked like a woman who'd woken on a bus to find she'd missed her stop—angry-frightened, like Norman in the middle of the night.

'Rosemary?' Louder still the third time and the question hardened. No longer *Which one are you*? Now: *What are you about to do?*

A second nurse had come around the corner and each looked ready for anything—wondering, I suppose, whether Rosemary might be working with the women in the street; about to tear into the surgery, rip the blinds from the windows and drag the baby-bit bin through the streets of Rockhampton to make a scene and the evening news.

Rosemary pulled her pink gown straight. Everyone was looking at her now.

'It's okay, darl,' one of the nurses whispered, and Rosemary turned to her first.

'I'm sorry,' she said. Then, 'I'm sorry,' to me, to the girls still waiting for their own names to be called. 'I'm sorry,' again, to the mothers reaching now to take small, shaking hands into their firm and capable own. 'I don't want to do it,' to no one in particular.

'You don't have to,' I heard myself saying, standing, wobbling a little as I took her arm. My hands were shaking but my eyes found hers. 'You don't have to do it,' I said again, louder than I'd ever heard myself speak. She would stay! My heart began to trot as I pictured her at Magpie Beach, growing and glowing and bringing new life to us all.

I could see the baby snug as a bug in a blanket, bottle feedings shared. A swing strung from a lemon gum. A little girl in scuffed pants, picking strawberries and shelling beans and showering the world around her with all the bells and glitter of her joy. Or a little boy perhaps, knee-deep in puddles, hours into a book beneath a tree. Crabs in buckets and worms in pockets, piggybacks and bedtime stories. Christmases and birthdays. Years of magic rolled out before me like Solomon's carpet.

It may have been seconds or minutes. Between nurses, Rosemary had been led away, and I scooped our bags like parcels and ran to catch up, my heart still cantering like a pony.

CHAPTER TWENTY-EIGHT

Rosemary

'What made you change your mind?' Lily asked me, and I told her I didn't know but that wasn't really true.

There was a nurse at the clinic, the one who let us in, the same one who took me through to change out of my clothes. There was a robe on a chair and it was one of those one-size-fits-all things that you put on like a hairdresser's cape, but it had arms that looked like neck holes, and long ties that went through slits in the seams and wrapped around you, and I put it on all wrong and got in a tangle, and the nurse had to help me get out of it and then back in again, and I was so flustered and frustrated that I began to cry.

'Slow down,' she told me. 'Take a breath and start again.'

She had cold hands, but the hug she gave me was as warm as chocolate.

'You're going to be okay,' she said. 'It's your right, your choice.'

I told her it wasn't the right time, and she said, 'It never is,' and that was it: that's what changed my mind.

Back in the waiting room I thought about what she'd said: that it was never a good time—for all of us there in the gowns. I could see it was too soon for the teenagers, but I wasn't a teenager anymore. What if this was it for me? What if there was never going to be a better time? What if this was my one chance and there never was another? Looking back, would this time actually have been right? And the other things the nurse said: that it was my right, my choice. It was up to me. I'd felt that getting pregnant was a dead end, that I'd be stuck in Maggie Beach forever, but I felt a door swing ajar beside me and I saw a whole other way that I was free to go.

I could keep this baby, let it grow inside me, if I wanted.

Slow down. Take a breath and start again.

I could still leave. I would just take this little jellybean away with me, before it grew so big that people realised two of us were leaving. I could raise this child all by myself, far away from Maggie Beach, far away from Eddie, who'd never need to know he was the father.

Would that be so terrible? Would it be any worse than what I had been about to do?

He'd be hurt, but he'd move on, meet someone else and marry again. He would have other chances, I was sure.

'Are you going to leave him?' Lily asked.

Meg was focused on the road ahead, nibbling the inside of her bottom lip, the way she did when she worried. I told her not to. 'It'll all work out, you know.'

'Not by itself it won't,' Lily said. She was right of course.

I was glad that Meg was driving and Lily had taken the front seat. I needed time to grow my thoughts. I lay down across the back and watched the tall signs and balconies of the city as we left it, and the gum trees close enough to the side of the highway as they sped past in a crackly blur after that.

I would be the mother my own never was. Hold this child tight and love every piece of it. Take it to the park, to the beach, to the library, by the hand. But first I would need to take it far away.

I knew enough about Melbourne and Sydney to know that the things that mattered there didn't matter to me, and cold weather expenses would make the states around them harder to afford, but there were other places, far away and warm. There were buses to Brisbane, and there were buses from Brisbane to Darwin and to Perth. I could do it.

Mum once told me to make sure I always had a bit of money set aside. I think I only followed her advice because she gave so little of it, and I knew she'd never had a penny of her own before Dad died, so maybe I kept it to spite her, too, in the beginning. But then I kept it out of habit and just in case. I'd been tucking away fives and tens for years. A roll in the toe of a boot that lived in a box under the bed. It was in my pocket now. They'd given it back to me when I hadn't expected them to. It was a start.

Something fluttered in my stomach. Not the baby (it was far too soon for that), but the seed of a plan was sending out thin white roots.

Hope was taking hold.

CHAPTER TWENTY-NINE

Meg

Eddie had been right about the traffic. There was only the occasional lorry which shook the Kingswood as it passed. I drove for two hours beyond Rockhampton, then Rosemary told me to pull in to a rest stop and she took the driver's seat. We left Lily sleeping, earlobe folded and chin resting on the sling of her seatbelt, and stretched our legs in trading places, tightening the straps on the tarp that tucked the horses in the trailer.

It was less than an hour then to Theodore, and we slipped our shoes back on and collected the bits we'd taken from our handbags: tissues and glasses and lolly wrappers.

The motel Eddie had booked was just past the fuel stop on the run into town. A long double-storey with two parking spots in front of every spinach green door: one each for the unit downstairs and its twin above. There was a bottle shop at one end and a restaurant at the other. 'You'll have to book if you want dinner tonight,' the girl on the front desk told us, and Lily snorted but she went ahead and made a reservation.

'We won't want a late night,' she said.

Once we'd found our room, Rosemary disappeared into the bathroom and locked the door. Lily and I understood her wanting to be alone and didn't worry it might take a sinister tread. We knew she would come back to us when she was ready, and in the meantime we settled in to wait.

Lily tutted at the crust of calcium in the kettle, but she made tea and we sat together on the big double bed with our shoes off while she dragged us up and down the television channels and found a film that hadn't long started. Rosemary knew its title when we told her later, though by then Lily and I had both forgotten it. When it finished, Lily levered herself off the bed and buttoned her cardigan.

'Red or white?'

'Either,' I told her.

'But which would you prefer?'

I didn't mind.

A little whistle escaped her teeth. 'Right then.' When she rapped on the bathroom door, we heard the thick swoosh of Rosemary sitting up, waking to chill water and a scum of soap.

'I'm just popping out to get a bottle of wine,' Lily called. 'Will I get you anything?'

'I'm right, thanks.'

'Right then.' *Right as rain*, my grandmother used to say.

There was the squeak of a tap and the blast of hot water bringing the temperature back up, but it was still a while before Rosemary came out, and Lily and I drank wine out of teacups Lily wiped out with a tissue she found in her handbag, while we watched a teatime quiz show on the television.

We had our dinner early. Lily did most of the talking, wondering what to order from the chalkboard, whether we should have a glass each or another bottle of wine. Rosemary bounced hints and hesitant little questions away like small stones off a racquet. She wasn't ready yet to join in, so there was no mention at all of the little baby assembling in our minds now that we knew it grew inside her like a cashew. We talked instead about the drive, wondered what the market would be like, how many horses we might hope to sell, who might buy them, whether we might get a chance to wander around the other stalls ourselves.

Teeth were brushed and nighties pulled on turn by turn in the mustardy light of the bathroom, and we were in our beds by nine o'clock, Rosemary and I sharing the double while Lily took the rollaway that someone had been in and set up.

'Does anyone want to read?' she asked.

I would have liked to but didn't want to say, so the lights went out in a sequence of snaps and pings.

'Did you ever want children?' Rosemary asked us then.

It was velvet-black in the room, its curtains wide and thick enough to let road-weary travellers sleep late into next mornings and right through sunny afternoons. The pillows were crinkle-clean and crackle-soft. Sheets pulled tight and blankets scratchy.

'What makes you think I haven't got them?' Lily said.

'Do you?'

'No.'

I felt the shake of Rosemary's giggle.

My brother and I used to share a room. We used to giggle in the dark, whisper across the lava of our bedroom carpet and stuff our faces into pillows so laughter wouldn't bring an angry parent in the middle of the night. Sometimes we'd share a book and torchlight and the Wild West of Louis L'Amour.

'I never wanted them,' Lily said, though there was a stillness to it that made me wonder if she might have, once upon a time and long ago; if *Helen* might have been a baby's name.

'I've never much liked them,' she went on. 'Always up to something they shouldn't be.' There was a pause in her breathing and the dull clunk of a cup reaching a saucer on the floor. It could have been water or wine. 'Dirty little things.'

It was a strange word to use, I thought: *dirty*. Men in raincoats and hairs in pies. Children are grubby; their faces want scrubbing, hair brushing, feet wiping; they're biscuits in bedclothes and dogs up where they shouldn't be, but I'd have liked a grubby little boy or girl. I'd have let them dig in the garden, run along barefoot, lick the spoon.

'I never really thought about it,' I said. But I had.

Rosemary reached across and took my hand. It was kind enough to put a lump in my throat, but I wanted desperately to pull away. I wished myself outside, under a big sky, cold and on my own. More pressing, though, was the feeling that I didn't want to hurt her feelings, so I left my hand in hers and only squeezed my eyes shut tight.

'Well, it's a bit late to start now,' Lily said with a chuckle. She was right. It was all water under the bridge, and I half-remembered a poem my grandmother taught us about a mill turning. If she hadn't actually made us learn it, she'd recited it so often that we did.

'I was never that interested in sex or any of that,' Lily said quietly. 'I dozed off more than once.' Rosemary giggled again and my hand was freed. 'More to the point,' Lily went on, 'do *you* want children?'

Did Rosemary want children? The child that grew inside her, did she want it? Would she keep it?

I waited a long time for Rosemary to answer, but she didn't. She just turned away, untucked the top sheet with her feet and pulled fistfuls of hairy blanket, and her knees, into a curl.

After a while, Lily began to snore softly. There was chatter on the street. Taps turned on next door. I lay there alone in the dark and worried the corners of my grandmother's poem until it peeled from memory like a label soaked.

Learn to make the most of life,
Lose no happy day,
Time will never bring thee back
Chances swept away!
Leave no tender word unsaid,
Love while love shall last;
'The mill cannot grind
With the water that is past.'

'That was nice,' Rosemary whispered, so some of it, at least, must have been out loud.

CHAPTER THIRTY
Lily

I remember the weekend we took Eddie's horses to the market. Rosemary and Meg took turns driving us there. It was such a long way.

The field set aside was a sea of folding tables and pop-up shelters, and we struggled to get the horses out of the trailer and across to the spot they'd given us. Not because we couldn't manage them between us, or because we didn't know where we were going; there just weren't enough of us. Someone needed to stay with the trailer, and someone needed to stay with the stall, but it took two of us to carry each horse. It was like that riddle where the farmer has the chicken, the fox and the bag of grain to get across the river. He can only take two at a time, but the chicken will eat the grain, and of course the fox will eat the chicken if either pair are left alone. I don't remember the answer, but there's a lot of back and forth involved. The solution's not obvious, and it wasn't for us. If I remember rightly, we roped in a fella who painted Elvis on clocks.

People came in droves, and they all had a good look. We had to tell them to keep their sticky fingers off the saddles, even though Eddie had given us cards he'd laminated that told them not to touch. There must have been close to a hundred stalls that day. I'd never seen anything like it. Everything you could think of—so many candles!—and a little van selling Tibetan dumplings, of all things.

The horses were gone by lunchtime, but Rosemary didn't want to go home. 'Can we stay another night?' she asked us. She was like a child.

'We can do what we like,' I told her, but we couldn't really. If we could have done what we liked I don't think any of us would have gone back to Magpie Beach. But we had to. There was Norman to be taken care of, and Eddie to be fussed over, and I suppose Meg's scratty cat and kittens would have needed something.

We did stay another night, though.

We took the trailer back to the hotel and we each had a bath and a change of clothes, another bottle of wine while we waited for the sun to set, then we headed to the pub on the main street. I don't remember its name, but I know we stayed there till it closed.

There was a band set up in the corner and we danced till we were dizzy. We weren't going to dance at all to start with, but some busty redhead got us on our feet, in a line with all her friends who'd come in for the rodeo. Girls in fancy boots with tassels on their blouses, all over the cowboys in their big hats and their dirty jeans. Oh, I was so cross at that redhead for making a scene—making everyone stare at us and clap and egg us on—but looking back I'm glad she pulled us up. Once we joined in, no one was bothered that we didn't know the steps or which way we were supposed to turn. I forgot all the things that were waiting for me at home, the salt and the dirt and Norman's illness and the awkward business of that little girl. There we were, the three of us arm in arm, tapping our heels and yee-hawing like Annie Oakley, like we hadn't a care between us.

It was one of the best nights of my life. I never told them that—Rosemary and Meg. I should have told them. I should have thanked them. It had been such a long time since I'd laughed like that and let myself go.

It really was a night I'll never forget.

CHAPTER THIRTY-ONE

Meg

We pulled off the Bruce Highway at three in the afternoon. 'Don't tell him anything,' Rosemary made us promise. *Don't tell him what nearly happened. Don't tell him what we did.* We sold the horses, that was all.

It was more than Eddie's minding us staying away that extra night, and it was more than Rosemary's not having told him we were going to and, unable to reach him, not yet having told him that's what we'd done. For all Eddie knew, we were dead in a ditch beside the highway, but it was more than any worry we might have caused him. When Rosemary told us to tell him nothing, we knew what she meant. Don't tell him about the bath bomb she bought at the market and used in the afternoon. Don't tell him about the people we met, and laughed and danced with. I think we were all afraid that on a knife-scarred kitchen table, in the light of an ordinary day, it would all spoil like cheese. The word *secret* wasn't spoken but it was known. It was decided hours before we drove across the packed mud at the end of the lane.

I half-expected Eddie to come tearing onto the porch in yesterday's clothes, dark circles under his eyes and fear curling his fists, demanding to know where the hell we'd been as he took the steps in one crooked leap and dragged his wife out of the car and into his arms, but Eddie wasn't there and the secret we kept ground under our heels when we saw all the people. So many of them, in uniform, in white paper suits, and two men waiting for us in a plain blue car.

'Mrs Rosemary Lamb?'

They weren't local, and they eenie, meenie, miney, moe'd us with bobbing heads until Rosemary put her hand up.

'Can you come with us please, madam.'

They'd taken Eddie early Sunday morning.

I wondered if they'd flashed their lights and shouted at him, called him names like they did in American movies. I wondered if they'd spread him across the hood of their car and read him his rights. I wondered if they'd handcuffed him between them, if they'd had their sirens blaring all the way to town. I wondered if they'd let him phone his parents. Who else could he have called and what must he have said? *I didn't do it.*

'Sweet Jesus,' Lily said.

Tape wrapped around the cabin's balustrades, and the open sides of Eddie's shed were closed off with great sheets of milky plastic.

Of course, we knew before they told us that they'd arrested him for Jessie Else's murder.

CHAPTER THIRTY-TWO

Meg

The police didn't release Eddie's name, but the public knew it soon enough and people came then, but not for the magpies, and even though there was no beach. Angry wheels spun and cans and bottles flew from moving windows. They spat and shouted vile words and streaked them into violent sentences they sprayed on our homes in the anonymity of night. One man threw a wad of his own shit at Rosemary's kitchen window. I knew it was his own, because I watched him do it, squat like a dog next to his idling car. He would have been in his forties, with thick-rimmed glasses and grey socks.

'Bitch!' he shouted.

They all thought Rosemary must have known what Eddie did, even though he'd only been accused of doing it. No one knew for sure, but Rosemary must have known, they thought, when she did his washing, unblocked the sink, dragged the bin all the way up to the highway every Wednesday night.

The journalists came back, lobbing their questions one after another like snowballs.

'A quick word, if you don't mind.' Not caring if I did.

'Did you know the Accused well?' *Did I*, as if he were dead.

'Can you tell us a bit about Eddie Lamb, Mrs Cooper?' *Eddie*, not *Mr*, and I was no longer a Local Character. I was Mrs Cooper, 'a neighbour who thought she knew the Accused well'.

They only printed cuttings of the little I said, and they spliced them together so 'I don't believe he did it' became 'I can't believe he did it!' *Don't* and *can't*, two letters between them, and an exclamation mark, and a world of difference.

'I know him very well and he's a good man,' I told one of them.

NEIGHBOURS LEFT SHOCKED was her front-page headline. '*I thought I knew him*,' she quoted me as saying. '*I thought he was a good man.*'

I still thought he was.

The library grew busier around me.

'Nasty business with the Elses' little girl,' people said.

'It's all happening down your way at the moment, isn't it?'

Do you think he did it? were the words they wanted.

'Do you think he did it?' Catherine asked. 'Does he ever hit the Cole Girl?' (Back to being the Cole Girl.) *Does he look as if he has it in him?*

I shook my head. I shook my head at all of them, but that only made it worse.

'Why are you protecting him, Mrs Cooper?' one of the journalists asked. 'Don't you think the Elses deserve some answers?' As if I had them.

They didn't chase Lily the way they chased me. Perhaps they felt I owed them more: a few quotes in exchange for all the help they'd brought me in the past. Perhaps it was simply because Lily laid low for the weeks it took the journalists to move on. Other stories came eventually, and they followed—'like vultures,' Lily said. A father and son went missing on a fishing trip. A toddler drowned in a backyard pool, and the journalists wielded their pens and blamed the parents.

'They never see any more than they want to,' Lily said, and I pictured my own mother picking up a paper and picking Eddie and Rosemary apart with pointed tongue. *No smoke without fire*, she would have said. *Look at his face—look at those eyes—I wouldn't trust him to post a letter.*

'Truth will out,' Lily said.

It wouldn't matter who thought what. Gossip wouldn't stand up in court. All that would count then would be the facts, and 'they've got nothing', Eddie told Rosemary.

'There's nothing here to find!' Rosemary told the detectives who kept coming back to look.

But: 'There's something,' Catherine told me quietly between the library stacks one morning. 'You know I can't tell you, Meg. You know I'm not supposed to know, but there is more to it.' And she rested a hand on my shoulder and shook her head as if to say *Don't fight this battle*.

Was it only then that I began to doubt Eddie's innocence? Little things kept me awake. Little memories troubled me like stones inside a shoe.

The avocado tree he'd known about. 'You've just got to get up and in a bit,' he'd said, then quickly changed the subject.

The way he scraped grey dirt from under his nails with the back end of a knife much longer than necessary.

The first time I'd seen the Kingswood, parked beyond the clearing, not so long before he brought Rosemary to live in Magpie Beach, but weeks before he had his house, or his shed, or any idea that someone might have noticed.

'Into all sorts of trouble,' Leonie had said, fingertips on picture frames, the night of Rosemary's party. *Especially Eddie.*

Rosemary had a letter from the chocolate factory, with a cheque attached and apologies enclosed. They were cutting costs and wouldn't need her anymore.

'When it's all over, I'm sure they'll have you back,' Lily said, and Rosemary nodded the way she did when she felt there'd be no point in disagreeing.

Tom and Leonie came by every Saturday and took her away with them to visit Eddie.

'We're managing,' Leonie offered when I asked, but the puffy grey beneath her eyes told more of the story. It was a frail and quiet Tom who rode beside her. His thin frame stooped, shoulders folding like wings into the rattle of his chest. He was tired, Leonie told us. Though he still went into the shop, he sat on a chair in the office while the Coulter did the butchering and ran the counter, and only scratches and space remained to the left of the younger man's name on the window. Tom's own, which had stood for so much in Winifred, had come to stand for something very different.

'It's a difficult time for all of us,' he said, and Leonie pursed her lips and looked high into the trees to keep from crying.

Lily came by most afternoons, while Norman took his nap. There would not have been a place for him among us. No plan passed between Lily and me, but we moved to close the space around Rosemary like sisters, and in the absence of the real thing, I like to think we were enough. My brother and I had been close; 'thick as thieves', our grandmother had called us. We had the intimacy of a history shared, memories iron-forged, and depths of understanding, and what had grown between Rosemary, Lily, and me was not that, but it was root-strong. We were like three wild figs wandering up the same tree. The fingers of our stories wove around each other, those we told and those we never would. There was strength in our being together, and there was sunlight in the higher branches, even if there was dirt between our toes.

We watched crackling midday movies on Rosemary's small television, and made each other tea and coffee without a need to ask how anybody took theirs. We chatted plenty, but often sat with books in our laps, in silence or light sleep.

Lily left by sunset at the latest. Sometimes we walked her home, but she never asked us to, and she never asked us in. We never made it past the doormat where she kicked her shoes off, toe to heel, and bent only to spray them. She must have brought the plastic out to wrap them later because we never saw her do it.

'Right, thanks for that,' she would say, or, 'See you tomorrow then.' Both meant the same thing: *I shan't invite you in.*

Those were weeks of waiting.

'Have faith,' Lily was fond of saying.

We thought the police would turn up something that would prove that Eddie hadn't done it. We thought there'd be some test they'd do with strands of his hair, or a sliver of his fingernail, or with his spit or worse, mismatched against whatever they'd taken from poor dead Jessie Else with cotton buds and tweezers; but if they did, it didn't send him home.

We hoped someone would remember seeing him on February fourteenth, but no one did. He told them he'd been buying timber out at Boone, but the men in the timber yard didn't remember his having been in. It was all cash and there were no receipts. He'd picked Rosemary up from his parents' late in the afternoon and he had the timber with him, they all said, but that didn't prove he'd bought it just that morning. It didn't prove he hadn't set it all up in advance to make his day seem unremarkable and to hide some other truth.

'He was acting normal,' they said, but that didn't prove he was. It didn't prove a thing, and who were *they* anyway? His mother and his father and his wife.

There was a doctor who'd said at the time she'd seen a man with a girl who looked a lot like Jessie Else, on Valentine's Day, in the centre of town. She didn't mention a limp, but the man had reddish hair and Eddie's build. They were holding hands, the doctor said, and police appealed for the man to come forward, if it wasn't the man that everyone thought it was, so he might be eliminated from their inquiries. But nobody came forward, and words changed so that it went from 'holding hands' to 'being led away'.

That was something like a piece of evidence (if it were him, if it were her). I couldn't understand why no one would come forward if it had been them.

She'd been hit across the back of the head with something heavy, the *Courier* said. Eddie had an axe and a hammer and a mallet. Eddie had a toolbox and plenty of wood lying around.

She'd been strangled then with butcher's twine, tied so tight the coroner had to cut it from her throat. Ordinary butcher's string that anyone would use to truss a bird for roasting, or tie greaseproof paper over steaming puddings, but Eddie was a Lamb, born into a family of butchers.

And after all of that, the cause of death, they said, was suffocation. A big hand or a pillow or a plastic bag. No need to say that he had all of those.

What came before the something heavy? we all wondered, though I tried hard not to. There were two fingers missing, Catherine told me, long before she knew to tell me nothing. There was terror in that little girl's last moments, maybe hours or days of it. They were angry hands that killed her. I'd never seen Eddie angry, but that didn't mean he didn't have it buried in him somewhere.

My father's rage was barely underwater, but other men check theirs well in public. Rosemary's father was a model citizen. A week after they'd scraped him off the highway, I'd stood beside Catherine on the library steps and watched his funeral pour down William Street. Eighteen cars rolling no faster than a steady man could walk, with their headlights on low beam. Shop doorways filled with staff standing as we did with our heads bowed. *A loss this community will feel deeply*, his obituary said. There was no mention at all of his temper. No one spoke up or against him, but I suppose there was no need, no purpose to be served. His wife stopped wearing scarfs and heavy make-up, and a couple of years later she flew away so suddenly that someone else returned her library books—two unread and one unfinished, a card still marking the page she'd got to.

'Are you still set on leaving?' Lily asked Rosemary one afternoon.

We'd just switched off the television set. It was time to straighten legs, set cold cups in the sink and walk her home.

'I can't now, can I?' Rosemary said. 'It'll look like I think he did it.'

'But you don't, do you?' The shock in Lily's voice surprised me.

Rosemary didn't answer right away. She busied herself with the tap and a squirt of washing-up liquid.

'You don't, do you?' Lily pressed.

'It doesn't matter, does it? If I leave him, it'll look like I do.'

'Have faith, love,' Lily told her, and Rosemary turned towards us with a weak smile.

Rosemary didn't need Lily's reassurances. She needed help sanding and painting her front door when someone sprayed CUNT across it. She needed the right shade of nail polish to cover the words she found scratched on the bonnet of Eddie's car. She needed company, and someone to fetch her groceries, and a place to hide at two o'clock in the morning.

They set a date for the preliminary hearing in September. We were sharing a slice of winter sun with steaming cups of coffee at our elbows when the courier came. He drove carefully and wound the window closed before climbing spider-like out of his car.

'Rosemary Lamb?' He was looking straight at her (even those people who hadn't known her before knew her by then), but she still threw a hand up in the air. She looked so young sitting with her knees together and her toes pointed in, though her nails were no longer painted.

The courier held a clipboard at arm's length and Rosemary's hand fell to the hem of her shorts as she clambered to her feet.

Her signature was short and exchanged for an envelope. 'Well, this is it,' she said as the young man drove away.

She tore open the envelope with shaking hands. Pulling from it a clean white slip of paper, she read in silence and gave us only the date that had been set: 21 November. Then she folded the letter back into its creases and jammed it roughly into her back pocket, but she didn't sit back down.

'I'm going to have to tell him about the baby.'

Lily and I exchanged a glance and nodded. November was still two months away and she was already swollen hard like a tin can past its use-by date. For a while yet she might have Eddie believing she was eating poorly under pressure. It's what we'd been assuring her people would think, but we were already lying when we said it.

'November.' Trying it out like a married name. 'We'll know then, won't we?' There was a crust to her voice, like bread that had been soft a couple of days before, but if Lily picked up on that she spoke as if she hadn't.

'It'll come right,' she said, and that was all Rosemary needed.

'For you, maybe,' she snapped.

'And what do you mean by that?'

'It's not your husband, is it?'

There was a pool of silence and then, 'Truth will out,' Lily said, not for the first time, but you could tell from the crease between Rosemary's eyebrows that it was what the truth might be that troubled her the most. She looked at Lily for a long moment, readying her thoughts and steadying her voice, before she spoke again.

'What if he did it, Lily? What then?'

It was more of a challenge than a question.

'You know he didn't.'

'No,' Rosemary said. 'I don't. And neither do you. Why are they still holding him? Why haven't they sent him home?'

'They just don't want him disappearing,' Lily said.

'And why would he disappear if he was innocent?'

Lily shrugged. 'People panic, don't they? Look at you, now. They've got nothing on him because he didn't do it. You know he wouldn't hurt a fly.'

I remembered the set of Lily's jaw the morning we'd left for the winter market when Eddie had said Norman could have stayed with him. She hadn't wanted Eddie anywhere near Norman then, and yet here she was, defending him. I wondered was it faith in Eddie's innocence that kept her lifting Rosemary's chin, or was she supporting loyalty to a promise made? For better or for worse, a wife stays by, and on, her husband's side.

'I don't want it to be him,' Rosemary said, 'but someone did it, didn't they?' She was asking both of us, telling us: 'They did it here.'

She looked around as if someone might be camped out now, just waiting for another opportunity.

'But you weren't here,' Lily said airily. 'You didn't even live here then.'

'But we came. Right after. And it was Eddie's idea.'

'They've got nothing,' Lily said again.

But Rosemary was already shaking her head. 'You know that can't be true. They couldn't have kept him this long without something.'

'They're just trying to rattle him,' Lily argued. 'They're trying to scare you—and it's working, isn't it?'

'And you think what?' Rosemary shot back. 'They're just going to stand him up in court and point at him and tell the judge, *He looks suspicious—we think he did it*?'

'You've seen too many movies,' Lily scoffed.

'I've seen enough to know they couldn't keep him if they didn't have something that tied him to it tight, and they're not going to tell us what that is until they have to. They're not going to take any chances on our stories changing, things being covered up. For all they know, I'm in on it. Someone did it, Lily, and they think it was Eddie. Why do they think it was Eddie? *Why?* What do they know that they're not telling us?'

Lily pursed her lips and shook her head, but Rosemary went on.

'Her little head was smashed in.'

'Stop it,' Lily whispered.

But Rosemary was only getting started, her voice lifting the weight of it all. 'Her arms and legs were broken.'

'Stop it!'

'They've said it might have gone on for days. What else did he do? Haven't you wondered? Put yourself there beside her?'

I had. The time between the taking and the ending had crammed itself into some of the darkest dreams I'd known. I'd pictured Jessie's terror, heard screams rent from her broken body, and woken shaking in a chill of damp sheets. I imagine her parents did little else, and the wondering that filled the cracks between the knowing and the not may well have been the worst of it.

'If it turns out it was Eddie . . .' Rosemary's hands were raking through her hair, shaking now with fear and anger and frustration. 'Jesus Christ, I hope it wasn't, but if it was'—the last of it was sobbed—'how could he have lived with himself?' Broken, finally, she collapsed back onto the step. 'For fuck's sake, how could I have lived with him?'

'Have faith,' Lily said one last time, but it was quiet and tired and I didn't see how Rosemary could now. Faith isn't something you can pick up off the ground and wipe clean on your apron. You either have it or you don't.

CHAPTER THIRTY-THREE
Rosemary

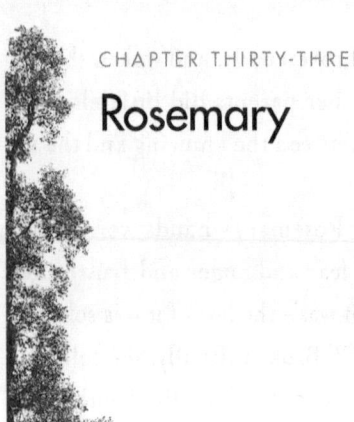

I was eight, maybe nine, when I first went to the Galaxy. I'd seen the building with no windows on the corner, and sometimes sounded out the backlit words and sentences that appeared randomly, but I'd never really wondered what they meant, why they changed so frequently, or what could possibly be going on inside.

Mum took me to see *An Officer and a Gentleman*. It doesn't take a genius to figure out that there began the casting of my fantasies. I don't know how she got me in. It had sex, swearing, suicide, and an R rating, but to be honest none of that struck me so much at the time. I don't know that I even followed the story, but I remember how the theatre and all the women in it were transformed. I remember the sticky nicotine-yellow of the bathroom in the opening sequence, and from there on everything slowly washing clearer and lighter until, in the final scene that everyone holds close, there's Richard Gere, whiter and brighter than a Napisan commercial, with everyone around him clapping and cheering, and all the women in Mr Breadsell's audience came apart at the seams.

I watched Mum dabbing at her eyes with a wad of toilet paper for about ten minutes. It was a different sort of crying from the sort she did in the bathroom at home. This one she seemed to be taking pleasure from. It was giving her something—feeding something inside her. She didn't say anything much until we were out on the street.

'How do I look?' she asked then.

I told her she looked beautiful.

'What did you think?' she asked me next.

'I loved it,' I said, and she squeezed my hand, but it wasn't the movie that I'd loved. It was the circus of it. The magic of a spell cast.

We walked home. It wasn't far. We didn't talk much (we never talked much), but when we stopped to cross Rosella Street, she took my hand and said, 'You're my special girl. You know that, don't you?'

I didn't, but I nodded that I did. Tears were welling in her eyes again, and all that toilet paper had blotted her lipstick down to pink.

Those first few weeks when Eddie was gone, I'd have given anything to hear her say it again: 'You're my special girl. You know that, don't you?' Even if your mum has never been that sort of person, she's still *your* person; you still like to think she'll be *that* person, if it comes down to it.

I thought about telephoning her, but what would I have said? 'I miss you'? I didn't miss her. Not literally. There was no gaping hole where she'd been and suddenly wasn't; she'd not been there for years and, even when she had been, she hadn't really, not like Cher in *Mermaids*, or Shirley MacLaine in *Terms of Endearment*. But she was missing. I would have trusted her to take my hand and help me across the road. I would have listened if she'd said, 'Rosemary, here's what you must do,' and laid it all out plainly in steps from one to ten for me to follow like a recipe.

In the end, I wrote a letter late at night—many nights—long after Meg's light went out. I pulled the mattress off my bed and lay on it under the window with the little reading lamp I could click off in a moment if I heard a car, and I wrote page after page.

I thought it would be easier to write than talk about it and it was. I started by telling her about the baby, and then I told her how Eddie didn't know, and why I'd kept it a secret, that I'd been planning to leave but now I felt I couldn't. It all came out like a fever. I don't know if I ever actually thought I'd send the letter, but it did help to write everything down.

I'd forgotten I liked to write. I'd liked English and I hadn't hated school to start with. When I was twelve, I wanted to be a teacher. The sort of teacher that everyone wanted. I imagined I'd ride to school on a motorbike, sit on the edge of my desk and tell the students to call me Roe, not Miss. I liked the sound of Roe when I was twelve. I don't know where it came from, and I don't know where it went. I was going to be the sort of trusted teacher Dolly Doctor meant when she told girls where to take their troubles. I would not drive a boxy little car or carry my books in a basket. I would not take deep exaggerated breaths or scratch angry lines through anyone's story with a red pen.

But somehow I ended up at the factory instead. I'd stopped caring about being a teacher by then. I cared more about movies than I did about anything else. In exchange for chipping an hour and a half out of any ordinary day, I got to peep through a crack in a door and share somebody else's. There was nothing I wanted to do more, and between my Blockbuster membership and the Galaxy, I lived a fantasy life of rotating scenes in my head. While I was failing a history test or making Michele and Dan's bed or scrubbing gluey egg yolk off their children's plates and faces, and later, when I drove the sweeper around the cocoa-dusty factory, whenever I was doing the sort of everyday thing that I could do with my mind somewhere else, my mind was about as far away from Carney County as it could get. New York, Paris, Montana. I didn't know where in the world Montana was, but I spent a lot of time there in a flyaway summer dress all running-river wet around the hem. I was Ruth in *Fried Green Tomatoes* and Vivian in *Pretty Woman*, and Hilary (of course) in *Dying Young*, where I kept Victor in remission so we could drink red wine and dance night after night in the house with the draughty kitchen window.

It's pathetic. I know it's pathetic. Did I know it at the time? Maybe. Deep down. (Maybe not even that deep.) I don't know how or when or why I let go of my own actually-possible dreams. I could have focused on my studies and gone to teacher training college. I could have learned to ride a motorbike. But somewhere between *An Officer and a Gentleman* and marrying Eddie, I let go of it all.

CHAPTER THIRTY-FOUR
Meg

We didn't see Lily for a couple of days. We noticed her absence, but if either of us worried, it wasn't out loud. There were plenty of other things to be worrying about. Tom was in hospital again. They'd taken him in an ambulance and were talking of keeping him there to manage his pain. Leonie was struggling on her own. She and Rosemary had been trying to contact Eddie's brother in Europe, but so far they hadn't found him.

'He needs to come home now,' Leonie said, as if he might put everything back the way it was.

When a couple of days became a few, and a few became a week, noticing darkened a little. I imagined Lily on a slippery bathroom floor, impossibly bent and blocking her own exit, begging help from a man who could no longer. So, on a grey and windy Friday afternoon, Rosemary and I took the track across the headland.

The proper house was quiet and still. The door was always closed but the house seemed heavier than usual, like a cake that hadn't risen. A thin drift of sand blew around it, and cobwebs grew like shadows in its corners.

There was no answer to our knocking on the door or to our calls and shouts. We cupped our hands to better peer through windows either side, hoping for a crack between curtains, but all we could see were three burnt matches, and the crusted currants and crisp-dried wings of insects dead on sills. The plastic on Lily's shoes had begun to turn the bluey white of cataracts.

We circled the deck like wolves, and around the back saw that someone had done their best to hammer storm shutters on the tall glass sliding panels that faced the ocean. It wasn't the season for storms. They were banged up raggedly, so it wasn't hard to pull one off—fingers under an edge not flush and a bracing foot against a frame.

'I think they've gone,' Rosemary said, her face pressed up tight against the glass, like Aunty Molly at my grandmother's, but I didn't think Lily was hiding. I saw it too: the floor swept, counters wiped, and chairs tucked in, a blue cloth hanging neatly from a tap, a single glass upended on the draining board.

But where would they have gone? 'I'm too old,' Lily had said. Wasn't she? Wasn't Norman? She'd tied the shoes to his feet and guided him to the Lambs', and longer and longer it had taken them until she'd stopped bringing him altogether. 'It's too much,' she'd told us then, so how could she have taken him anywhere else?

'I guess she'd had enough,' Rosemary said, and the look that passed between us stirred my stomach like a spoon.

I don't know what made us think to try the front door, knowing Lily the way we thought we did: the woman who wrapped her shoes and buried her purse at the bottom of her handbag, locked a car door with her elbow, couldn't stay long, wouldn't stay late; but of course, it was unlocked. How else could she have let us in?

The cold hall smelled of lavender and disinfectant and something rotten that made Rosemary pull the collar of her shirt across her nose and mouth.

Did I call her name one last time? Perhaps I did.

There was a door on either side, bedroom to the left. I remembered the flutter of curtains from the long-ago night Norman had wandered off. And I had seen the pipes and drains and water tanks of bath and toilet to the right. Straight ahead, a sickle-shaped glass panel in a wooden door filtered the light we'd let in when we'd torn the shutter off, and that was the door we opened to the sun-baked stench of sweat and urine.

'Jesus!' Rosemary choked.

We made to throw that wide corner of glass open and let great gusts of sea air clear the house, but someone had splintered doors and windows with stout nails that locked them to their frames.

We might have left then, shut the house back up and wondered what to do about it later, but for the faintest sound.

I held a hand to quiet Rosemary, who'd just drawn breath to speak.

To our right, and strung across the room, hung a honey-coloured curtain. Threaded on a wire by someone not quite tall enough even on a chair, so that there was a wide space between hooks and ceiling while the too-long fabric puddled on the floor.

Breath came from behind it.

It was Rosemary who lifted the curtain back, one hand pressing flannel to her face. Sunlight seeped in, colouring what hid behind, the rich, sweet caramel of late afternoon. An empty plate, a bucket on its side, the filth within it soaked into the thick edge of a mattress, and on that, skin and bone and barely alive, was Norman.

'You're flesh and bone!' my grandmother used to say. She meant: *You're not eating properly. Your edges aren't as rounded as I think they should be. You're not looking after yourself.* More specifically: *Whoever's looking after you isn't doing as good a job as I would.* But it wasn't true in the way it was true for Norman, that afternoon. You could see the shape of his teeth through his cheeks. The whites of his eyes were yellow, there were brown smears of dried blood beneath his nose, and when he opened his mouth his tongue hovered like a bobtail's.

It was Rosemary who ran to call an ambulance. There was no discussion, no questions as to who should do what. In a moment she was gone, and I was filling the glass at the sink with an urgency the plumbing was unused to.

Norman's back was sticky against the arm I snaked behind him, and when I tipped the glass to his peeling lips the water caught in his throat so that most of it ran into his ears and pooled in the hollow of his neck.

I told him it would be okay. I told him an ambulance was coming.

His hair was clumped around his head, knotted with bits of scalp like something snatched up out of a drain. A torn sheet was tangled around his legs, and there were things I'd not have noticed if he'd had pyjamas on: bruises on his collarbone and around his wrists and ankles; a puckered scar that crept across his chest, no neat white kisses telling it had seen a nurse or needle. There were dark memories of old scabs on his forearms and, around his groin, fresher wounds the pinky white of uncooked pork, some soft and green.

There were maggots on the mattress.

'It's going to be okay, Norman,' I told him more than once. 'You're going to be okay.' But not for a second did I believe it.

CHAPTER THIRTY-FIVE

Meg

It was a long time before the ambulance arrived. There was no phone at Magpie Beach, so Rosemary drove out to the service station on the highway. I don't know what she said when she got there. I don't know if they recognised her, or if the paramedics knew the story behind where they were heading.

She ran back across the headland and was waiting for them on Lily and Norman's porch when they arrived, coming up from Bingham on the road that brought them all the way. They complimented the weather as they tramped inside with a stretcher clattering between them, and they talked to Norman kindly, lifted him gently and put him to sleep with a sharp and shiny needle.

While the woman strapped him safe inside the yawning ambulance, her partner leaned across the front seat to radio the police. 'We have to report it,' she explained; because of Norman's scabs and lesions, because he was naked and starving and lying in a mess of his own excrement, on a mattress on the floor, in a house in the middle of nowhere.

If not us, they wanted to know, who looked after him? 'Where is she now?' they asked us then.

'We don't know,' Rosemary told them.

But actually, I did.

I had recognised the smell, like fruit and green ground-up beef left airless in the sun, sweet and sour and old and unwashed, stirred up thick beneath the shit and soft-cheese smell of Norman.

Lily lay in the darkened bedroom beneath a blanket I like to imagine came with her from Calcutt. You couldn't see it was Lily, because there was a plastic bag over her head, tied tightly about her neck with string and bloated full of breathed-out air and vomit, but her teeth were in a glass of cloudy water on the bedside table. Crossed on the smocked breast of her nightdress, her hands were the colour of cooked liver, but I knew the rings on her fingers, the crucifix stuck to her chest, and who else could it have been?

The paramedics didn't touch her. They didn't even take her pulse.

'The police will be here soon,' they said. 'Will you be alright? Do you want us to call someone to stay with you?'

'We'll stay with each other,' Rosemary told them, and the paramedics shared a look. It wasn't until later that I realised they'd expected one of us to go with Norman.

'Make sure you don't touch anything.'

What would we have touched that we wouldn't have already? If anything wanted taking, wouldn't I have taken it in all the time I'd had before they got there?

CHAPTER THIRTY-SIX

Meg

We went to visit Norman in the hospital, took him fruit he couldn't eat, a magazine he wouldn't read and flowers that the nurses put in water. We didn't know what to say, but we told him we were sorry. We hadn't known. How could we have known? But we should have. I did think that we should have.

He's a clumsy thing, Lily told us.

Bruises easily.

Doesn't always see the step.

He lay in a wide, hard bed pinned to tubes that dripped a life-of-sorts into him while others drew away his waste. Unblinking, unswallowing, and uncaring. The mattress squeaked and crackled when the nurses rummaged under stiff sheets to tend him, clicking and tutting all the while.

Who would do such a thing? What sort of woman would do this to her husband?

'He's been through a lot,' the doctors told us, diplomatic and discreet. We weren't to expect much in the way of a recovery.

The scar that streaked his chest came from a clean flat blade, they told us. Because no one came, who else was there to tell? The lesions that spotted Norman's forearms and the soft puckered skin of his groin came from the glowing tips of Lily's cigarettes. There were light ticks of scars beneath his fingernails, plum-grey with age, and made—they said—by sharp things driven in. Pins, perhaps, or cocktail sticks. (Two guesses were enough; we didn't fish for more.) She'd bound his wrists and ankles, and choked him more than once or twice.

Who *would* do such a thing?

Holding Norman's thin pale fingers, I remembered them tanned the sweet red of a ginger nut and powdered with the dust of Eddie's horses. I remembered his milky blue eyes cornered creamy white from squinting smiles.

'Make sure you behave yourself for Mr Lamb.'

Don't make a fuss. Don't tell.

I remembered the night I'd found him wandering in the dark. 'Please help me,' he'd begged, and I had taken him back.

But for all the questions, everyone knew who'd done it. There was nothing suspicious about Lily's own death, only the mess she'd left behind. Hers was suicide: overdose or suffocation or drowning in vomit, she was dead, and she had killed herself. The details didn't really matter at all.

But who was she? This woman who'd starved and tortured her husband, and left him to rot from the inside out, like a kitten still-born in the bush. Not the woman he'd married, that was clear. Not that girl with the sweetheart smile and baby's breath tumbling from her veil. Not the little girl with a blackberry moustache who skated on the river in her winter boots. Not even the woman who'd laughed in a line of cowboys dancing, not so long before. This other Lily stood away behind a curtain, stiff and still and out of sight.

One kindly pastor offered her a prayer. With bowed head at the foot of Norman's bed, he cast a blessing after Lily's soul and invited Rosemary and I to join his silence. It had been a long time since I'd prayed. I closed my eyes and pictured Lily in the pink dark. I saw her pressing pill after pill from blistered foil, standing by the sink so she could fill that glass time and time again, and then she'd rinsed it. What else had she thought to do? Was the plastic bag chosen ready and waiting? Had she measured and cut the string to tie it? Had she told Norman goodbye? Had she meant for us to find them both moved on, or had she killed herself in order to save him?

No one held her hand as she was dying. I don't know that she deserved it, but I would have held her hand. No one should die alone.

My deepest regret is that Sonny did.

He died at home and in pain, some time between four and five on a Saturday afternoon. I'd gone for the doctor, who'd followed me back with needles that would have helped but were too late.

It was raining when the doctor left, and it was getting dark, and reluctantly he let me keep Sonny for one more night. I sat with him right through. I watched him change colour, felt the stiffness come and then subside, held his hand then and whispered secrets until the sun came up and dust motes danced in shafts across the bedclothes. I told him everything there was to know, but he'd known it all along.

They came to take him in the morning, and I do remember that I tried to stop them, but they stroked and stuck the slate run of my arm until I couldn't hold on any longer. 'Sleep a while,' they told me. What else was there for me to do?

'Is there anyone we can call?' they asked.

Sergeant Scanlan came for me days later. Had I been expecting him? Had it been arranged? It was raining lightly, and the policeman drove carefully on wet roads while I stared blindly through the spotted windscreen. He spoke but I barely heard him; I'd spent days weaving a basket around myself so that the world came to me vaguely now, like a lake lapping behind a legion of trees.

I did not know how to be by myself.

Peas in a pod, Mum called us.

'Double trouble,' Sonny said.

Paired in heaven, I believed, and put on earth to save each other.

No one spoke of Sonny. Who could have said a word about him but me? No one knew him like I did. But without his hand in mine, I found I could not speak. The pastor said he was a fine man and a hard worker, and he was both those things but so much more.

Others were there. Men who'd shared a shift. They shook my hand and told me they were sorry. 'If you need anything,' they said. 'If there's anything we can do.'

How did I get home? It was almost dark again by the time I got there, and when it was, and when the rain stopped and the humming and the croaking and the chattering began, I sat on the lowest rocks and begged the tide to take me.

More days, and a woman came and handed me his ashes in a stoppered urn. 'If you have a jar you'd rather . . . ?'

But I had only jam jars with lids that didn't always match. I took the urn she handed me. Did I thank her?

More days. Then came the night I took the ashes he had been, out onto the rocky headland, and I threw them as high as I could into a wind that swept him out over the ocean that he loved almost as much as he'd loved me.

And he was gone.

And I was left alone.

Rosemary patted me awake gently. 'It's time to go,' she whispered. Visiting hours were over. We never went again.

CHAPTER THIRTY-SEVEN
Meg

Sergeant Scanlan sent now-Senior Constable Pike to find me. He stood awkwardly outside the caravan, leaning across the cinder block Eddie had set there for me rather than standing on it. His hat was back in his hands, but he hadn't the nervous look on his face this time.

More than eighteen months had passed since he'd come to ask me whether I'd seen Jessie Else, neither of us imagining that when time and weather turned her up, I would be the one to see her first, and I wondered, knowing now how close he'd been back then, what he might wish he'd asked me.

More, I think.

Less of the had I known her, had I seen her, and more of the *anything else at all*.

'Sergeant Scanlan thought you might be able to help us,' he said this time. 'They don't seem to be in the system.' He shrugged as if it happened often, but the way his fists turned his hat like a steering wheel suggested that it didn't. 'Their names,' he went on, 'well, they're not—weren't—who they said they were.' He took a short breath then, and held it while he tidied his thoughts. 'We need to find out who they were, Mrs Cooper. Sarge said you might be able to help. Off the record,' he added. *In secret.* I owed Mike Scanlan that, and much, much more. He wanted me to help him look through Lily's things. Help him figure out if she was Lily-short-for-Lillian, and whether there were next of kin who could be called to come and sort the mess of Norman out. 'You were friends, weren't you?'

'Do you want me to fetch Rosemary?' I asked him, though I doubted she was home. I'd seen her set off earlier to visit Tom in hospital. A few short weeks, doctors had warned them, weeks ago.

Pike shook his head, and I watched his jaw stiffen as his teeth set. Had he been the one to ask Eddie his questions? Had he too readily accepted answers that would have crumbled with a nudge? 'Did you know her? Have you seen her?' Anything else would have cast a better light. If he'd lingered just a moment longer, probed a little deeper, caught some small inconsistency or something too familiar. Had he thanked Eddie for his help when he should have taken him in for further questioning? Did that keep him awake at night?

'Would you help us then?' The shadow of an accent, and I knew something of him, this Senior Constable Pike. His mother had come to the library often, brought him for his picture books and, later, for books with words like *train* and *pterodactyl*. She had the same flecks of hazel in her eyes and Irish lilt, though his was faint. Catherine told me they'd all gone home to Ireland, when the strength of family was needed.

'I was sorry to hear about your mother,' I said.

He gave a tight nod but his thanks were warm, and I thought: *You will be good at this, after all. This will be what shapes you. You will catch something that others miss, and something will not happen because this happened to you.*

We walked single file, scattering lizards like beads. A brown snake wove a whisper of a trail across the path and as I stopped to let it, Pike put a hand on my shoulder in surprise to stop himself. He hadn't seen the snake. He didn't know why we'd stopped all of a sudden and I wondered how many miles away he'd been.

'Is this it?' he asked, knowing of course that it wasn't but needing to fill the space.

Another twist, another turn, and there stood Lily's house against the blue and I wondered—not for the first time—what it was the man who'd built it painted here, away on this fierce little point where the ocean must have spat at him the way it salt-burned Lily and the patches of her English flowers.

Such a short time it takes to leave a place feeling deserted. Birds had dropped long green-white streaks down windows. There was a grimy film of salt dust on the front porch, the honeyed crust of a cicada lay on the mat that begged us to wipe our feet, and cobwebs tangled the cheddar hunks of Lily's shoes. Pike nudged one to stop the front door closing, but fresh air did not thin the smell inside.

'Don't touch anything,' the paramedics had told Rosemary and me, so we'd sat together on the edge of Lily's creaking deck and stared out over choppy water, waiting for the second ambulance and the police who kept us out there while they took their photographs and measurements and eventually zipped Lily into a stretchered rubber bag.

She still stained the bedcover. The pillow a nest for her head.

'Shall we start in here?'

Touching everything, Pike began by pulling out a bedside drawer. Creams and tissues, prayer cards and peppermints.

I opened Lily's wardrobe to her winter coat and a rail of dresses that I knew.

'Let's take everything to the table in the other room,' Pike said, so he knew there was a table. He must have been before, though he'd not been in the car that came to start with.

I didn't know what I was looking for. Names and dates and details, Pike had said. 'Bank stuff, insurance stuff.' There was stuff in Lily's pockets: details of the day she'd worn the coat, had a cold, seen a coin and picked it up. Pike must have noticed the loss about me because, 'I'll finish off in here,' he said. 'You check the other rooms.'

There was stuff in the bathroom: soap in a margarine container, a towel on a hook, a toothbrush in a mug and salt in a greening spoon. A roll of paper hung on a string between two nails on the back of the toilet door, and a small, laminated verse unseen by men who leave doors open. Romans 12:20: *If thine enemy hunger, feed him; if he thirst, give him drink: for in so doing thou shalt heap coals of fire on his head.*

'Anything?' Pike called.

Was it something?

'No.'

More stuff in kitchen cupboards: powdered soup and long-life milk; a biscuit tin, a teapot, ants in sugar and, in a drawer, a large, square photo album, the blue-black of deep water, gilt-edged, its corners stubbed. This I pulled out and up onto the kitchen counter, feeling some guilt as I eased it open, prying eyes expecting Lily's life in pictures: friends and families, first days, front doors, weddings and holidays.

Not expecting what I found.

Instead of photographs, the album was swollen with newspaper clippings, some full pages folded into quarters, others cut and splayed, all long-ago yellow, with bolder headlines faded to blood-brown. Many had been attacked with pens and pencils. Pictures scribbled on so hard that holes were torn in faces. Words and sentences angrily underlined.

Pike carried through a shallow case and set it on the small round kitchen table, snapping it open to reveal a bed of red-and-blue-trimmed aerograms, frost-windowed envelopes, and handwritten notes. 'Bingo!' He nodded at the thick book in my hands, 'Anything?'

Everything. But I couldn't answer.

Cutting upon cutting told the story of seven little girls across two states. Seven little girls, each taken by a man who'd promised something wonderful then driven off the quieter roads and left them there when he was done, lost and afraid, in tatters and in tears, their little worlds torn up and tangled around their ankles.

Seven stories, similar enough that '*anything else*' must have led someone to tie one man to all of them, and there was his picture, ringed in furious pencil in *The West Australian*, wanted for questioning. A younger, brighter Norman, but not named Norman, as it turned out. His name was Trevor Haxby, and pages later, head down, collar up, Lily—short for Lillian or Elizabeth? we had wondered, when, after all, her name was Helen.

Had she known? Reporters speculated. There was a page on wives of criminals, what made them stay, how many turned a blind eye and the other cheek.

For all the nurses' wondering how Lily could have done the things she did to Norman, no one thought to wonder why. What tiny seed had grown into such fury. What she was punishing. What she had stopped.

The West Australian had a tip that they'd returned to England. Scotland, someone else suggested, and I stopped reading then.

Some small inconsistency. Something too familiar.

Pike glanced up as I reached into the kitchen cupboard, but he was poring over a letter with fine paper and an airmail envelope, shaking his head and pulling his bottom lip in between his teeth. He nearly had it. I could tell from the sweat on the back of his neck, where a nervous thumb was kneading flesh.

This would not keep him awake at night.

Not any longer.

I knew the weight of a packet of biscuits; the dull thud that comes when they slide to the side of a tipped tin, and this one rattled. A pony and a thistle on its lid, and of course it rattled, though I set it very gently in the young policeman's hands.

CHAPTER THIRTY-EIGHT

Lily

When we left England, I knew there was something else. Honestly, I thought Norman had been having an affair—someone at his office with one of those skirts slit right up to show her stocking tops, taking notes in meetings after hours and grabbing at each other in stationery cupboards.

There'd been a finding-out of something. I knew that much. There was an angry man on our doorstep late one night; the name of a woman Norman was warned to stay away from. So I said, *Yes, let's go to Australia and have a fresh start*, and pretended it was all about the opportunities. Never mind we'd neither of us been before and weren't sure it would suit us. I held his hand and my head up high, and off we went—here we came.

When we got to Adelaide, there was something fierce in him to start with and I liked that. He kept his arm around my waist and laughed with his head flung back and his mouth wide open. We ate out in restaurants and made new friends. But after a while there was a restlessness about him. You know when you ask someone if they're alright, because they don't quite seem themselves, and they tell you they're fine—they just have a lot on their mind? It was like that. I could tell that his eyes were beginning to wander, and after a while (late nights in the office and straight into the shower when he got home) I was certain he'd found himself another bit on the side.

I began to snoop. I went through his briefcase when he was in the bathroom of an evening, and one day, while he was at work, I took one of the kitchen stools upstairs and had a good look through the things he kept on the top shelf of his wardrobe. There was a shoebox I'd never seen him take down, but I'd come in to find him putting back there, once or twice. Receipts, he'd told me when I'd asked, but that's not what it was full of, actually. Mostly, they were photographs of children. I didn't know any of them, and I don't know where he'd been to take so many. Changing rooms, it looked like; swimming baths and department stores. The children were all ages and there was nothing inappropriate, not really. They all had on their underpants or bathing suits.

I just thought it was an odd sort of hobby. I'd known a woman whose husband collected Nazi memorabilia. She didn't like to talk about it in case people thought he was a Nazi (which he wasn't, of course). I'd heard of husbands putting on their wives' shoes and dresses when they were home alone, which on its own didn't make them homosexuals. Norman liked to take and look at pictures of children. There wasn't necessarily anything more to it, and I told myself there were worse things he could be doing. I didn't want to tell him that I knew. I didn't want to push him to explain. I thought that would embarrass us both, and I didn't want to know any more about it. So I pushed the shoebox back into its corner, and I didn't wonder why he took or kept those photographs. I only trusted that they hadn't been developed at the local chemist.

I didn't find anything to do with any woman he was seeing. Though I was quite sure he was seeing someone, he was careful not to leave me anything of her to find.

There were times the phone rang, and Norman told me not to answer. There was another husband spitting threats from the doorstep late one night, and another evening Norman came home with a split lip and a cut on his cheek that should have had a stitch or two.

It began to crumble then, what we'd built around us.

I didn't sit by like a dummy. It got to the point where I asked him outright what was going on, but he swore that there was nothing.

'Of course it's not nothing!' I shouted at him. 'You've been up to something!'

'You've been watching too much daytime television,' he sneered.

I told him not to be so condescending. 'I wasn't born yesterday.'

'Clearly,' he said, calm as custard, and he dragged his eyes from the very top of my head right down to the tips of my toes and back up for good measure, with a look on his face like he'd smelled shit on his shoe.

'You want to leave?' he asked, so quietly it was almost a whisper. 'Go on,' he said. 'What's stopping you?'

He was only asking to be mean. Where would I have gone? What would I have done? I didn't think I'd weather the shame of going home without him, and I didn't think I'd survive here on my own. Better to survive an affair, I thought, and those that would come after, because by then I realised that was the lot that I'd been cast.

Keep Calm and Carry On the posters used to say, and the mummies and the aunties and the nannas would make pies without butter and bake them full of crabapples and we'd sit around the table all together with blankets on the windows and we would do better than keep calm: we'd laugh and sing and, if there was fuel enough for a lamp on, we might play cards. We British invented soldiering on. So that's what I did. I soldiered on.

His late nights continued, and the phone kept on ringing at odd hours.

I didn't think to link any of it to the photographs, or the stack of children's clothing catalogues that had grown beside the bed, until the police came to tell him not to park outside the school. There'd been complaints.

'This doesn't concern you,' he told me.

But it did, and so I listened, and I took the coat someone said he'd been wearing and I hid it at the bottom of the garden, and when they'd finished looking, I took it out to the quarry and I burned it, and I burned the underwear in its pockets too.

It was down to me to save my name, before he dragged it through the dirt.

We left for Perth not long after that. It was quite sudden again, the need to seek better opportunities. The work that Norman found didn't pay as well as it had, but it was enough for us to get by. There was a downturn in the economy, he kept telling me. 'It's another recession,' he said. Didn't I read the newspapers?

Oh, I read them.

I took a job cleaning houses. I wasn't above it, and the money was good and all cash in hand. Here and there I took a little something extra, but nothing anyone ever thought to worry me for. One diamond earring. One fifty from a wad of notes. A hundred from a wallet. A dress or a jacket. I did for three families, and they were all filthy rich. The stuff they had beyond what they ever could have needed was mind-boggling. Clothes they'd never worn, all with the tags still on. Cars they never drove, houses they'd never even seen. We'd not been poor, and I'd had some wealthy friends over the years, but I'd never known anything like this.

We had quite a lot in savings, and I withdrew tens of thousands from the bank. Joint accounts, but Norman's was an easy signature to forge. It took a long time because I took it all in bits—no more than five hundred in a week, but every week, and I bundled it by thousands into zip-lock bags I hid up in the attic with the Christmas decorations.

I knew the whole mess would begin again, and when it did, I wanted to be ready.

He swore black and blue that this time would be different. The promises he made and broke would curl your hair, and when you've promised to trust someone, they expect you to believe whatever they tell you, don't they? Even when you've caught them lying that many times it's a joke. They say, 'I swear to you! I swear on my life!' and if you challenge them, then you're paranoid and hysterical. 'Listen to yourself! Look what you've become!' Past the point you learn you're married to a liar, there's not much use in questioning what they say. So you stop. You stop questioning, and you stop rooting through pockets and checking the time. You stop sitting up when you hear the front latch click. You pretend to be asleep. That's what you do. That's what I did. I'd turn myself over to face the wall, close my eyes tight, and hope that it would all just go away.

But of course, it didn't.

I came home one afternoon to find him crouched in a cold bath, sobbing like a big baby, one almighty mess of snot and tears with scratches all over his arms.

'Help me. Please. I don't know what to do. I don't know what to do.'

It was the first time he'd asked me for anything. He needed me, and I can't tell you how gratifying that moment was. I felt ten feet tall and as strong as Atlas. It wasn't: *Stop asking questions, this doesn't concern you. Give it a rest for God's sake woman!* He hung on every word I said. He didn't know what to do, but I did, because all those nights he'd worked late, or gone to bed early with his catalogues, I'd been watching crime shows on the television.

When they took him away in the morning, he said everything I told him to say, and he did everything I told him to do. And when they brought him back, I knew we didn't have long. This time, there was too much to say he'd done the things he'd sworn he hadn't. They'd be back before tea with a warrant and handcuffs, but I was ready. I had the car packed in the garage, clothes and jewellery and anything of any value boxed up on the back seat or crammed into the boot, all our zip-locked thousands tucked in with the spare wheel underneath. The car was fuelled up ready to go, and all the curtains drawn.

He was still crying when we drove away.

'Don't look back,' I told him. 'Keep your eyes on the road ahead.'

I thought we'd be happier here, I'll admit. Starting out on a clean slate for the twilight of our lives. We called each other by our new names, took them on so completely, it's how I know us now—Lily and Norman. Some things, there's no going back from. Alone in a little house on the coast, just the two of us, with Norman out of temptation's way and no one to bother us, I thought we'd take long walks, build a garden, sit in the shade and play backgammon. I thought we'd enjoy each other's company without distraction. I thought I'd matter, like I mattered in those first years back in England, and the first few months we'd had in Adelaide.

Norman was happy enough to start with, grateful to be anywhere other than prison, but he got bored soon enough and started wanting to be off by himself. 'I just need a bit of space,' he said. 'I can't stay cooped up here with you every second of the day.'

Cooped up.

'I'm just going for a drive.'

Liar.

'I'll be back in time for tea.'

And I was expected to stay home and cook it for him?

No more.

He needed his wings clipped.

'Have some cocoa,' I said.

The holes we dig.

The lies we live.

CHAPTER THIRTY-NINE

Meg

They lowered Tom into a coma from which he never regained consciousness. He did not live to see his son released. If he was told the charges against Eddie had been dropped, it was in whispers and prayers that may or may not have found him, but I like to think they did.

Perhaps in sleep he saw the tape that tangled around the house beyond the headland; the police whose hands reached into its narrowest cavities, whose boots stood on the steps of shovels to turn every inch of its surrounds.

Within hours of opening her biscuit tin of change, they found Jessie Else's little backpack partially burned and buried beneath a clump of English flowers that hadn't grown; and they found more than a ring trapped in the patch of shade-cloth cable-tied to filter the flush of the kitchen sink. Without it, two little fingers might have made their way into and out to sea.

Maybe Tom understood when Leonie pressed her lips close to his ear and breathed the news. Perhaps, after all, it was a mist of some weight being lifted that released him.

'He knew you didn't do it,' Leonie promised Eddie, but that might not have been true. I'd hoped he hadn't done it, but to say I never doubted would have been a lie. Even his wife had thought he might have done it. Most of Winifred would have bet their pensions that he had.

NEW SUSPECT IN THE ELSE CASE was the headline soon enough. There was no mention of Eddie. No one buried the bones they had so worried. The *Courier* didn't write about the months he'd spent in jail, or that he was now free and had always been innocent. They didn't tell the public they'd been wrong.

There was no shame at all.

No one came out to clean Rosemary's windows, or scratch *I'm sorry* on the side of Eddie's car. There were no reporters waiting when Rosemary brought him home a quieter man.

Eddie's brother finally reached out. Sorry he'd been out of touch so long and so impossible to find. Sorry, but he wasn't coming home just yet, things were busy and complicated, and his life was over there, but, 'Well done, bro!' he said. As if Eddie had won best in show.

'Dad's dead,' Eddie told him, but nothing would bring Shane back.

'His own father's funeral.' Eddie shook his head, anger time-worn into disappointment. 'I can't take it in,' he said. *That my father is gone. That my brother does not care. That a man I'd treated kindly killed a child and let me take the blame. That these people I grew up with thought I'd done it—believed I was capable of that.*

But truth will out.

'How well did you know these Haxbys?' Sergeant Scanlan asked Rosemary and me.

These Haxbys, whose records were found quickly in the system.

We hadn't known them at all. What was there to say? That she'd been someone else to start with? That she'd flattened coins on a train track as a girl, and chased the coal wagon, and cut wild rhubarb with a stolen pocket-knife, and kept a field mouse in a box beneath her bed.

Would they have cared that she made burdock soup, and daisy chains, and perfume out of rose petals and rainwater? Would it make a difference if they knew about the river that froze in winter, or the brother whose school was bombed in the Blitz? Did they need to know that she cried the first time she saw the ocean, or that she learned to dance in borrowed shoes and a cold church hall?

They wanted only to hear about the woman she'd become—and what did we know of her, our Lily? That she was blunt, uncomfortable, and lonely; that she liked her coffee hot with cold milk on the side; that she scoffed at happy endings, looked after her pennies, hated thunderstorms and the thought of spiders in her shoes.

We didn't want to know *this Helen Haxby*.

But Eddie did. Eddie wanted every detail, and the newspapers and magazines were full of them. They printed pictures of Norman taken in better days, when his back was straight. In a time when he'd caught the train, and worn a belt and shoes with proper laces. It wasn't a young man in their photographs. He wasn't so far from the man we knew that we wouldn't have recognised his picture printed clearly. If we'd read a piece that asked us had we seen him, we would have realised. We would have rung the number. We may not have told the tax office, or the Department of Immigration, but once we'd read beyond the *Have You Seen?* and found the why, we would have told.

But back when they were looking, the pages that were folded square and read at breakfast tables passed through inky fingers in other states. People shook their heads in Western and South Australia, but of course they hadn't seen *This Man* because he was no longer there.

The house beyond the headland belonged to a woman wealthy enough to know it only as an item listed on a piece of paper years before. Her ex-husband bought it in Brisbane, with a view to drinking and fishing with friends. Then came an affair and, on a lawyer's mahogany desk, his weekends away were swept out of sight and kept out of spite. His wife had moved on and interstate and, 'I'd almost forgotten it was there,' she said. Living as she did in Perth, now, in a suburb where big houses backed on to a river, where there were private docks for private yachts and room enough for caterers in kitchens and money enough for a cleaner to come in three mornings a week.

'I couldn't fault her work,' the woman said, 'but obviously this has come as a tremendous shock. I'd never have imagined!'

She'd never have imagined Helen Haxby might have listened in to conversations, gone through papers filed in the cabinets she polished, understood the potential of what she found: a house beyond a headland on the other side of the country, fully paid for and shut up tight and never checked for squatters.

I'd never have imagined.

It's what they all said: neighbours, friends, and colleagues. Journalists interviewed them all, and they interviewed the parents of the girls Norman had assaulted. Wanted for further questioning in Adelaide, but they'd wanted him for more than that in Perth. Questions they knew to ask by then ran deeper than *Did you know* and *Where were you?*

The girls were women now. Their faces blurred or covered by cascading hair. They asked that their real names be kept from strangers, but it didn't matter what their parents called them, only what this man had done, and he'd done plenty—more than Lily had ever suspected enough to cut and paste. They numbered more than seven. There were girls who hadn't told, and some whose people-they-told hadn't wanted anyone else to know.

The police took Norman—Trevor Haxby—back to Perth as soon as he was well enough to travel, which was sooner than it would have been for the man they'd thought he was when they'd tucked him up in hospital in the first place: the abused husband. *Who would do such a thing?*

After all, when they found out what he'd done himself, 'The strain might be too much,' was not a thing they said.

No nurses waved him off. They bundled the few things he had into a plastic bag that swung from the handle of his chair, and a policeman wheeled him out into a mob of microphones and cameras. Norman kept his head down and his hands together in a blanket on his lap while they threw their questions at him like eggs, not snowballs. They wanted more than his attention. They hit him squarely every time and covered him in shame.

'Haxby? Haxby!' they shouted. 'You can't hide from the truth! The public has a right to know!'

But despite everything the public knew already, I felt sorry for the man I watched through a battering swell of damp shirt backs and lashing tongues. When I closed my eyes, I saw him only lost and scared in a dark and messy soup of bats and gum trees.

'He deserves everything he gets,' Catherine said.

I had no doubt she was right, for all that Trevor Haxby had done to those children; still, it was hard to see Norman in this harsher light.

The Knew-the-Accuseds never say, 'He was my friend.' That part is set aside. Interviews full of 'I had no idea', because that is the only safe thing to be said. If they did not know, they could not have helped, and they are one of us.

But in the quiet away from tape recorders, they must unpack and mourn the friendship, if there was one. Could haves and would haves send a shiver, but care leaves some indentation, as in snow or sand or even mud. There is something that lingers longer than a shadow. Companionship that warmed and company enjoyed. There is grief that comes with *He was my friend*.

I wondered how his victims would feel when they saw him on the television, beaten and broken and brought to his knees. *Eye for eye, tooth for tooth*, the Bible says—the old one, brimstone-burned and waved in anger—*hand for hand, foot for foot, burn for burn, stripe for stripe*, but I don't know that it works as tidily as that. Sometimes more feels better. Sight for an eye then, tongue for a tooth; arm for a hand, and leg for a foot. With burns upon burns and more stripes than a tiger, would it comfort them to know he'd suffered?

What of the Elses? What thoughts flooded them when they watched Norman on the evening news, arriving in Perth flanked by plainclothes officers who carried him down the aeroplane steps and wheeled him across the rain-slicked tarmac? They knew now with whom their little girl had spent her final hours, if not entirely how. Norman was not talking, and who else would tell? Not-knowing spawns imagining, but maybe knowing-every-bit-of-it is worse.

'He doesn't look as if he has it in him, does he?' Rosemary said, as we looked at his photograph between us, a double-page spread in a magazine she'd picked up with her groceries, already ringed with a circle of tea.

She was right, of course—he didn't look as if he had it in him, and he hadn't for a long time.

'I'm sorry,' he'd said the night I found him. Six weeks after Jessie Else went missing. The night I took him home and handed him back to his wife.

'No more,' she must have made him promise in Adelaide, and again in Perth. Promises he broke. So, in the salt-whipped house beyond the headland, she'd put her foot down hard enough to crack a tile, and made sure, promise or no, that Norman did not work as well as he'd have had to if he'd wanted to catch a little girl and keep her still long enough to do what had been done to Jessie Else.

'I'm sorry,' he'd told me.

But sorry for what?

Certain things had not been done to Jessie Else; things that had been done to all the other little girls; things they had been taken to be done with.

Not all truths come out. What's done is done. For better or worse, Norman would take the blame, because for all the coals that Lily heaped upon his head, she had cared for and protected him as well. The anger in her pockets made her scratch, but for a long time she had combed his hair, brought him to Eddie on her arm to sit on warm steps and feel the breeze blow through a shirt she'd pressed and buttoned. When she took him home, she sponged the red dust from his creases, boiled the kettle, and set good meals before him.

There was anger in her pockets, but once Jessie Else was found, and Eddie was arrested, and Rosemary's chance at a Life Like That began to slip away, there were other things, lumpy things that could not be lost in corners. Fear and shame pushed pins beneath an old man's fingernails, pressed the flaking stubs of cigarettes into papery skin.

'Have faith,' she'd said. *In me,* she meant. *Have faith in me, Lily, Helen Haxby, wife, secret-keeper and pin-sticker. Friend.* For all her bitter words, she was a loyal friend; and for all the secrets she kept, she stood by every promise.

'I won't do it again,' Norman told her, the night I took him home.

Perhaps she promised him the same thing, waiting by the kettle in the creamy light of early morning. 'I won't do it again. Don't run away. Don't you leave me here alone.'

Why would he? How could he?

'We're alright, love,' I hear her tell him. 'We're safe out here. No one's coming.'

But oh, how her cup must have rattled on its saucer.

CHAPTER FORTY
Lily

She was just where they said she was, in the car park outside Woolworths, rattling her tin under everyone's nose. Why ever would she have come home with me? For a kitten? For a puppy? To tell you the truth, I'm not sure I remember which, but a greedy little girl she was. She ate a whole packet of biscuits on the way, and they all had cream fillings.

What it was Norman sought in their company, I never understood, but they took his sweets, and his hands, and they climbed into his cars and ruined everything.

Oh, I know it wasn't their fault. It was his, all his, but still, there was something about that little girl, that day, which set my blood simmering. It was Valentine's Day, and that brought enough memories on its own of days I'd never get back—cards and dinners and bunches of flowers. I'd thought we'd grow old together properly, not the way we were, hiding in a salt-crusted box miles away from everything.

And there she was in the middle of the footpath, in my face and in my way.

'How many boxes do you want?' she asked me. Not: 'Would you like to buy some?' There was that sense of entitlement that so many youngsters have these days. They push in, and push past, and look you right in the face demanding your attention and assuming your interest. I just wanted to knock her down a peg, that's all.

'Shouldn't you be in school?' I said, and her face fell, and I liked the way that made me feel.

There was no one else around. It was the middle of a Monday morning. I'd just come out with my shopping, and it was starting to rain. I said, 'Your shoes don't look like they fit you very well,' and her face fell even further, and I felt better than I'd felt in years. 'Your mum mustn't care very much that your toes are all squashed like that.' That's when she started with tears in her eyes, so that's when I mentioned the puppies or kittens, I really don't remember which, but the promise of a cuddle from a bundle of them put a little smile back on her face.

Not too many people passed to see us chatting. I told her I'd buy every box of cookies she had as long as she helped me put them away, and as a bonus I wouldn't call the police to report her truancy.

I didn't plan to keep her. I was just enjoying that little taste of being nasty.

We had the driver who never talks. I'd thought I'd ask him to wait half an hour and run her back to town. I didn't think he'd mind, and I didn't think he'd charge me the waiting time. He could have his sandwich and read his book. I'd seen him do as much before. But she sat so quietly in the taxi—her mouth was too full of biscuits for talking—I could see he'd barely noticed her and wasn't at all interested in who she was, or why I had her with me, and I began to wonder how good it might feel to be just a little bit nastier.

I shoved her out quickly when we got home, and I paid the driver through the window, so I don't know if he even realised there'd been two of us in the car. Old women often mutter to themselves, don't they? And there's a lot of focus needed on the road when it's raining.

There was the whistle of a kettle boiling as we started along the path. I thought I'd maybe catch her finger in a drawer, that's all.

And I did that.

I bent another one back a bit. And then I bent it back a bit more. I didn't think I'd go much further, but I was so very angry, and the scissors were so very sharp.

Afterwards, I knew I'd let rage get the better of me, but what's done was done, and sometimes you just have to get something out of your system, don't you? Though I'd not known it was in there till that day.

It was the next day we took her up into the bush. Norman had to help me, even though he didn't want to. It needed the two of us, and: 'It's not like I've never had to clean up your mess,' I told him.

She was a chubby little thing, but still not terribly heavy, and once I'd tied her up a bit it was easy enough to get her in a bag. I wore my gardening gloves, so they wouldn't get a print off the plastic if they found her, which of course I hoped they wouldn't, but I'd seen enough crime shows to know there was a chance someone would stumble across her eventually—a dog walker, or a jogger, or teenagers staggering off the beaten track to take drugs and have sex.

The bag tore with the weight of her inside it, so I pushed the bundle into a duvet cover, which I worried might be traced, but it never was. We got the whole thing into the wheelbarrow and covered it with sticks, and we pushed it as far as we could—which wasn't very far. We carried it then between us, though I did most of the heavy lifting. Norman wasn't much help, even when it came to digging a hole. We settled on an old tree, in the end, and burrowed between its roots like wombats.

'This is yours,' he said. But it wasn't.

'This is because of you,' I reminded him. I had to remind him often. Show him cuttings of the things he'd done. All of it was on him, every move we made. Every rock he hid beneath, I'd had to throw. This was just another one.

'I'll tell the police,' he threatened once or twice. 'I'll tell them what you did.'

But I knew he wouldn't, because he knew I was the only thing that stood between him and a life in prison. And he knew, because I'd told him, what they did in there to people who did the sort of things he liked to do with little girls. Still, I helped him let it go. Made his cocoa a little bit stronger, of a night. There's so much you can get without a script. A bit of this, a bit of that. (More than a bit, does wonders.)

Was I sorry?

I felt sorry for her parents when I heard them on the radio or saw them in the supermarket. I ran into the mother once. We came up face to face and she looked me right in the eye, and for a split second I thought she could see the guilt in me—see what I'd done, what I'd taken from her—and I felt something then, and bile rising in my throat, but I don't know that I'd call it sorry. I was scared I'd be found out. I would have died of shame to have it all dragged into the open.

I know what I did was wrong. A sin. I lost my temper, plain and simple.

I have reflected, and I have prayed.

All that hate. I will say that I kept it better-focused after that.

CHAPTER FORTY-ONE

Rosemary

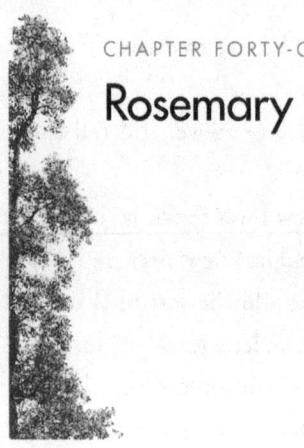

Half of me wondered if I should have gone ahead with the procedure when I'd had the chance; when Lily-who-was-really-Helen and Meg and I were in Rockhampton, and the baby was a cluster of cells and I'd had an appointment and a story to cover all the questions Eddie might have asked.

I'd waited too long. I'd waited for Eddie. I'd felt I owed him that much, but now it was too late. I was seventeen weeks pregnant, and the baby was too big to keep a secret. It was the size of a pear now, and it was ours.

'You should have told me,' Eddie said.

'She didn't want you having anything else to worry about,' Leonie told him, but she wished that I'd told her, I could tell.

They were over the moon, the pair of them.

'You've made me the happiest bloke in Queensland,' Eddie said. Not the happiest bloke in Australia, *the happiest bloke in Queensland*, which was bigger than the world to Eddie. He talked about having a second baby not too long after the first so they could play together. 'No good waiting till you're too old to kick the footy about.' It's what Tom had said. Everything Tom had ever said or thought was chiselled in stone after he died. Tom would have liked this, Tom did it this way. Of course, we were going to call the baby Thomas, but I wasn't to tell Leonie in case it was a girl.

'She'll be disappointed,' Eddie said, and there was a little bit of accusation in it, as if it was somehow up to me. 'It doesn't matter what we have, as long as it's healthy!' he told other people, but it was always him, he or the little fella, and the paint he bought to do the room was pale enough, but blue.

'It'll be a boy, don't you worry,' Leonie told us. 'Every firstborn Lamb's a boy.' As if it mattered. As if we needed a boy to herd or hunt or take the throne.

I got my job back at the factory, and I went to work, and I came home. Sometimes someone asked how I was doing. Was the baby moving much? Had I felt sick at all? Did I know what I was having?

Yes, yes, and yes. Right from the start I knew I was having a girl. Mother's instinct, Meg called it. She stroked my belly as if it were a cat and brought me flasks of watery soup and herbal tea when I was sick.

'Just check what's in it first,' Eddie tried to insist, but I never asked. Meg's teas, pastes and potions always made me feel better. Maybe it was just the love and care she put in them for me, when Eddie's and Leonie's love and care were always for the baby.

It was partly Tom's dying that sent Eddie back to being a butcher. The town began to dribble in again with their purses and their pensions (which, thinking on it now, was some sort of an apology, I suppose), and Leonie asked Eddie if he could step in and help out. 'Just for a couple of months, love,' it began. 'Your cousin's struggling on his own.' But, really, Eddie didn't need much persuading back into his apron. He was pretty keen to get his foot back in the door.

Prison had given him a lot of time to think, he said. It made him wonder what he was doing with his life, what he wanted out of it, and where he wanted to find himself a way down the track. He took a good look at himself, he said. I suppose he took a good look at me, too.

'Where do you see us in ten years?' he asked.

I couldn't begin to answer that.

'What do you want for yourself?'

'I'd still really like a dog,' I said, but with a baby on the way I knew he'd tell me that it wasn't the best time.

'A puppy needs a lot of attention,' he said, as if I didn't know it. As if I hadn't dreamed it through and planned its walks and tricks and where it would sleep. As if I didn't keep a shortlist of the names that I might give it on the fridge.

'You've got Dolly now,' he said, meaning the kitten Meg had christened because I had so little interest that I'd called it Kitty-Cat.

Another peg in the ground.

His woodwork went back to being the hobby it had been in the beginning, when he'd dreamed of it growing to be something more. He dragged the horse he'd been so close to finishing into the corner of his shed, and it stood there naked without its mane or tail or varnish, and the shallow hollows of its eyes empty and blind.

'Later,' he told me when I wondered if he'd turn his tools to finishing. 'I'm not in the mood for it,' he said.

Instead, he set to work on a cradle for the baby, short and stout like the one in the Jesus and Mary scene they set up in the foyer of the library every Christmas. After that, he made a highchair, then a set of bookshelves for Leonie.

'I'm redecorating Shane's room,' she'd announced, and Eddie spent a weekend ferrying his brother's old clothes, books, CDs, and footy trophies to the Salvos. 'There's no room for all his junk,' Leonie said. Because he'd not come home when Tom was dying, but not just because of that. When she and Eddie were done, and the life that Shane had left behind was gone, the room was blue.

I knew it was only a matter of time before we moved back into town. With all Eddie's driving back and forth, and with Leonie on her own now and the baby on its way, it would make sense and be decided.

The butcher's window was repainted, *Coulter and Lamb*, and every customer seemed to be a long-lost friend.

'I saw Nat Murray today,' Eddie would tell me over dinner, and I was expected to care.

'Cal Brown's pregnant again. That'll make four!'

Why would it matter to either one of us how many children Cal Brown had?

'You'll never guess who came in this morning!'

I never did.

'I thought we could ask Donny and Jules over for a barbie, maybe Sunday?' Eddie suggested one evening.

'Who are Donny and Jules?'

'You know! Donny and Jules!' He looked at me like I was losing my marbles.

I still didn't know who they were, but I faked a rush of memory. You can blame anything on being pregnant. You can forget things, break things, cry for no apparent reason, dry-retch in public bathrooms with no one thinking you've been drinking since breakfast. You can certainly chalk up a few forgotten names and faces.

I didn't know who Donny and Jules were until they pulled their baby out of its car seat and handed me a big dish of potato salad. I recognised her then—Julie Wilson. She sat behind me in year ten maths. She used to dig fingernail-sized bits of devon out of her sandwiches and spit them at the back of my head using the shaft of a biro as a blowpipe, and now here she was, all grown up and expecting dinner.

Donny was older than Jules, and he and Eddie had been in the same year at school as well. I suppose that was what they had in common enough for Eddie to want them as friends. He must have asked them to bring their wedding album with them, and once we'd eaten we went through it together.

Did we remember this guy? Did we remember that one?

I remembered some of the girls in the photos, and it wasn't with fondness, but Eddie was having the time of his life, and he and Donny dragged up story after story between them. There was the time this one punched that one; the time that one hid in a cupboard for a whole science period; the time another cut the better part of his finger off in metalwork.

I sat quietly with their baby on my knee. It was gurgling like a drain, with a milk arrowroot biscuit dissolving in its face.

'Well!' Jules began every sentence. This one ended up going out with that one. That one married this one. This one was supposed to marry that one but carried on with another one in secret and everyone found out, and they ended up moving to Sydney.

'No way!' Eddie said, and, 'You're kidding?' and, 'Did you hear that, Rosy?' He and Donny drank beer after beer, taking turns to fetch two at a time from the kitchen. And with every one he downed, the looks that Eddie shot me got sterner. He wanted me to join in more, talk more, laugh more. He wanted me to make Donny and Jules feel welcome, so they'd want to come again, so they'd invite us back.

'Do you like it out here?' Jules asked me.

'It's okay.'

'So have you got any names picked out apart from Tom?' (Eddie had told them that, then.)

Not that I was going to share with her.

'Do you ever see Mad Meg?' she asked. 'Did you ever see the old man that killed little Jessie? How far is it to his place? Did you talk to him ever?'

I didn't want to give her any answers. I knew she'd take them to her peachy, puff-sleeved bridesmaids; they'd hear every detail of her afternoon at Maggie Beach, and she'd answer all their questions. What was I wearing? What state was my kitchen in? Was I drinking? Did I smell? The colour of my toenails, the pictures on my walls, how close Eddie and I sat together: it would all be dumped in front of them like dead mice on a doorstep.

There were a lot of Wild West tumbleweed silences between us.

'I remember you were always so shy,' Jules said. 'We used to call you the Ghost.'

'You used to call me a lot of things,' I reminded her quietly.

As they were leaving, she handed me a book from inside the car. 'I thought you might need this.' She laughed lightly.

Need, not want.

What to Expect When You're Expecting. I had a copy on my bedside table which I read every night, copying bits I thought I might go back to into a notebook I'd bought specially.

'That's great, isn't it?' Eddie said.

'I've already got it, but thanks,' I told her and handed it back.

'No, you haven't,' Eddie said, and when I opened my mouth to remind him that yes, I had, he said, 'You haven't *got* a copy—you've borrowed one from the library,' and he sniggered.

'Well, you can keep this one,' Jules said.

I could keep the copy I had, as long as Meg renewed it every three weeks. 'I'm good, but thanks,' I told her again, then, because Eddie was giving me another look: 'It was really kind of you to think of me.'

She was still holding the book at arm's length, and I was reminded suddenly of a time at school when our hands had touched as we were both reaching for one last paper bag of popcorn on the almost empty counter of the canteen. I'd drawn my arm back, but she'd kept hers zombie-straight, with a look on her face as if it were up to its elbow in a cow's arse.

'Thanks, freak,' she'd said. 'I needed a shower.'

Eddie had his back to the car. 'Just fucking take it,' he mouthed at me, but I didn't want to, and I wasn't going to. His face was pig-pink with VB and frustration.

'Pregnancy, hey?' he joked, as he turned back to face his new friends, one hand in the air, miming a stabbing knife and squeaking the *Psycho* theme, while he reached out with the other and took the book from Jules.

When they'd gone, he was angrier than I'd ever seen him. 'What is wrong with you? No wonder—'

'No wonder what?'

But he wouldn't finish.

'They're going to think you're a fucking lunatic,' he spat. That was what mattered to him: what they would think of me, of us. Of him.

After prison, and after Tom died, and with a little Lamb on the way, Eddie cared what people like Jules and Donny thought. Nat Murray, Cal Brown. Never mind what they might have thought all the while he was in prison. He didn't let that bother him. This was his second chance, his do-over, his afterlife, and he had both hands around his bowl like Oliver Twist.

I should have left when I had the chance. I needn't have waited. I should have taken a case on wheels and a bus to Brisbane. Never mind what people would have thought; they were going to think it anyway.

CHAPTER FORTY-TWO

Rosemary

I waited till Thursday, because Meg was at the library and Friday was Eddie's day off in lieu of Saturday. On Thursdays he finished at four but wouldn't be home before six. He'd spend an hour on the horses at the TAB, then check the box at the post office, and maybe pick up a couple of things from Woolworths, which was right next door.

The oven was still warm when I put my head in it. I'd spent the morning baking pies and the rack was greasy on my cheek and smelled of pastry. The only note I left was square and yellow and stuck to the fridge. *PEPPER STEAK & ONION. WRAP AND FREEZE.*

It was one of those old ovens with the door that opened sideways like a cupboard. If it had been one of the modern ones that pull down, I don't think I'd have been able to get close enough from the front for my head to fit all the way inside. For a pear, there was a lot of padding around it.

I heard Dolly pouncing around on the deck, chasing a fly and pushing up against the screen door. There was a kookaburra somewhere—two kookaburras, calling to each other. The clock was ticking, the gas was whispering, and I closed my eyes and concentrated all my thoughts on breathing deeply.

It didn't take long for me to lose consciousness. I couldn't say how long, exactly, but not as long as I'd thought it would, and I don't remember dreaming.

It was Eddie's voice that brought me around.

'You've got a letter from Mary,' he said.

The words came from far away and I didn't register at first what had happened, what I'd tried to do, but then I felt a wash of guilt and shame, and I was six years old and on the edge of getting into trouble. There was a sinking feeling in my stomach, but that might have been the baby or the gas or the two not mixing.

'You've got a letter from Mary.' Louder the second time, and I opened my eyes, but everything was dark, which frightened me, and I banged my head on the roof of the oven jumping up.

Eddie had his back to me. He was taking the top off a beer, and he said something else, but I didn't hear it, only the rattle of bottles in the door as he closed the fridge. I was looking at my watch and wondering why I wasn't dead. I'd been on my knees with my face on the baking tray for three and a half hours.

'Don't overdo it, love,' Eddie said. He was looking at all the pies. There were twelve of them scattered around the kitchen. The note I'd left had fallen to the floor and stuck to the bottom of his shoe. He turned and saw me then. Just backed out of the oven with grille marks on one cheek and burnt crumbs in my hair, I must have looked a mess.

'Jesus,' he said. 'You'll wear yourself out.'

I already had. All that frying and stewing and baking and making.

'We're out of gas,' I told him, and then I burst into tears.

CHAPTER FORTY-THREE
Meg

Rosemary grew full, her stomach pulling at the buttons on her shirt. She took my hand and pressed it hard—harder than I ever would have thought to press—into her side, and I expected dough and stuffing but instead felt rocks and pebbles. 'Just wait,' she said, and I waited awkwardly. They call it kicking, but the baby didn't kick; she shifted like anyone might reposition in sleep, tucking tighter into a blanket in the middle of a cold night. Eddie and Leonie expected a little boy, and Rosemary let them, but she knew it was a baby girl. Sugar and spice, and all things nice. I felt some part of her roll beneath my hand, and I must have said something, because Rosemary laughed.

'It's pretty cool, isn't it?'

There were other times I felt the baby stretch a leg. 'That's her foot,' Rosemary told me then, and I really felt the little heel, and imagined tiny toes curling, uncurling.

One morning Rosemary placed my hand where baby had turned against the top of her stomach, and I patted the little back and imagined the day when I might get to hold her on my knee. 'Aunty Meg,' Rosemary called me. I would read that little girl stories. I would knit her cardigans in any colours she chose. I would love her.

I didn't see Eddie very often. Gone were the gentle taps of hammer on chisel. Gone, too, the constant hum of the sander. There were no more rocking horses. He was the Butcher now, and he drove into town early most mornings. He and Rosemary still took their coffee on the steps together, but they didn't have the time they used to. Between her pulling up in the Kingswood, and his climbing in and pulling out, there wasn't more than an hour.

Every now and again, Rosemary dropped Eddie at work so we could go to the cinema, but it meant a lot of fuel and driving, so we only went when there was a film she really had to see. Most days we spent time together in our own faraway worlds, reading quietly, cushions at our corners and cups between our knees. Our friendship had spread beyond Tuesdays.

While Eddie seemed to be enjoying a warmth of fresh acceptance from Winifred, Rosemary presented her coldest shoulder to the town. For the way it had behaved in Eddie's absence. For its refusal to acknowledge any wrong.

Once a month, Eddie's country music wove its way through the trees, but it didn't cast the spell it used to. There was no dancing in the moonlight, no romance in the shadows, no wishing upon stars. When the music started up it was a different scene it coloured.

Men with easy laughs smoked Eddie's sweet tobacco on the porch. Men with wives who'd bother them at home with 'Turn it down!' and 'What time are they going?' brought beer and bourbon, and pizzas in boxes, and they took each other's money around a table Eddie built from scratch and covered with green felt all in one day.

There were four of them, and they drove out together and left at one or two o'clock in the morning, shouting their goodbyes because there was no need to shush and tiptoe. Rosemary would be working. There was no one to wake with a slamming door or a farewell toot of the horn but me, and I wouldn't say boo to a goose, Eddie told them. 'You shouldn't believe everything you read in the papers!'

They laughed harder than ever at that.

One evening, Eddie came to see me. He was holding two beers, and I took the one he offered me. 'Rosemary's working,' he said, but I knew that already, and he knew I knew.

We sat opposite each other on chairs that lived outside the caravan, either side of a table I'd found and mosaicked with broken dishes.

'I need a favour,' Eddie said eventually. He smiled then, and the knowledge that I'd do whatever he asked of me without a moment's hesitation chilled my calves like a spring tide.

'Some of the blokes are off fishing for the weekend, taking the swags and a few beers.' They came out to Magpie Beach for poker, but they weren't the type of friends who'd come all the way at ten o'clock on a Friday night just to pick him up. Not yet. 'Any chance you can drive out with me, bring the car back and pick Rose up from work in the morning? She's off on Sunday, so I'll be good for a lift back.'

'It's a one-off thing,' he said, hoping that it wasn't.

'Of course I can,' I told him. It wouldn't be the first time I'd picked Rosemary up from work in Eddie's car. Not long before, he'd dropped her off and then forgotten that he'd have to go back for her in the morning. He'd thrown up twice outside my door when he'd staggered over to ask me, embarrassed and apologetic, when he needn't have been either.

I'd enjoyed driving out there as the sun came up. The road that ran south of town was little used, and I'd stopped for an echidna which disappeared into the long grass on its verge.

Rosemary had skipped across the slowly filling car park with a smile flooding her face when she saw me. 'I wish you'd told me you were coming,' she said, as if knowing in advance would have meant something to her. As if she might have looked forward to finishing work in a way that was different from usual.

'We should go for breakfast!' she'd announced, and we'd driven up to Marlow Beach, where there was a van that sold bacon-and-egg rolls to take away.

'Do you ever think about just getting in your car and driving, picking a direction and just setting off?' Rosemary asked me that morning. We were sitting at a picnic bench on the grass that fringed the sand, watching someone's dog sniff its way along a string of seaweed.

'I don't have a car,' I told her. 'I'm driving yours.'

She laughed. 'It's not mine either. It's Eddie's.'

That was that, then.

They came over together, late Friday afternoon, to make sure I'd not forgotten. I was just finishing the windows, rubbing streaks free with newspaper, and Rosemary steadied the arm of the chair as I stepped down, though there was nothing of a wobble.

'Come early,' she whispered.

'There's plenty of fuel,' Eddie said.

Rosemary stepped back and behind him, shifting from one foot to the other. She was dressed for work already in the custard-coloured shirt, which was big enough to cover her stomach, but needed a safety pin now at the neck. Hidden from Eddie, she raised three fingers, then flashed all ten and five, mouthing: 'Three fifteen'. She did it twice, would have done it three times if I hadn't stopped her with a nod, and when Eddie turned at that, she brought her fingers to her chin as if she'd just found some lost crumbs or a smudge of soup left from her lunch.

Three fifteen was more than a bit early, but I didn't question it.

CHAPTER FORTY-FOUR

Meg

I rode to Milligan with Eddie at nine o'clock.

'I'll be right from here,' he said, pulling up and climbing out at the top of the rise that ran down to the boat ramp. 'It can be a bit of a tricky turn at the bottom,' he told me, though we both knew that it wasn't.

There was a tag on the bail of his new reel, and I reached across and snapped it off.

His friends were down there already. Waiting by their tinnies, rods leaning against their eskies: one, two, three, four in a row at the end of the squat little dock that sat beside the boat ramp like a Mars bar. I imagined they'd jig for squid on the way out. Put their lines in closer to the mangroves.

I watched Eddie trip down the shallow hill, his swag bumping on his back, and I watched them welcome him into the fold, a couple of them looking up and around while he waved loose fingers vaguely in my direction, telling them what? I doubt it was the truth. These were men whose wives were on the P & C; neighbours who brought each other's bins in and mowed each other's lawns, and celebrated children's birthdays at the barbecues on the edge of the lake. It would have cost Eddie to tell them who it was behind his wheel.

I drove the Kingswood back to Magpie Beach, and sat up most of the night smocking a tiny dress, sinking into sleep from time to time but trusting the alarm I'd set to wake me up at half past two. And at half past two, I brushed my hair and teeth and set out to pick up Rosemary.

Half a moon shone grey-white on a dry and empty road. Cicadas whirred in the bush, and night air washed against me as I drove with windows wound right down and the radio playing softly. As the hour rolled over, a request show began, and I turned off the highway and started along the factory road that bordered the south bank of Lake Carney. I slowed right down in case of kangaroos, hoping I might see the ball of another echidna. This was their time, their place.

A woman called in to the radio station, requesting a song played at her wedding, needing to remember the best day since her divorce had come through that morning. Funny the things that stay with us. It was my aunt Mae's wedding song as well. She and our new uncle Ken swayed barefoot while we all stood in a ragged ring around them. She'd ruined her shoes in the car park, and the hem of her dress was puddle-grey. By the chorus, other couples had begun to dance, and my mother pushed me into the glittery light where my brother caught me and saved me the humiliation of being alone. I suppose she would have danced with our father, if either of them had been sober enough to stand.

Was I singing along when I noticed the patch of sky ahead glowing a dull, bruised orange? For a moment I thought the sun was rising, but it was the wrong direction, too early, and this sunrise flickered like a candle in a draught.

I had just enough time to realise the factory was on fire before a string of cracks cleaved the still night, and flames shot high, cannoning burning chunks towards the stars. Blazing debris splashed into the lake and fell blanket-muffled in the bush. Hard edges rang as they landed on the road ahead.

I pulled the car up like a horse, blood pulsing the length of my neck. The engine stalled, but the radio kept playing.

Smoke matted that purple-gold sky, and clouds of embers drifted to settle like snow. The trees ahead were stark now in silhouette, as fire raged beyond.

I don't know how long I sat in the flame-licked treacle of that night.

Cars and trucks screamed down the road that ran along the far side of the water. Still mine was the only car on the quiet side of the lake. The town would wake to sirens, people asking their partners groggily, 'Do you hear that? Must be a big accident somewhere.'

They always came quietly when they came to us in the night, their blues and reds colouring the rubble on the front grass like splats of paint. If a man beating his family was worth waking a neighbourhood, then ours would never have slept.

Spot fires sprang up around me, trees crisp-crackled and collapsed in clouds of flaming dust, and then I saw her jogging along the verge towards me. There was no doubting it was Rosemary. One hand pressed against a stitch in her side, while the other supported her stomach, and with no arms free to swing for balance, her foot slipped on the verge every couple of strides, and the bag on her back threatened to push her headfirst into the ditch.

I was so shocked that I didn't even start the engine. She had to run all the way to the passenger-side door.

'Let's go,' she panted.

Her mouth was bleeding, but still I didn't move right away. It was all I could do to speak, and I'm sure it was barely a whisper.

'I thought you were dead.'

'I am,' she said, and she smiled weakly. Two of her teeth were missing. Her lip was quivering. Her hands were shaking. 'Meg, we have to go now. Please.'

I turned the key with clumsy fingers and dragged the Kingswood into a three-maybe-more-point turn.

Rosemary reached across and killed the headlights. 'Until we get onto the highway,' she said. She shrugged the pack from her back and dropped it in the footwell, and she slid right down on the seat, bracing herself on her elbows and tilting her chin to get her breath back.

I knew she wasn't coming home, but still I hoped all of that short and darkened distance to the highway, where I snapped the headlights on and the indicator down. She reached over for the second time and flicked it up, turning us right, away from Magpie Beach, away from Winifred and Carney County. South, towards Brisbane, Sydney, Melbourne and the rest of the world.

'Please, Meg,' she said. 'This is the only way.'

While I drove, Rosemary took a zip-lock bag from the glove box and pressed a wad of sterile gauze into her mouth. Then she threw her bag into the back seat and climbed after it. She pulled a roll of banknotes out of her sock, swapped her boots for sneakers and the custard-coloured top for a Rolling Stones t-shirt I'd never seen her wear. She tucked her ponytail into a plain grey cap.

'Where will you go?' I asked.

She thought about telling me. It was in the pause that hung in the dark space between us in the time it took her to answer, but, 'I'll be okay,' is all she said.

'If you need—' I stumbled on my words like I hadn't for a long time.

'I know,' she interrupted, with a hand on the back of my seat. Perhaps she was reaching for my shoulder. 'I won't be coming back,

Meg,' she said softly. 'You understand.' It wasn't a question. It didn't need to be.

The odd car lit us up coming the other way, and when it did, she dipped out of sight. Her shoulder and chin shone in the rear-view mirror, in the sliding white, like a side of bacon whipping through Tom's—now Eddie's—slicer.

'Say when,' Tom used to say, lifting a slice off the scales before he pushed the button, and winking his good eye. I didn't know what Eddie did. I hadn't been in for a long time.

Those were the days, my grandmother would have said. It's what Lily used to say when she remembered Calcutt, but they were days I didn't really cherish at the time. Slipping the bacon in its pearly paper packet into my basket, and unwrapping it at home to lay slice by smooth, pink slice in a pan for a man I loved with all my heart and to whom I owed everything. Happy isn't enough. We should cherish more.

I wished Eddie upriver with a fish on his line, and a dripping beer, and two or three more hours before his sky caved in.

At five o'clock Rosemary sat up and busied herself checking and re-checking the seat and floor to make sure nothing of her was forgotten. She reached forward then and hung a thin chain lightly round my neck, lifting my hair to clasp it carefully.

'I was waiting for your birthday,' she said, 'but we've been friends more than a year now, so I must have missed it.'

Friends.

I didn't thank her. I couldn't, but I didn't need to, and I didn't need to glance down to know it was a charm I'd touched at the market in Theodore. A moonstone set in a hammered silver sun.

I would have driven her anywhere, but she asked me shortly after to pull over.

There are so many things I wish I'd told her in that last hour and a half, and in the ten minutes we spent together on the highway's dewy verge. Words that haunted me in the sleepless weeks that followed, but which I couldn't find in the grey light of that early morning, though I scratched and pulled and tried so hard to press sentences together.

I cherish the memory of her small hand in mine as we waited for lights to find us; sweet expectation on her face in the swoop of cars that didn't stop; the shadow of her thumb passing over the tarmac like a bird.

It was a semitrailer that finally slowed to pick her up. It took a lot of road to stop completely, so she had to run as best she could to catch up and climb in. The hug we shared was years too short and our goodbyes spilled shallowly on the grass.

'Your turn next,' she shouted as she pulled herself up into the cab. She hung there from the handle, one foot inside and out of sight already, while the other dangled mid-step, its lace undone.

My turn to leave, she meant. Magpie Beach and everything that kept me there, and everything I'd be as long as I stayed.

I would have left right then and there. I would have run and climbed up and into the cab beside her if only she'd beckoned. But she just waved, and the heavy door slammed shut behind her, and the semi hissed and revved and eased itself back on its way, and I watched its red tail-lights grow smaller and smaller and finally disappear completely, swallowed by distance or a dip in the road, and Rosemary Lamb was gone.

CHAPTER FORTY-FIVE

Meg

There was time enough for me to refuel the car and think of what to say. Questions would tumble in. Where had I been? How had I known? Because I had not crowded the car park with inquiry the way others would have.

I slept through the explosions I would tell them. I saw the aftermath as I drove to pick Rosemary up, but by then the car park had been blocked by steaming trucks and men in thick yellow suits, and I just knew, I would say, and I turned Eddie's big car around and I drove home to wait for the news to find me.

It was Sergeant Scanlan whose knock rattled my door a little after ten. He wasn't in his uniform.

'Do you know where Eddie is, Meg?' he asked. Soft as cotton, knowing what had happened, and the news I would be given before day's end. Knowing better than anyone what it might do to me.

I told him about the fishing trip, the launch at Milligan, the plan to fish the mangroves then head out and up the coast, and

Sergeant Scanlan nodded and swallowed so deliberately that it made a noise.

'Meg—'

'I know,' I said, and he smiled, sad and sweet and sorry but not sure that I did.

'I'm supposed to—'

'I know,' I said again.

'But—' He looked around to clear his head, to make sure he was certain of what he was about to say, that telling me first wouldn't bring a slide of trouble. 'I've a bit of bad news, darl,' he began. 'Can I come in?'

A bit of bad news.

He was too big for the caravan. Like Alice when she ate the cake. He sat on the end of the bench that ran around the table, and with his legs stretched out, the soles of his shoes touched the drawer under the oven.

'You'll have heard the explosions?'

I shook my head, ready to lie for her already.

'Well,' he went on. It didn't matter.

It was a bank of gas cylinders used to power the sweepers and the forklifts, so they wouldn't belch out petrol fumes around the chocolate. Some valves may have been faulty; they were investigating. 'But it's early days,' Sergeant Scanlan said. Answers would be found among the smouldering rubble. 'Chances are someone was having a smoke, not thinking smart,' he said (or thinking smarter than they ever gave her credit for). It had only been a small fire to begin with, but the where-it-was had led to where-it-went.

It had taken hours to tame the fires that spread, but there were only patches of bush smoking now. Much of the factory was gone, he told me, and he was very sad to say that Rosemary was gone as well. Missing at this stage, 'but there might not be much to find', he warned me, and a story came back to me unbidden, from one of my grandmother's cloth-spined books: a little girl called Harriet, who played with matches and sent herself up in tiger-striped flames, her startled face crosshatched in pencil smoke. All that was left of her in the end was a neat little pile of ashes, and a pair of scarlet slippers.

'I'm so sorry,' Sergeant Scanlan said.

'That's more than a bit,' I told him.

The police brought Eddie home some time later. Their tyres crunched the distance from the highway, and I stood amid the lemon gums and watched two uniformed officers help him out of the car. One patted his shoulder gently as they walked him into his kitchen. Maybe he pulled Eddie's chair out and cleared a space on the table before them. How many cupboards did they open before they found cups and teabags?

Is there someone we can call? Did they need to ask, or had they called already? Leonie's car came soon enough, and I was glad that she was there with Eddie, because she understood the pain, and she knew that this day, and the storm of tears and rage and questions that would fill it, was only the beginning. Nights would fall, and Eddie would sink into many bourboned sleeps, but grief doesn't settle like an ocean.

It's waking up and finding they're not there. It's lying in bed and having that dawn and settle on you morning after morning after morning, like dust. When you come upon a forgotten pocket and slip your hand inside it with a shiver of Christmas morning, hoping for what? The gift of a torn receipt, a cable tie, a button? Something more of them to keep, to have. It's that. It is the shadow of a still guitar, a hat on an empty chair, fishing magazines and the debris of an ordinary day: little piles of bolts and coins and useless scraps of paper. *The mill cannot grind with the water that is past.* Looking upstream. It is that.

What if he wasn't dead? Do you think missing him would have felt the same? Rosemary had asked me once. Had that been the start of it? A breadcrumb torn and dropped and followed later?

I understood. It would be easier for Eddie. He need not wonder why or where, how, or how he might have done things differently, how he could possibly put things back the way they were before. There would be casseroles and hotpots for Eddie Lamb the Butcher, whose wife and unborn child died in the Factory Fire. One foot after the other, he would move forward, and he would begin again.

Not-knowing would not finish Eddie off.

CHAPTER FORTY-SIX

Meg

As it turned out, they found two teeth and a wedding ring, but if the lack of bones raised an eyebrow, it wasn't high enough to stop Rosemary being officially declared dead.

'We take our break at three,' one of the other cleaners told the *Courier*. 'Thank God we were all together in the crib room,' which was about as far away from what they called the garage as you could get—though of course they were not *all* together.

'She kept herself to herself a bit,' they said.

Sergeant Scanlan's guess had been correct: the fire was started by a cigarette, or by the match that lit a cigarette (the newspaper was vague, and people weren't that interested). There was insurance. Building would be done, new sweepers and trucks bought and stored in a safer space. The factory would make less chocolate for a while, but it would go on to make more than it had before. How and when this would be managed would not rustle newsprint while there were better details to be pecked at.

TWO LIVES LOST IN FIRE was Monday's headline. Everybody knew about the first, but they paid the cover price to read about the second. Local woman Rosemary Lamb was seven months pregnant.

An Afterlife for Rosemary Lamb

In the photograph Eddie gave them, Rosemary is pushing her hair up out of her eyes, squinting in the bright light of a late winter's afternoon. She is smiling straight into the lens, her shoulders cocoa-coloured and her cheeks a little sunburned. There is nothing to tell it in the background, but I know—because I took the photograph—that she is standing outside a bar where she will go on to dance with cowboys on a floor of crackling peanut shells.

When it was decided by those who make such clear decisions, that there would be no more of Rosemary to lay to rest, the *Courier* was tasked with inviting all her friends and family to a service at the Baptist church on Lakeview. There would be a tree planted afterwards. What sort of tree, I wondered, and who made that decision? Rosemary loved golden wattle, and the snapped-leaf smell of peppermint gums, but I don't know that anyone else knew that.

Early on the evening of the night before, I went over to the Lambs' cabin to sit on the steps where I'd so often sat beside Rosemary or watched from a distance while she lost herself in a book, or bent to paint her toenails. I wanted the company of where-she'd-been; the shade of how it felt when I was with her.

When Sonny died, I felt I'd lost all that I'd ever been. My strings were cut, and I collapsed. I could not stand without him.

But it was different after Rosemary.

I had been left behind, but I had not been left. She had not taken with her the blue of the sky. She had splashed colours that would not wash away, and left choice on my table like a dice in a cup.

Your turn next.

Words I fingered like shells in my pocket.

The timber was warm beneath my bare feet. The sun had poured most of its colour down behind the trees and the mozzies were out. Perhaps I was half-expecting Eddie; it was that time of the afternoon, though he'd spent a lot of nights at his mother's. I'd been avoiding him, afraid I might give something away under cross-examination, but what was there for him to question? As each day passed, I'd come to breathe a little easier, so I did not scurry home when I heard a car approaching. I waited on the step and watched as it swung an arc of light around the clearing and parked with its back to me, its single occupant as still as stone for minutes behind the wheel.

It wasn't Eddie's car. It wasn't Eddie.

The door opened slowly, and bright sneakers at the end of dark blue jeans tapped the ground as if testing its stability. Rosemary's mother hadn't changed much in the years that she'd been gone, and I recognised her profile even in the gloom.

Joanna Cole had always been a woman who turned the heads of other women's men. Her clothes were ironed, buttons carefully left undone. Pendants rested low. She wore make-up and earrings and highlights in her hair, but she couldn't hide the furrow on her brow that wondered who I was and what I was doing on this deck that wasn't mine. She didn't know me, and I felt myself sit up just a little bit straighter because of that.

'Eddie not here?' she called out.

I shook my head.

She wandered a little, here and there, around and about, and eventually came close enough to share her thoughts.

'By God, this place hasn't changed.' She squinted at her watch and then noticed the day's paper on the step beside me, folded to page five, where there was a short piece covering the details of the next day's service. It was the same picture of Rosemary they printed every time.

Joanna picked it up, and she looked at that photograph for long minutes—for all the time it took Eddie's car to pull in next to hers, and all the time it took him to join us on the deck.

'Not like you to be on time,' he said.

They exchanged a weak hug. Brief and broken by limp pats on shoulders.

'Eddie, love.'

'How've you been, Jo?'

'I spoke to her just last month,' she said quietly. 'I didn't imagine anything like this would . . .' She didn't have to finish the sentence.

'She didn't say she'd spoken to you.'

'No, I don't suppose she did. How are you coping?' she asked, but Eddie didn't answer.

'You remember Meg?' he said instead.

'Yes, we've met before.' A tight smile, a sharp nod, and I felt my shoulders soften.

'She was a good friend of Rosemary's.'

A look of surprise swiftly covered.

I began to stand, but Eddie put a hand on my shoulder and pressed me gently back towards the step, wanting company or a witness or just help to dilute the conversation. I didn't know how well he knew Joanna, but I knew he didn't like her very much.

She returned to the newspaper while Eddie took the key from under the lavender and disappeared into the house. He didn't ask if she wanted a glass of wine, so she couldn't say *No, thank you*. It gave him something to do. It would give them something to set between them in place of the woman who would have filled that space.

'So, you were friends?' she asked.

I nodded.

'Close?' She turned to look at me, trying to test the depth of my friendship with her daughter, needing me to confirm it with a password, a wink, or a coded handshake.

'Very.' Only one word, but with it a flush of pride as blue as a ribbon.

Eddie wouldn't be long inside. She had maybe two minutes, not enough time to cast a line and reel it slowly. She had to ask outright.

'Is she really dead?'

Until then, I was beginning to think Rosemary might have hitchhiked all the way to Melbourne, a daughter drawn back beneath her mother's wing.

'They found her teeth,' I told Joanna.

'I know that,' she said, 'but they didn't find anything else, did they?' She smoothed the newspaper in her lap like a napkin in a fancy restaurant.

'Her wedding ring.'

Joanna gave a snort like a horse impatient with its saddle. 'And that's all you're going to tell me.'

I thought about giving her more, but I didn't know that she deserved it, and I'd promised Rosemary I would keep her secret. Keep her safe.

'That's all there is,' I said.

'Ah, but is it?' She drew a thick breath slowly as though sucking through a filter and she held it, and my eye, for a long, still while.

My brother and I used to fill boring waits with stares, unblinking across bus seats, church pews, and dinner tables. All siblings know the prickle of dry eyes. I held my breath as Joanna held her own, and I cleared my head so she could not see inside me.

Her eyes were more green than brown, and quite beautiful, though I'd never noticed before. I'd never looked; if I ever had she would have looked away. But I remembered the sketch on Rosemary's wall, Joanna's angles softer than they were in real life. 'She wasn't that much of a looker,' Eddie had said, but she was.

Eventually, she exhaled sharply, as if to snuff the candles on a cake.

That's that then.

'She didn't really belong here, did she?' She didn't expect me to answer, but I wanted to. I wanted her to understand she wasn't even close to knowing all there was to know about her daughter.

'She made it feel like home,' I said.

Eddie banged back through the screen door and handed us each a glass of Rosemary's wine. *Chateau la Boîte.*

They exchanged facts—traffic, weather, real estate—and then, 'Why are you here, Joanna?'

I was wondering the same, but grief made Eddie bold. Why had she wanted to meet him here at Magpie Beach? Why not pay her respects with everyone else at the ceremony tomorrow?

'Honestly, I don't know,' she said. 'I just wanted to see . . .' Another broken sentence. 'I'm sorry.' It was thicker than sorry for dragging him all the way out here for no real reason, and I wondered what it was exactly she was sorry for. There were so many stages for her to regret.

'Do you want to go inside?' Eddie asked, nodding back towards the door he'd not long come out of. 'Do you want to look at her things?' It sounded watery. 'You can have a wander round if you like,' flicking limp fingers towards the shed, the barbecue, the rocky path down to the compost bin.

'If I'd known . . .'

If ifs and ands were pots and pans, there'd be no need for tinkers. Perhaps I said it out loud, because both Eddie and Joanna were looking at me once I'd thought it.

Joanna shook her head, pulled her lips into her mouth, then ran a hand through her hair in a manner that was every bit her daughter's. 'I really am sorry.'

Eddie dug a booted toe into the ground. 'I know you are.'

She set her glass on the newspaper and centred a bracelet on her wrist as she stood to leave. Fumbling for something to say, she double-checked the time of the service, and then she apologised one last time, but it was puddle-shallow now. 'I'm sorry for your loss.' *His* loss. She reached out and cupped his cheek briefly in the palm of her hand. He did not lean into her touch, and perhaps that cut it short, but he walked her to her car and waited while she climbed inside and wound the window down. She trapped his hand beneath hers on the window lip, as if she had something she wanted still to say but wasn't sure whether, or how, to say it.

'It'll all work out,' she said finally, patting and releasing his hand. 'For you, I mean.'

There was a whoosh of aircon as the engine started, and a whine as the window glided closed. Keen wheels spun slightly, and she was gone.

I followed Eddie into the kitchen, where he apologised for the dishes in the sink, the milk carton on its side on the table, and the cat's bowl which was a scribble of ants. He took the glass from my hand and refilled it from the box on the counter. I didn't remind him to put it back in the fridge.

Rosemary was everywhere: rings and hair ties on the windowsill; notes and quotes dragging magnets down the fridge, and a list of names I doubted had been for the baby (Barney, Edward, Lucy, Zak); a gossipy magazine folded back on itself. I couldn't place the actor in the story, though his face was familiar enough. Rosemary would have known him and every movie he'd ever been in, who he was married to, and what he was reported to be like 'in real life'. 'You know this one, Meg. Think!' she would have said to me, as if it were important. She'd have fed me clues until I had the taste of an idea and told her he was the astronaut or the baseball player or the murderer-after-all, and that would have been enough for her to hand me his name like a little trophy.

'I'm sorry too,' I said.

'I know you are, love.' Eddie sucked his teeth and widened his eyes to keep himself from crying, but still the tears spilled through his lashes. 'But don't be,' he said. 'Be glad you knew her. She loved you, you know.'

I covered my ears with my hands because I didn't want to hear any more.

'This'll need returning.' I saw his lips move as he handed me the book: *What to Expect When You're Expecting*. Slow breaths and years of habit led me to flick through the pages, and I caught Rosemary's bookmark as it slipped. It was an old postcard, its colours faded and corners brittled by time, but I recognised the pale stone building in the photograph, the rack of pillars at its entrance, and the tall clock tower. I knew where the card had come from, if not who'd sent it, and I slid it back inside the book before Eddie might notice and want to keep it for himself.

He sat down with a sigh. 'She'd have been a great mum, you know.'

I knew.

'Not like . . .'

So many sentences never need be tidied shut. I nodded and sat down beside him.

'She nearly left once, you know,' he said quietly, and my heart froze. It was a thoughtful look he gave me. Deliberating: would he say what he was about to, or would he keep it to himself? There was wondering in it, and I didn't want it out loud.

Keep it, I pleaded silently. *Please keep it.*

He looked down at the stubby in his hand and scratched at its label with a thumbnail.

'She came to our place really late one night,' he began, and confusion must have flickered on my face. 'Joanna,' he said, and I let my breath go quietly.

'Before Rosemary was born,' he went on. 'We still had the farm. I must have been nine or ten. Mum and Jo were best friends back then. Our families were really close. We used to go camping together. Shane and me were fast asleep, and there was this hammering on the front door. I remember getting up and looking down the passage, and there was Aunty Jo, crying on the doorstep. She didn't have her girls with her, and I can remember wondering where they were. Mum was crying too, and there was a taxi with its engine running. Dad went out and paid it, and brought a suitcase back in with him, which I thought was weird, but Mum had already taken Jo through to the kitchen, and Dad waved Shane and me back to bed.

'I didn't really think about it again till years later. Jo stayed the night. I suppose Dad drove her home in the morning. It didn't seem like such a big deal at the time. Grown-ups argue. Everyone's parents spent the odd night on a couch. Things were always stitched up in the morning.'

He went to swig his beer and realised it was empty.

'Mum persuaded her to stay with King, I guess. I'm sure it wasn't that hard. Where did she think she was going? How did she think she was going to manage? She had no money, no trade. No experience doing anything other than working in the shop. King took the photos and ran the machine that developed everyone else's.

'It's a nice idea, isn't it?' he added, flicking the lid off another beer with the tail edge of a knife. 'Just fucking off. Life's not like that, though, is it?'

It was a Lily thing to say, and I shook my head, *No, it isn't*, but I'd begun to wonder if it could be. If it might be.

'I don't think Mum has ever properly forgiven herself. For stopping Jo leaving that night, you know? But no one knew what King was really like, then. He was your regular "merry old soul"!' He made quotation marks with his fingers, and gave a sour little laugh.

'The next thing, Jo was pregnant again and they all got to see how jolly he was once the baby was born.'

'Rosemary?'

He nodded. 'She might have stayed with him, but she wasn't faithful. You know that. Everyone knew it soon enough. As soon as Rosemary could sit up straight, you could see it. But Joanna never admitted it, even to Mum. And King stayed with her, I'll give him that, so maybe he believed her, but I doubt it. I think he was just lazy, and it was easier for him to go along with the lie. In public, anyway. In private he was something else.'

There were four empty bottles in front of Eddie now.

'The phone would ring in the night, and we'd hear Mum talking to Joanna: "Take the baby. Lock the door. Tom's on his way". And Dad would bolt off and Mum would wait up in her dressing-gown till he got back. It went on for years. Mum went sometimes, but it was usually Dad. No one trusted King around a woman when he'd been drinking. Dad said he was shagging anything that moved towards the end, and it wasn't all consensual, if you know what I mean.' Eddie sneered even as he looked disgusted, almost apologetic. 'Her life would have been so different if she'd gone,' he said.

'Whose?'

He shook the question away. 'Well, there would have been no Rosemary, would there? There'd have been none of this.' He waved his arms at the home around him. 'None of that.' His eyes falling on the book I still held in my lap. *What to Expect When You're Expecting*.

I worried that something too familiar might be pointing the shadow of a finger at his own wife's disappearance, and hoped it was only his seeing Joanna again after so many years that had nudged these memories up.

He drained a fifth bottle and dragged a hand down his face.

'You need to sleep,' I told him.

We both knew what the next day held, what was set to be let go, and it was deep dark now; night had fallen like a curtain. I stood up to leave, gathering the bottles to take with me.

'What I've never understood,' Eddie said, as I reached for the door, 'is why she didn't take Rosemary with her when she finally did go. I don't know why she left her here, when there was nothing here for her. Why do you think that was, Meg?'

He didn't often use my name, and it kept me there with my hand flat on the flyscreen.

'I don't know, Eddie.'

But actually, I did. We portion blame like berries. We keep some for ourselves, we give more or less to the person who deserves it, but the little left can end up in the most unlikely places.

CHAPTER FORTY-SEVEN

Meg

I set Rosemary's postcard—the one I'd tucked back between the pages of *What to Expect* in Eddie's kitchen—on the table. *Brisbane* on the front in yellow bubble writing, balloon-like in a too-blue sky beside the clock tower. I hadn't needed it to know which city's hall the building was. *Officially opened in 1930*, the small print on the back told me, but I knew that already, and that in front of and either side of its columned entrance lay two lions cast in bronze, though in Rosemary's postcard they were hidden in the shadows of towering palms and a statue of King George up on his horse.

I took my own postcard from the book beside my bed. The postcard I'd kept for years. The card that had survived when so many other special precious things had not, safe in the book that I was reading, in the bag that I had with me the day I lost my home, and everything within it, in a sweep of rain and mud. The card that was old even when I found it, trapped in the library book Joanna Cole's pasty daughter returned the week after her mother moved to Melbourne.

The City Hall lion, his paws together and his head so slightly bowed. One of a pair, its own fine print read. *Modelled on the bronze lions of Trafalgar Square. Unveiled in 1938.* I knew it by heart.

The messages on the backs of the cards were almost identical.

March 2, 10 am, don't forget!

Mark your diary! 10 am, March 2 x

Even without them, even ignoring the date, there was unmistakable sameness. The soft grey-black tails of *f*, *g* and *y*; *1973* postmarks faded like tattoos; the same initial curled in both cards' corners: the *P* that could have been an *A*.

The same address: 16 Rosella Street, Winifred, Qld.

To Joanna Cole.

Either card arriving on its own might not have drawn too much attention, a reminder easily explained away, even with the kiss. Still, I imagine she was sure to be the one to check the letterbox.

I took the back of an opened envelope for a scrap of paper, and I worked from Rosemary's twenty-first, which was the only date I knew.

She was born in 1973, but not until September. In February, Eddie would have just turned nine, and Joanna Cole was already pregnant when she woke him up in the middle of the night with her hammering on the door—a train ticket in her pocket, and her bags in the back of the taxi that idled behind her in the dark. Her girls were fast asleep in their beds, with no idea she'd be gone when they woke up in the morning. Would she have made it, if she hadn't stopped to say goodbye to her best friend? If Leonie had said, 'Go on, then,' would Joanna have gone?

If ifs and ands . . .

What had Leonie said to make Joanna stay?

Better the devil you know?

Candles snuffed and blankets folded, did she shine a harsher light into the corners of her friend's affair? Tell her life's not like that? Draw a finger through the dust of dreams, drag the sheets back to reveal the stains on the mattress underneath; handprints greasy on the window; fruit flies drowned in the dregs of wine sticky in the bottom of their glasses?

How long had they been apart already? Were secrets beginning to feel dirty?

Could she really leave her children? They were not boxed possessions she could send for in a week or two and were not quite old enough to follow by themselves. King would not have let them go to her. He was not a man who would have let her have them and, as Eddie said, she had no skills to trade.

'What will you do?' Perhaps that was all Leonie had to ask her. I wonder did she stumble on her words, as I had?

Had Joanna known yet that she was pregnant?

I leafed through the book Eddie had returned to me. Rosemary would have been the size of a grain of rice, perhaps an olive, safe in her mother's womb, tucked beneath a blanket on the Lambs' couch. The man who would be her husband, still a boy, asleep in a blue room at the other end of the passage.

Things were always stitched up in the morning.

'It'll all work out, you know,' Leonie might have told Joanna. It's what Joanna had promised Eddie, and what Rosemary had often told me when she saw me worrying threads and corners.

('Not by itself it won't,' Lily was fonder of saying.)

I don't know that Rosemary would have wondered any more than I did about the card she found, wherever it was she found it. Either one by itself was nothing more than a reminder from a friend. Wherever would she have caught an idea that its curling hand belonged to her real father?

P or A.

Don't forget!

He had not just been passing through. Rosemary was not the product of one night with a stranger. He had a name her mother knew and must have thrilled to hear on others' lips, feel the shape of on her own. A delicious special-secret something, and there had been enough between them for Joanna to have packed her bags and grown a plan to join him.

Did she let him know she was not coming, or did she let him wait for her in the square beside the lions and King George upon his horse? How long might he have waited, checking his watch against the clock on the tall tower? Would he have settled on a bench eventually with his head in his hands? Called her from a public telephone that afternoon or the next? Would she have answered?

How many letters did he send Joanna in the weeks that followed? The squeak of the letterbox bringing her a spidery chill higher than the butterflies whose wings must have fluttered so deliciously in the beginning.

I don't believe he knew there was a baby. If he'd loved her enough to plan their future, then he would have come back for her if he'd known they had a child.

Eddie was right: Joanna's life would have been so very different if she'd gone. But she'd stopped to say goodbye, chosen to stay, and sealed the envelope of Rosemary's own chance at a Life Like That.

What had she been expecting?

CHAPTER FORTY-EIGHT

Meg

Rosemary had never been a Baptist, but there was some connection with the sister who was tasked with organising something. A brother-in-law—the tall, thin husband of a woman whose children sat quietly either side of her in the front pew—delivered the eulogy. He described Rosemary with clear, kind words, but they were pencil drawn when she was full of colour.

'Always up for a laugh,' he said, but he didn't mention that she laughed loud and often with her head tipped back, and feathers in the lines around her eyes; or that she found the brightest humour in the simplest things.

'Bubbly,' he called her, but he didn't tell how her words embraced you as she spoke, and made you feel as if she'd rather be with you than anybody else. He didn't tell how she was always ready to join in, and take a turn, and be herself, and never once expected any less from you.

'Young,' yes, but there was glitter in her youth, lift in her step, a future in her eyes.

'She loved life,' he said, but she loved so many other things as well. She loved tawny frogmouths and carrot cake. She loved thunderstorms, and romance novels, and Richard Gere; the camphor smell of kitchen cupboards, and the brush of velvet. She put her boots on the table and bare feet in puddles. She was the top hat when she played Monopoly, never took the last biscuit or the first, walked under ladders and left food out for possums. Her favourite colour was green.

There were more than a hundred mourners, according to the *Courier*. I recognised some of the women she'd worked with who'd come to her birthday party. I knew Mr Breadsell, Theresa from the Pink Fig, Catherine and Sergeant Scanlan, Leonie and Nola and Joanna. There were more strangers than friends, but Eddie drew strength from their handshakes, their pats on his shoulders, and the cappuccino froth of words that bubbled on their lips.

The hole in the park had been dug already and a silver wattle sat beside it in a fat little mound of soil. We stood in a loose ring around it while the pastor read a passage from the Bible.

'There is a time for everything, and a season for every activity under the heavens . . .'

Three men lowered the young tree into the ground, but Eddie held the shovel and helped scoop the soil in and around it, and it was Eddie alone who trod it flat.

'A time to tear down and a time to build, a time to weep and a time to laugh, a time to mourn and a time to dance.'

Who would Eddie go on to dance with? I wondered, and I may have stared too long at the women who stood alone, their fingers interlaced, heads bowed and eyes closed in prayer—or maybe only wondering whether they had time enough for a sandwich before they were expected back at work.

Rosemary's mother left as soon as the Bible snapped shut. Leonie took her arm and offered soft, sad words that might have made another stay awhile, but red lips mouthed, *Too late*. Too late for a drink. Too late for lunch on Carney's deck. Too late to rekindle a friendship that was nothing now but brittle sticks and ash. There was no room for

Leonie in the life Joanna had carved for herself in Melbourne. There would have been new friends, old friends after a while, but it was too late for Leonie to be either.

If I ever saw Rosemary again, I willed there to be warmth between us still and not the frost that hung smoke-white and crystal-cold between Joanna and Leonie. The water passed, a river frozen solid. There would be no skating, no holding hands, no spring thaw. The mill would not turn again. It was hard to imagine a time when they might have known each other's thoughts and habits and told each other everything (but not everything).

Eddie came between them and slipped his arm around his mother's waist.

'I've a plane to catch,' Joanna told him. She gave him a limp hug, then she crossed Lakeview and stepped out of the heels she wore and into the car she'd hired. There was no backward glance. No smile or wave. She pulled out and disappeared into thin traffic.

Others followed. Street parking began to clear, and those on foot trailed like ants towards the pub, reappearing on the deck that overlooked the lake with pints of beer and glasses of wine, in twos and threes and fours until they spread into a colony of cheers and chatter.

I stared across the park towards the bench the Rotary Club had paid for and cemented by the path. They called it Mrs Carney's bench, and a plate there marked her time and task and suggested she was buried underneath, but I knew she lay in an unmarked plot outside St Anthony's cemetery. They had considered moving her, but in the end they'd let her be, and that was just as well, I thought; she had been through enough.

Her fields were empty now and the bench was empty too, bleached to bone away beyond the geese and reeds, and standing in the sharp light of that late morning I decided that the stone Rosemary had cast would skip and travel. Shadows would lengthen, times would change, Mrs Carney's plaque would smooth to wordlessness, and the little tree just blessed would grow, but I would not be there to see it.

A time to be born and a time to die, a time to plant and a time to uproot.

It was my time.

CHAPTER FORTY-NINE
Meg

It was a waxing moon. There weren't so many stars to see for all the cloud, but it was bright enough, and the rocks were still familiar beneath my feet. The ocean lay like the back of a spoon, with barely a lip of foam, but there was no temptation to scramble down. I only wanted to see it, to know it and be close to it, one last time. To save it.

It was the last night I would spend at Magpie Beach. In the morning I would drive away in the little car Catherine had sold me for much less than she might have taken from someone else. 'We've been meaning to get rid of it,' she'd told me, but I didn't know if that was true. 'You're doing us favour,' she'd said when I first slipped behind the wheel, but she was the one pressing a kindness.

One of Eddie's friends had come with a truck to take the other car away. There would be no fixing that one, only a pulling-apart. I had cleared the weeds around it and run a cloth over it, and I had sat for a while in the passenger seat with the ghosts of journeys taken.

I was ready to say goodbye.

So many things had changed in recent weeks and months. Eddie's back and forth had grown more forth than back, and he'd taken a little more with him to Leonie's every time. Rosemary's baskets were gone. The fairy lights had come down, and the porch was empty.

Beth and Amy had been boxed in straw and delivered via the library to a woman with a brood of her own. Silence now as I passed the henhouse. No worried fluff of feathers, no gentle rumble of dream.

There was no more cause for wonder as I walked. There was no chance of passing Rosemary in the night. There was no moth-flecked light outside the house across the headland, and I walked right up to and around it. Everything was gone but the doormat. Lily's flowerpots lay soil-less on their sides and upside down, their contents long since sifted through.

There were boards on all the windows. *Stilton and Haines Real Estate* plastered in glossy paper strips across the timber with a Brisbane phone number no one was likely to see. Someone else would buy the house one day, someone with a hobby or a habit that needed tucking out of sight, as in time someone would fill the space that I had taken on and around the cream-grey slab Sonny had laid. Eddie's house was up for rent. People would come again to Magpie Beach. Vegetables would be grown and chickens cooped, kettles would boil and cakes would rise, mangoes would be picked and pickled, fish caught and storms weathered.

'Was there a note?' the police had asked, the afternoon Rosemary and I went looking for Lily, and Rosemary had told them no, but I'd been lying when I shook my head.

Tucked beneath the lamp at Lily's bedside, it was addressed to me and I did not share it.

It was not long. *One last favour*, Lily had begun. *There is a thin path that begins beside a short stump.*

The clearing was darker than I'd known it other nights, but bright enough to see the ring of bush that crept around it. There were six or seven tree stumps, severed long ago, blunt edges weathered smooth and frosted with undergrowth, but Lily's path was wider than she would have known it, trampled flat by officers in boots, and it was easy enough to find.

Ten minutes along it, Lily wrote, and she told me where I must dig when I got there.

I could have followed it under a warm sun, but night-time felt in keeping with secrets, and it was to be kept secret. Lily was very clear on that.

Leave it some time, she had written, but I didn't know why. I didn't know then what would happen, what would be found among the things she'd left in places she must have known someone would look; and then I knew enough to know no ground could be turned over without those same someones noticing. Withholding evidence, they would call it then. So, I kept Lily's favour a secret and it became a secret of my own, and I left it some time (more time than Lily would have meant for me to leave).

I would take what was buried with me in the morning or burn it before sunrise. *Do with it what you like*, Lily had written, *but don't leave it there to rot.*

Ten minutes is five or fifteen depending on your stride and hurry. It is an egg boiled the way you like it, bread cut and buttered, a tap and a crack and a pinch of salt. In no time at all the little path spilled onto sand, as Lily had written that it would, and in a huddle there I found the patch of pigface she'd described. On my knees, I pushed flat hands beneath its blistery leaves until I felt the stones Lily had set there.

My heart beat hard, and my hands were shaking, but I pulled the tangled roots free with a gardener's care, and dragged my fingers deeper; picturing *Jamaica Inn*, lighthouse lamps snuffed on stormy nights, shipwrecked men clubbed like seals on wild beaches where crates and barrels washed up and were looted.

It wasn't buried deep or hard to find. A box wrapped tightly in a plastic shopping bag. Tape wound around to keep it dry and all together. I didn't for a moment consider opening it there. I needed to be home with the door closed and curtains pegged tight. After all that had passed, I could imagine too many things she might have felt she needed to pass on. I bundled the box into the sack I carried on my back, and I lay the pigface like a net upon the worried soil, where it would take, and I retraced my steps back to Lily's clearing and from there took the easy path that cut across the headland, home to the quiet hollow of the caravan.

I cut the plastic carefully. There was strength still in its binding. It had not been underground so long as to have been weakened, and when dusted off its colours were still bright. Inside was an ordinary shoebox. Its corners were squashed and the sticker that showed what size and style had been stripped away and left a raw, grey patch of cardboard. It hadn't been chosen to weather any winter, only to wait a while for dust to settle and crowds to clear.

I poured tea and found my glasses and a biscuit, and I let the shoebox wait a little longer, as it must have sat wrapped and ready on Lily's own kitchen table. As I imagined it sitting in the sand while she troubled the pigface with her trowel.

Cup, plate and scissors on the table, I lifted the lid. Beneath it, a head of crumpled newspaper, and a letter with my name, taped to a thick wad of fifty-dollar notes, tightly bound and cling-wrapped like a sandwich. I'd never seen so much money. The cash I had came in brown envelopes and fell out in fives and coins. I smoothed the page of *The Carney Courier* flat upon the table, but it was nothing. BRILLIANT BAINSY

BOWLS HIS WAY INTO CENTRAL QUEENSLAND CRICKET TEAM, advertisements and a strip of weather. Underneath it, and wrapped carefully in tissue, what had Lily chosen to secret away? A cornflower-blue-and-white brooch that I'd never seen her wear; a bracelet of small ivory elephants; a pair of earrings that might have been her favourites, crystals and summer-yellow stones gathered in knots; a commemorative coin boxed on a bed of royal blue velvet; a ribbon won for spelling; a delicate ceramic robin wrapped in a time-softened handkerchief with *K.A.* embroidered in one corner; *Wuthering Heights*, well thumbed and with a pressed flower and a prayer for St Anthony slipped between its pages; a tiny bottle of sticky yellow perfume; a stiff paper crane; a cardboard coaster and a champagne cork; a stack of tickets from the Galaxy, torn but tidied straight and paperclipped together; and a box within the box of small, square photographs. Calcutt, of course, in silvery grey: its viaduct; a frosted pond; a snowman and the length of a back garden; a child in gumboots swinging between two adults; a field with distant steeples; a sleeping dog; a Christmas table backlit by a wide, white window; a cake with candles; socks and buckled shoes beside a hedgehog and a saucer of milk. Memories, swept like crumbs from a counter, but collected in a careful palm. In Lily's hands, hours would have rippled around every one. The champagne cork—a meal shared, an arm around her waist, moonlight and dancing. There was something of the woman I'd known in the photographs (the river I could better imagine frozen, the brother whose face I now knew, the fields she'd tumbled through), but Lily alone held what came before each moment captured, what happened afterwards. I would never know whose careful fingers had folded stiff paper; could only imagine the prayer known off by heart; could only wonder: Why the robin? What history had the jewellery? From whose pocket had the handkerchief been taken?

I knew something of the coaster's either side, remembered Lily tucking it into her bag, as if it were theft, as if anyone would have cared or noticed, the second night we spent in Theodore. One side branded with a beer that Rosemary might have drunk, if she'd been drinking, the other ringed with Lily's own red wine. The barman called her Princess, and she drank a little more than she was used to, and let herself be pulled into a line of dancing, and the warmth of company and the kindness shown and the far-enough-away.

And the movie tickets—for every film that Lily, Rosemary, and I had seen together—trapped in order, first and oldest at the top: *Wolf*. I remembered that morning, the rain that fell like curtains over awnings, the voice Rosemary had raised to be heard above it, the cake we'd shared while we waited afterwards for Lily. What errand had she run? I wondered now. Not that it mattered. Not that any of it mattered anymore, but I wondered, when Lily lay her head in the filtered light and slippery plastic of that bag, in the crackle of her dying breaths, the hum of medication shutting all things down, when she knew she was leaving it all behind—Norman to be found and crucified, every secret to be unravelled and exposed, friendships to be tested—did this box she'd buried give her comfort? Knowing there was this walnut of proof that she had been here. She'd had this other life, been someone else before all that she'd become, and done, and hidden. The proof of it boxed and buried, the essence of who she'd been to start with.

My memories, she'd called her stories once. Two words she'd powdered with apology, as if Rosemary or I would think less of her for having them than we would of someone who kept none at all. Over cake and coffee, she had hooked them out of holes and corners where they'd sat for who knew how long gathering dust and cobwebs, and she'd crocheted such a picture for us. Still, the blanket was hers to keep.

'You can't take it with you,' my father used to say. He meant money, winnings blown on takeaway chicken and bottles of brandy. *Easy come, easy go.*

What can we take with us in the end, but the hope that we've left a memory with someone who will care enough to keep it?

CHAPTER FIFTY
Meg

It was the butcher's van that drew up, mid-morning. I'd been ready to go since first light, but it seemed honest to wait until they came to take what had been borrowed, and I needed the station-calm of someone on a platform as I pulled away. The raised hand of a solid goodbye.

Eddie swung down from the driver's side, and Leonie and his cousin climbed out after him. It was a fine day, and they stretched their necks and tipped their chins to the sun like turtles.

'All set?' Leonie called out.

I was. Mrs Robinson was already trapped in the car, likely asleep in the rubble of our belongings.

'Any idea where you're off to yet?'

I was wary of suggestions and struggled to find something to say that would nudge the conversation on to other things.

'Have you got everything?' I asked Eddie. From the house, I meant. Had he taken everything he was taking, now he'd made the decision to move back to town completely.

'There's only the big stuff left,' he said. 'Saves me a bit of Bugs Bunny using this thing.' He slapped the side of the van and it rang like an old dustbin lid, and for a long moment I was halfway down a hill that was my grandmother's front path, flat-footed and bare-legged, racing my brother and a great iron disc that wobbled and wound its way into a pocked and empty road. Last one to the far side was a rotten egg.

'He was going to rent something,' the Coulter said.

'Yeah, I'd forgotten about this old girl!' Eddie slapped the van again, but with more care and kindness.

It was a pointless conversation, but no one wanted to be the one to say, 'Well, this is it then!' and open the gate.

'Old'd be right!' said the Coulter.

'Now then, you!' Leonie laughed. 'It's bigger than your car, anyway!' And something in the way she said it badgered a memory. *It's bigger than your car, anyway.* Someone else had said that, or something like it. Someone else had wanted the same, and I struggled to remember who that was.

Leonie clipped her nephew's ear playfully, then gave a little yelp, remembering something close to being forgotten, and hurried back to the van, returning a moment later with a wicker cat basket.

'I knew we'd kept it after Tiger,' she said, handing it to me. 'There's a lead in there as well. I know, I know!' She threw a hand up in ready defence and pointed the other at Eddie. 'Don't you say anything! It was you who wanted to take the poor bloody thing for walks!'

'And how did that go?' asked the Coulter.

'Yeah, not well.'

Confetti chatter.

'It might make your drive a bit easier, anyway,' Leonie said, and another memory stirred: Mrs Robinson wrapped in a cardigan I was cold to be without, the night I found her wandering all alone on Marlow Beach and brought her home, driving carefully with the nest of her in my lap.

A memory layered; there was something beneath it.

Moonlight matted by mist. Police, fire and ambulance scattered around a body in the road. The accident I might have missed by minutes. The highway blocked by blue lights that slowed our journey home. It was King Cole's car parked on the scrubby verge.

I watched them scrape him, floodlit, off the tarmac. Too late for a siren, the whole scene played out in a terrible silence. Policemen stood to the side. Grey faces lit in flashes by the lights that spun above the cars they came in. They smoked cigarettes and shook their heads, hats high and back where sweaty palms had pushed them clear of foreheads. 'Move on now,' they called out when the road was clear. 'There's nothing to see here.'

But in the full moon there had been plenty, and the image of Roy Cole's hair, caught in the teeth of the bag they zipped shut over his face, fell into idle moments for months. The stretch of road he'd spread across stayed dark for weeks, until it rained.

But something still beneath it.

There was a thin root to the memory that I could feel. Something else moved when I worried it, like a ligament that holds a wobbling tooth.

Leonie was still talking, but I was focused on the van behind her, *Lamb & Coulter Quality Butchers*, and it came to me then, something snapped, and swinging free was a memory clear: Catherine's voice, library-quiet but clean as water: 'Something bigger than a car, anyway, Mike said.'

We'll find him! he'd assured the papers, but they never did.

It had started out as *Lamb & Son*. Resprayed and re-stencilled but it was the same van. It had always been theirs, and it had always been white.

'Meg?' Eddie shook my shoulder gently, and I must have blinked, but Leonie's was the face I sought.

I hit a cow once, she'd told us.

I could see the headlines and King Cole's Rotary portrait in newsprint. A hit-and-run, they'd called it, and I remembered Leonie's story after wine and beer and Baileys on Christmas night.

He was a big bastard. Made a helluva mess.

I think I spoke.

'What, love?' The Coulter leaned in.

It was Leonie. Leonie who'd run King down in the middle of the night, driven through him then back over him. 'As if he were a kangaroo,' Catherine had said, and speculated as to why he might have been standing out there on the highway. 'He was sober, you know,' she'd told me. Well, not completely sober, but he wasn't drunk, and, 'Why would you just stand there?' she'd wondered, as I'm sure her husband and his team had wondered too. As I myself had wondered. You'd jump out of the way, wouldn't you? You'd see the car coming and you'd throw yourself onto the verge.

But what if someone else who knew the car was coming gave you just a little push?

We don't want to hear about that now, Tom had said.

They'd sent Joanna home to King the night she'd come to tell them she was leaving. They should have wished her well and kissed her goodbye, but they sent her back to the life that they felt suited her, and better suited them, and in the years that followed, while she turned and turned like a cat in a corner, they came to see her husband for the man he really was. It was Tom and Leonie who Jo called in whispers from behind her bathroom door. They learned of the breaks and bruises, and they heard the names that people called that coffee-coloured, big-eyed baby girl. I wondered how long sorry took to find them, and how many times they'd offered it in the crooks of tired arms.

In the end, it had all worked out, but not by itself.

Too late, Joanna told Leonie after Rosemary's service, but it hadn't been.

The Lambs were the only family where no names were called across meat and potatoes. Leonie the only woman in Winifred who could have raised a boy to be the sort of man who'd see a pretty girl and only that; the sort of man who'd see the liquorice hair and wide, warm smile and watch her dance and think, *Now, there's the girl I'm going to marry*, nothing more and never less.

'Well, I guess this is it then,' Eddie began.

I'm sure I nodded. I'm sure I smiled. I'm sure I kissed the cheek he pulled me into one last time (*Take care of yourself. . . You too*), but it was his mother's eyes I met, as understanding spiralled like smoke between us.

'You do right by your friends,' she said softly. Seeing in it that I knew what she had done, and pressing me to keep another secret.

I only nodded. Already with a pocketful, what harm could one more do?

CHAPTER FIFTY-ONE

Lily

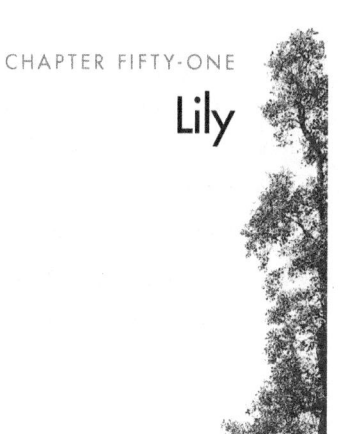

How do you keep a secret? You tell no one. But everyone tells someone, it's human nature, and your someone tells their someone, and they tell someone else. Secrets are never properly kept. Not forever.

This is not my confession. I'm not looking for forgiveness or understanding. I only want to tell the truth and tell it unreservedly. All any woman really wants, I think, is to be seen and heard.

'Hear me out,' men tell us, and we do, don't we? Even if we're not actually hanging on to every word, we hear them out. Even when we don't believe them, we let them talk, but they rarely return the courtesy.

In the early days, when Norman and I sat together at a table every night, I'd see him wincing sometimes like it was all too painful, to have to give me five minutes of his attention. He'd say things like, 'Is this going to be a long story?' and, 'Can you get to the point?' and I would be ashamed and embarrassed. Yet he would talk and talk and talk, about himself mostly. Things he'd seen that day, conversations he'd had, people who'd annoyed him. Talking and talking, telling me about this one at work, that one on the train, how best to tie a knot or grill a sausage, and I'd sit at the other side of the table thinking about all sorts of things but rarely what he was talking about. I'd heard it all before, but I'd never say that. I'd look as interested as he needed me to look, and I'd make all the right little comments to encourage the story along.

He never wanted to hear how my day was beyond *Fine, thanks* or *Not too bad*. So I might tell the postman about the mess the neighbour's cat made of my agapanthus, I'd give the teller at the bank the funny story I'd heard just that morning, and I'd tell the bus driver how I felt about the weather.

It was a lonely marriage. Perhaps I should have left him when I found out what was really going on, why he took those pictures and why he kept them, and the catalogues in the bedroom, but where could I have gone? I cared too much what people thought of me. I wish I hadn't, but there it is.

Looking back, it's easy to see the things I could have handled differently, should have handled differently. Like the song says, I've had a few regrets. I suppose I've had more than a few, but what purpose has it? Way leads on to way, doesn't it? If you'd turned left instead of right, just once, your whole journey from that point on would be different, and I wish it was some days, but I had a lovely childhood, and where I've ended up now, here at the end of it all, isn't such a bad place. I have felt seen and heard.

I am sorry that Rosemary and Eddie became so tangled up in the business of that girl. I didn't think that the police would take or charge him. I didn't know Norman had kept that little bracelet. I was angry with him when he told me, and angrier still when he said he'd lost it, and I suppose he must have dropped it over there, but I don't think it was on purpose.

They'll find everything they need to know Eddie had nothing to do with it. There'll be a mess of strangers through this house. They'll crawl beneath it, turn out all my drawers and pockets, dig up my plants. Lord knows there'll be enough to keep them busy with their tweezers and dusting brushes. Eddie will be sent home no worse for wear, and Rosemary can decide then whether to love or leave him.

I will leave this for you to find, Meg, and I hope that by the time you come to read it, you will not feel pressed to share. They will take these pages from you if you show them, and make no mistake, they'll bring you in close to ask their questions. You'll not like it, and they don't need every little puzzle piece, do they? Not when they've the picture on the box. Any little bits that don't quite fit together won't make any difference. What's gone is gone.

What's done is done, and so am I. I have set down everything I set out to share, and more. I have told my story. I hope one day you are able to tell someone your own. Whatever shame it is you ran from, Meg, it needn't underline the rest of your life.

That artist was right to build his house over here. The light really is lovely, even as it dims. I sit here now in the late afternoon with a glass of wine at my elbow and it feels strange knowing it will be my last. But I am ready to go. This will be it—this view, these last few lines. I will rinse my glass and take my walk and then I shall put myself to bed.

It is late and I am tired. I am tired of protecting Norman. I am tired of hiding, and I am tired of keeping secrets. I can only trust now that God will forgive what I am about to do—and forgive the things that I have done.

CHAPTER FIFTY-TWO
Meg

We all carry secrets.

Some we are given for safekeeping, wrapped in velvety trust. Some we have only an idea of: a glimpse of something like a sock beneath a washer, a look between people who should not be looking, whispers overheard, words torn from pages. They are pebbles in our pockets, and those we bury deepest are our own. Things we choose never to tell, pushed out of sight but never far from mind, and worried smooth by memory.

Of course, they cannot be seen. They're apparent only when the size or weight of one, or one too many, drops a shoulder and upsets our balance. People wonder then.

'If you want to keep a secret, you must also hide it from yourself,' George Orwell wrote, and I suppose he meant for us to keep our hands out of our pockets.

But that can be hard to do.

Some secrets destroy us. Too heavy, too hard, too much. Unhappiness can fester in the shadows of a high chin and the busiest of hands. A boy face down in a river, a woman in a field that once was green, another bagged in vomit.

And some lead us to put aside our own.

I left Magpie Beach, a hermit crab without a shell, though I knew the car would do for a week or more. Room enough for the seat to lie back. The space behind, a patchwork of books, boots, and plants in pots; a tray of late mango chutney, some canned food, sandwiches and a flask of soup; clothes and bedding in plastic bags, Lily's shoebox, and the chair with its mended arm, which I had become comfortable in and fond of. We take with us what we cannot leave behind.

Mrs Robinson found her own way into the wicker basket, which I lined with a sweater that would not hold another stitch. Her kittens were long gone to good homes or bad. Beyond Rosemary's, which Eddie kept, I had no way of knowing. She didn't seem to miss them when they disappeared in scratchy pocketfuls. The black one to a smallholder with mice, and the other to a friend of Catherine's whose daughters wanted a puppy. A kitten would do, the mother said. For now, I thought, but not forever.

I followed Rosemary south at least as far as I knew she'd travelled, and beyond that, I drove and drove, past and through small towns and those that imagined they were bigger. Brown signs promised lookouts and rest stops, yellow warned of things that might jump out at any moment, and green ones marked the distance still to go, though I didn't really know where we were headed.

I followed as far as the highway went before it became something else, something wider and more complex with choices too many to count.

I had money enough for a bond, a crisp reference from Catherine, and food to keep me going. Purchase enough to swing up off the ground. I would find a place to set a saucer on the floor, and push my chair into a shaft of sunlight. Somewhere I could call home. It is more than a teacup upended on a drainer; more than books on a shelf, a photograph tacked to a cupboard door; more than being safe and warm and dry. Home is the steadying of a heartbeat, the slow closing of eyes. It is where we empty our pockets, and where we are our truest, secret selves: busy, lazy, crippled by self-doubt; brimming with spite, broken, beaten, afraid.

Brisbane shone in the high sunlight of that blue-sky afternoon, and I was drawn along the roads that wound towards it. I found myself wanting to cross its bridges, lay a hand on the summer-warm backs of the postcard lions. The city's crowds tempted me closer. Room among others. I did not want to live alone again. Those of us who've done so know what it is to live unseen. I wanted to be greeted, to make space at a table, fill a kettle to the brim. I had remembered what it was to be counted and included, considered, heard and valued. Talked to instead of talked about.

What does she have there in her pockets?

I'd killed my husband, they said. Chopped him into pieces and buried him. Well, I didn't. He died of cancer. Too fast, but still slowly; and he was not my husband. This time I would tell it truthfully from the start.

Perhaps he ran away, people had reckoned in whispers. But we'd run away together. We did not want to be found, it is true, but we were not hiding from anything I ever heard rumoured. We were on no lists, we were not wanted. No one was chasing us for taxes or visas, debts or favours; broken bones or bonds or words.

'Why didn't you go home?' Rosemary asked me once. It was after dark and we were sitting together as we had recently begun to do, waiting for sausages to frill, for Mrs Robinson and Dolly to settle in one or other of our laps; waiting for the whole sorry mess of Eddie's incarceration to play out to the bell.

'This is my home,' I told her, although I knew of course which home she meant. The house with heights penned on its pantry door; where the bath was the colour of an avocado, and every other stair creaked on the way to bed.

'It isn't really, though, is it?' she pushed on. 'Are your parents still alive? Do you have brothers or sisters?'

It's best not to know some things, but I thought about it then, thought of telling her. My fingers curled around the smoothest of all pebbles and I was so close to the edge of drawing it out that my breath began to shorten, but I left it be.

'I had an older brother,' is all I gave her, but I'd had more than that.

I'd had a father I did not miss and did not bid goodbye.

A grandmother I'd loved.

A mother, for want of any other word.

Are all secrets secret-somethings or just things we do not tell?

'Should have done for you myself,' my mother used to say. 'Cheap bottle of vodka and a coathanger would have saved a lot of bother in the long run.'

'Are you stupid?' she used to ask me. 'Batteries not included?' And she would lean into her own smoky breath, fist clenched tight ready to knock my wooden head. Shave and a haircut. 'Is there anything at all inside that ugly lump?'

It is true that I struggled to make sense of numbers, which scrambled like tiles in a bag, while my brother's answers seemed to fully form themselves like bubbles on the tip of the wand that was his pencil.

'I'll help Meg,' he would say to stay her hand.

Boy genius, Mother called him, though by his own admission he wasn't really. He wasn't top of any class or even close, but he wasn't bottom. 'You're wasting your time on that chump,' she would tell him.

'You're a waste of everyone's time,' she would tell me. A waste of space. A waste of oxygen. A waste of money.

It is true, I'd needed operations when I was a baby. I needed special shoes and glasses as a child, and even though my brother promised these things were not paid for by our parents, I knew there were expenses that the government did not cover, so I worked hard to cover them myself. 'When you've finished that, you can get this done,' they used to say. 'Put your back into it. Pull your finger out.'

'You're too nice,' my brother told me. 'Too forgiving.' Cold nights he lay close once the bedside clock warned us the pubs were closing and all the boots and voices might come home.

'Go on upstairs and open a few doors,' Mother would tell them, if they wanted more than to piss from the back step, and my brother's hand would find mine in the dark just to let me know that any strangers straying would not come between us.

He would laugh at my imaginings, my wondering-whys and my loss of thread.

'Away with the fucking fairies,' Mother called it.

'Don't listen to her,' he whispered, and I carried that like a shield, and noticed things that others did not bother to.

'Still waters run deep,' Granny said.

'If you gave her a penny for her thoughts, you'd get change,' Mother scoffed.

'Give it a rest, woman,' Dad told her more than once, but that made it worse for me, so I'd wish he hadn't.

'Read,' my grandmother told me, and she sat with her big cloth-covered book open between us, long after my brother had moved on to Louis L'Amour.

I got there too. In time, he passed those little paperbacks along to me and many others. We had no library, but Gran had friends and we had neighbours and teachers who knew us well enough to know we needed doors to open, worlds to explore, and rabbit holes to throw ourselves into. Special precious books I tucked into the cube of cupboard that was my bedside table so the sight of them would not incite my mother. 'Get your head out of that piece of crap and pull your weight around here!' she used to shout, and sometimes she would have me watch her toss one in the oven.

But you can't burn every book.

I came apart when Granny died. Gently, she went into the night, the way she would have wanted, and I was happy for that, but I missed her raw.

It is true I struggled after school, but while my brother took an apprenticeship, he nudged me towards the local supermarket, where I worked well once the shutters clattered down and the aisles were free of customers. Shelves had the order that I would love later in a library. Campbell's next to Continental next to Heinz. I enjoyed the quiet and still of a daytime place at night, that feeling of abandonment and being left alone.

'It's not a real job,' Mother sneered. 'You wouldn't last two minutes out there.' In the real world, she meant, where her own movements were fluid, scanning groceries and opening doors and crossing busy roads.

'You're going nowhere,' she told me, when I thought for a time I might leave home and move in with my brother. 'What makes you think he wants you under his feet?'

It was true that he enjoyed his life apart. Still, he watched over me.

It was my brother who suggested the Worm and Monkey for my twenty-first. 'My treat,' he promised, and that was enough.

We were quiet around the table, peeling strips from coasters and trailing fingers through the condensation from our drinks, when he arrived. He was more than a little late, but no one minded. My father and my mother loved him more, but I did not care, because I loved him most.

His hair was shower-wet and sat in dark curls on his shoulders. He wore a shirt I'd given him for Christmas, and in his hand he held a single yellow rose. Five long steps from door to table, where he touched it to my cheek.

'Happy Birthday, little one,' he said, and I threw my arms around his neck.

'He's your fucking brother,' Mother growled. But he was so much more than that. He was my best friend, my north, south, east and west; the hand I held when everyone around us had theirs jammed into their pockets.

Peas in a pod.

Thick as thieves.

Up to no good.

'Sit down, Son,' Dad told him. 'You're making a scene.'

But Sonny only laughed. 'She deserves a scene!' he said. 'You know it's her birthday, right?'

'I know it's Tuesday,' Mother said. 'Half-price beer and steak.'

'I'll cheers to that!' Dad laughed and bottles clinked together in a toast.

It was that night Sonny told me he was leaving. Following a mate to Queensland, where there was work right up and down for fitter-turners. It was the next day that he took me for my passport photo.

We would not tell them, he said, because they'd spoil it. Break it. Stop it.

'How can they?' I wondered, but he promised me they would, and he made me promise not to tell.

'They'll wake up and we'll be gone,' he told me. That was the plan. When the time came, we would meet at midnight, in keeping with the darkest blue of secrets.

'Like in a movie,' Sonny said.

Or a fairytale, I thought.

Books were full of runaways: the Famous Five and the Boxcar Children, Oliver Twist. But it would have taken me years to find the courage on my own, and by then I think my sandals would have been too small and worn for me to run.

There was a storm the night we left. The rain was torrential, and the noise of it racing along gutters and pouring down drains was louder even than the thunder. Still, click of latch, tread on stair was loud enough.

'Where do you think you're sneaking off to?' Mother hissed, swaying in her bedroom doorway.

Shallow breaths and knees weak; bile rose in my throat.

'Away,' I told her without turning around.

'Go on then,' she said. 'Go on. Fuck off.'

But I did not move as she dropped down each step, one hand sliding down the smooth white rail, tethering the high that was not yet hungover.

'You,' she said. 'You.' She stood two steps above me, and ground the tip of her finger deep between my shoulder blades. I let her slap the back of my head as if it were my face. One, two, three times. Hair caught on her ring so that a clump of it tore from its roots.

'Found someone who'll fuck you, have you?'

I hadn't. I never had. I never would. But I did not answer.

'You walk out that door and you're dead to me,' she said.

And I nodded and she laughed, because she did not know yet who was meeting me around the corner, waiting in a taxi in the dark.

'Dead to me!' she shouted as I pulled the door behind me, but if anything came after, it was lost in wind and rain.

People will think what they want to think, no matter what you tell them, but palm flat and out of pocket, this thing I had not told was not as heavy as I had imagined.

He, my husband, and I, his wife.

Perhaps Sonny lied to save us from the rumours that would have found us if he hadn't, because Winifred was a meat-and-potatoes town even as we found it, where a surname shared and a hand held and an arm around a shoulder meant a thing tricky as butter to take back once spread. When someone thinks you something for so long, it is easier to become that other person.

Flesh grows around the seed.

He was the wool that kept me warm. He was the hand that kept me steady. He was the love of my life, but there was never any of the secret shame Lily suspected, and nothing more that either of us ever wanted from the other. He was my brother, and that was more than enough, in the dark, in the rain, in the end.

'I'll look after you, little one,' he'd promised, but I looked after him, too.

CHAPTER FIFTY-THREE

Rosemary

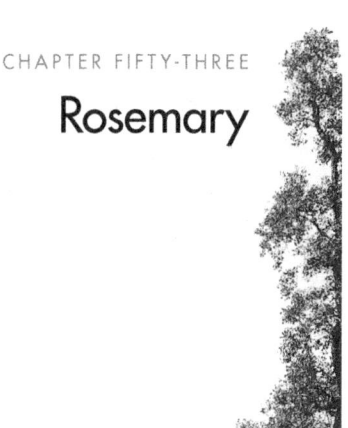

The first driver's name was Carl. He talked non-stop. 'It's nice to have a bit of company, especially on the night runs,' he said, and he went on to tell me all about his wife and children. It was reassuring that he had them, but I wasn't interested.

With my head up against the glass, nothing but dark and dead kangaroos whizzing by, I felt like Julia Roberts in *Sleeping with the Enemy*. She did the same thing—faked her own death to escape—but for her it was more of a running-away than the beginning-again it was going to be for me. I never wanted to be a runaway. I only wanted to be someone else, and Julia Roberts left too many loose ends.

I swapped rides and had some breakfast at a truck stop outside Gladstone, and Brian ran me to Bundaberg, where I knew I had the day to spend, waiting for the Greyhound bus that would take me back up the highway I'd spent half the night and all morning coming down.

It's not that I didn't trust Meg not to tell; I just wanted to cover my tracks. I wasn't sure I'd left enough for them to believe I'd died in the fire. I wasn't sure there wouldn't be news stories asking people had they seen me, and if someone had, I wanted to be sure they went off looking in the wrong direction.

I cut my ponytail off in the ladies' toilet, and I bagged it and pushed it into the sanitary bin. I bought the mildest of prescription reading glasses from a stand beside the CDs and the paperbacks, and when I got into town, I put my cap away and changed into a dress. I didn't have a lot of clothes with me. Only odd things Eddie wouldn't miss, and a couple of new things I'd bought in secret and been careful not to show him.

It was colder in Bundaberg than it had been back home, and I found a Kmart and bought a cardigan. I bought other things as well: cloth nappies and pins, baby singlets in different sizes, dummies and more clothes, Panadol and eye drops, antiseptic and antihistamine. I had a long list. (I had to buy another bag.)

At five o'clock, I found a pub that did counter meals and had a television, and I got fish and chips, a diet Coke, and a table on my own. The news came on at six and my heart was pounding like a mallet smashing schnitzel. A ute full of teenagers had rolled over on a farm, killing one and injuring all the others. A woman had been bitten by her neighbour's dog. And then the factory fire was shown, blazing in the night and smouldering in daylight, and my picture flashed up, but it was only small, set in the corner of the screen behind the newsreader. It didn't even really look like me. In it I was tanned and smiling. In the mirror above the sink in the bathroom I'd looked greeny grey and as serious as a heart attack.

The bus left just before ten o'clock. There were hours between stops and people curled up against the windows with books and headphones and pillows. I slept on and off, but I was awake when we rumbled by the turn-off to Winifred, and I realised then I must have blinked and missed the one to Maggie Beach.

The bus stopped in Townsville the next afternoon. It wasn't a long walk to the marina, but once I got there it took me a while to find what

I was looking for. There were plenty of people I could have asked, but I knew not to draw attention to myself. Even though she'd written that they would be, I didn't completely trust that *Muddy Duck* would be there until I saw it tucked into its little pen, and Mary pegging tea towels to the knee-high wire fence of its rail. She looked excited to see me, waving with both hands, and that was a relief. 'I'm so glad you came!' she said, and she took my bags and held out a hand to help me balance as I stepped onto the deck.

'You're so big!' she said, and there was a touch of worry in it.

'Come aboard! No shoes. Dip your feet!' Muddy called up from below, and then he was up the ladder and standing there in front of me. There was a bucket of salt water and a towel and I pushed my sneakers off without unlacing them and was embarrassed at the dirt between my toes.

'Well, didn't you turn out to be a dark horse?' Muddy said. I don't know how happy he was to have me there, but what he was set to do cost more than a favour, and I knew he was happy enough to have the money Mum had transferred the day after I'd called to ask her to.

I'd rung her from the plastic-hooded phone outside the post office.

'I'm really not in any trouble,' I'd told her.

'This'll come out of your share,' she'd warned me. My share of whatever she had left to leave us in the end, she meant. I told her it would be all I'd ever want from her, and I think she understood then that I wouldn't be around to ask for more.

'So, you're leaving then.'

I didn't answer.

'Does Eddie know?'

'About the baby? Yes.'

'About your leaving?'

'No.'

'Have you thought the whole thing through?'

I told her I'd done nothing but.

'And you're absolutely sure this is what you really want?'

'I really am.'

'Then don't let anyone change your mind.' I was surprised to hear her say that. I'd been expecting more of a lecture, but she just took Muddy's banking details and told me it might take her a few days. She was busy at work, but she'd do her best to get to the bank between appointments.

'Will I be seeing you?' she asked. *In Melbourne? Ever again?*

'No. No, you won't.'

'Is there someone else?' she asked then.

'No.'

'But you wouldn't tell me if there was, would you?'

Though I think I would have.

'There will be,' she said, which was kind, I thought. 'When you're through this next bit—which will be hard—you will find someone else. You'll be happy. Happier than you were before—than you are now.'

'Thank you.'

She was quiet for such a long time that I thought she might have hung up.

'You're going to have a very big secret to keep,' she said eventually. 'Make sure you keep it properly. Keep it to yourself.' It was a quieter voice she used, a careful voice. 'Those people who tell you they're good at keeping secrets usually aren't. If you want to put something away completely, you'll have to forget it's there. You'll have to let it be forgotten and let go of anything and everything that reminds you of it, no matter how much it hurts.' *No matter who it hurts.* 'Whatever lie you come up with, stick to it. Even if they doubt you, even if they challenge you, keep to your story, don't you waver. They'll believe you in the end if you give them no choice.'

No they won't.

'Good luck, love,' she finished, and there was a wobble in it, but as loose ends go, she's tied up tight enough.

We sat downstairs around the table in the belly of the little boat. Mary made tea, then a late lunch that might have been an early dinner, and Muddy spoke for a long time, in a low voice. He'd thought of everything, and everything that could possibly go wrong. 'Keep your head down this afternoon,' he said, though I had to make sure people saw me leaving the marina, so when I did, I shouted, 'Safe trip!' and, 'I'll miss you!' for the benefit of anyone who might have been watching, and then I had hours to kill quietly. There was no question where I'd spend them.

I bought a large tub of buttered popcorn and a Coke, and I took it all in, because I knew it would be a long time before I saw any of it again: the red-plum velvet seats, the squeaky wheel of the screen widening as the lights double-dimmed, the shooting sound and graphics of the Dolby logo. The boy who tore my ticket's name was Callum. I still have the half he let me keep. 'Enjoy the movie,' he said. He didn't mean it—he couldn't have cared less—but I did enjoy *Nine Months*. I laughed louder and harder than anyone else in the theatre, but I probably found it funnier because I was pregnant. I went straight in to Cinema 3 for *Waterworld*, which—knowing what lay ahead—perhaps I shouldn't have seen. They weren't great movies, but they were stories you didn't have to think too much about, which suited me fine, because there were so many other things on my mind there wouldn't have been room for something with a complicated plot.

The second movie didn't finish until late, and the few people I saw on my way back to the marina were heading home, climbing into cars or holding hands and walking with purpose. I would have looked the same to any of them who might have noticed me. I had my own place to be, and I was soon tucked in shadow on the high side of the grassy slope beside the main marina building.

I was comfy enough with my back against a tree. I watched a fishing boat come in and a homeless woman rummage through bins. I saw a couple of cats and heard a bird or a possum fixing itself for a night in the branches up above. I stayed there until three o'clock in the morning.

The gate securing the pontoon was wedged open ever so slightly with a fold of cardboard, and I slipped that into my pocket and let the latch click properly behind me. The boats on either side were shadowy and still, people inside them fast asleep or trying to be, while Muddy waited in the dark cockpit of *Muddy Duck*. He put a finger to his lips and helped me climb on board. I knew what to do. I knew where to go.

Mary found my hand and squeezed it as I pressed down the narrow steps and into the space they'd shown me the day before. There were no words exchanged, and I was asleep in minutes.

I stayed as quiet as a mouse and away from any windows in the morning. I couldn't use the toilet while they were away clearing customs, and if anyone came back with them I was to pretend I was there to surprise my friends and wish them a safe trip, but they came back alone.

Friends really did stop by at lunchtime, and I hid in the little matchbox bathroom. 'It's only for storage,' Mary told the woman when she asked to use it, and they walked together to the ablution block at the end of the pontoon instead, sharing stories of squatting over buckets on stormy seas. I sat on the closed toilet seat and puzzled over a crossword while they sat in the cockpit drinking rum and orange juice and balancing salami on their crackers. I could hear them chatting about the passage ahead, winds they might expect, reefs to avoid, sheltered bays they must be sure to visit, and ways to make their stores last longer. I didn't know yet what a passage was or what they meant by stores.

We cast off when they left. Once we were beyond the shelter of the harbour, Muddy cut the engine and Mary leaned down the steps and banged on the door to let me know I could come out, though I knew I could only move into the main cabin. The coast was clear, but only the coast below deck. We weren't out of the woods yet, Muddy would keep reminding us.

Their feet slapped on the deck above me. Ropes thumped and winches rattled. Sails flapped wildly then snapped tight and the boat tilted to the side so suddenly that I think I might have cried out. Cushions tumbled onto the floor and when I bent to pick them up, I fell into a seat on the downside of the table. Books strained against bungee cords, fruit and biscuits swung in hammocks, but there wasn't even a horizon to anchor me. I'd always thought of sailboats bobbing on the ocean, but we were carving through it. The wet noise of it racing past was deafening, and on one side of the boat the portholes seemed to skim the water. On the high side, it was like someone was taking great big fistfuls of sky and just rubbing them on the glass.

I stayed below deck until nightfall with a bucket between my legs.

Mary brought me a tall mug of soup and crackers left over from the afternoon with their friends. She helped me slide into my berth and I slept better than I expected to between the bounce and smack, and Muddy and Mary's swapping places every few hours between shifts at the helm.

By the next day we were in international waters and I was free to leave the cabin. I was shocked how calm it was up on deck compared to the noise and pitch and racket below. The ocean, a thick and inky blue, whooshed along the hull and pattered gently behind us.

All these words I learned to use: helm and head and port and starboard; galley and salon and sheet and cleat.

We passed days together in the cockpit, chatting and reading. Muddy taught me knots and the basics of sailing. Mary taught me how to live in a home that would not stop moving. In its own way *Muddy Duck* was like Eddie's parents' caravan, and the doll's house I'd had as a little girl, with a proper place for everything and everything in its place. Outside too big to come inside, and too few things to get lost or forgotten.

I took my turn at the helm every four hours from the second day, and I stopped feeling queasy on the fifth.

I liked the night watches, though I was never really sure what to be watching for. I liked being alone beneath the stars with nothing but the froth of ocean flying by and glittering with phosphorescence. I knew they were tiny animals, but they didn't look like anything but starlight.

One morning, Mary called me up on deck and there were dolphins off the bow and land on either side of us. Tiny pancake islands covered in palm trees. 'Louisiades!' Muddy called out, but I knew where we were already. He'd shown me how to take a reading from the GPS and plot a course with pencil kisses on the chart. He'd taught me how to be of use. 'She's crew, not cargo,' he'd said to Mary that first night, when I was not quite asleep but looked it.

There was always a lure trawling behind us and often we woke each other in the night with the cry of *Fish!* and all our hands were needed to turn the boat into the wind, drop the mainsail, bring the fish aboard and club it with a winch handle.

Everyone was woken when shifts changed: the whistle of the kettle, the slide and thud of the companionway opening up or closing tight depending on wind and weather. Muddy said passages were to be endured and not enjoyed, but I did enjoy it when the weather was fine. It was the first time I'd ever really felt part of a team, capable and valued, a cog in a machine. They'd called us a team at the factory, but it wasn't true. We only did the same thing at the same time for the same people and the same amount of money.

For a few days the sky was dirty purple and the ocean grey and broken. Squalls filled the rain tanks and rinsed us of salt. Those nights you couldn't see the bow for rain and spray, and even in Mary's waterproof jacket and pants I was soaked through to my underwear in minutes. Rogue waves came in sideways, crashing into the cockpit, and we buckled in turn into the harness in case one washed us overboard.

In the middle came one terrible storm, and Muddy steered us all the way through that. 'It's my boat,' he said. Everything was his. Mary and I hunkered down below, wedged into corners. It was like hiding in the footwell of a roller-coaster car. Even with everything closed up tight, salt water dripped and dribbled in, sloshing down the steps when we slid open the hatch to pass up mugs of coffee. Waves cracked like thunder on the hull, and it felt as though the boat would capsize or break in two at any moment, and I cried, secretly, into a cushion. Muddy worried that the bilge pump would burn out, but it didn't, and the third day wasn't as bad as the first, and the day after that was better still, and soon enough there wasn't a cloud in the sky or a breath of wind and the ocean was as level as concrete.

We opened all the hatches and portholes and pulled all the big cushions up on deck and into the sun to dry, though nothing ever dried completely, everything felt greasy—beds and clothes, plates and papers. It was the salt, Muddy said.

It took us twenty-five days to get to the Philippines. We couldn't stop at any of the places their friends had told them to be sure to, because of me. We couldn't take any chances. Muddy was alert if ships appeared on the horizon, and we were to wake him if we saw lights at night or if blips of any size jumped on the radar screen. I wondered sometimes if smuggling was something he'd done before, he seemed to be so good at it.

'Have you shown anyone the note?' was the first thing he'd said when we spoke on the phone.

Of course I hadn't.

'Make sure you get rid of it.'

That wasn't hard. I'd twisted it up like a lolly wrapper and pushed it into a can of Coke someone had abandoned on the shelf.

Plan B, he'd written on the slip of paper he'd tucked into the envelope with Mary's letter. *Leave a name and number and wait.* There was a phone number and I felt the tight thrill of a window opening. A thin white shoot thrust out of hope I'd thought was dead.

There was no mention of plan B in Mary's letter which I read out loud to Eddie. She must have known that he'd expect me to, because there was no mention of my letter to her either. All those pages that I'd written late at night while Eddie was in custody. I hadn't expected anyone to actually read them. I hadn't thought I'd send the letter, and even when I did, I hadn't expected a reply. Maybe a short note, a couple of paragraphs telling me to hang in there, things would all work out, but Mary's letter was long and newsy. She wrote about their journey north, the supermarket where she worked nights stocking shelves, a cut on Muddy's foot that had turned septic. Eddie hadn't been interested, but he'd pretended to be.

'You're never going to see her again,' he said. *There's not much point in writing back.*

But I did write back. And I called the number and left my name at the office of Townsville marina (which wasn't where Mary had told me, in her letter, they were staying).

Muddy didn't beat about the bush. 'There is a way you can do this,' he said. 'But it isn't easy and it's permanent.' He was firm about that. 'You won't be able to go back,' he said. 'Not for any reason.'

'I won't want to,' I assured him.

We sailed into Pabo Bay early one morning. Roosters were crowing, smoke rising beyond huts that stood in a clearing between a million palm trees. There was a cow on the beach and a couple of dogs. Two men waded through the shallows with a fishing net between them and, on seeing the sailboat, their shouts carried across the morning-misty water.

'Muddy Mary!' they shouted. *'Muddy Mary!'*

Children ran to the water's edge, and while we motored in close and anchored, young men paddled out in dugout canoes. Space was made for us between them, and we were ferried ashore, where we were met by Mary's parents, aunts, uncles, and cousins. It seemed like she belonged to everyone, and they passed her between them with hugs and thanks to God. They shook Muddy's hand and slapped his shoulders and they smiled at me as they chattered in Tagalog with Mary throwing in English here and there for me to pick up.

'This is Bella,' she said.

Eyebrows shot up and women touched their fingers to foreheads and hearts. I knew already that the name I was to take belonged to Mary's sister first.

'She's a teacher,' Mary lied.

'If you can read and write, then you can teach,' Muddy had said. We'd gone over the plan many afternoons. 'You have your baby, stay for a couple of years, learn the language, be of use, and then you leave as someone else.' He never said *Mary's dead sister*, but it was understood. 'Play your cards right,' he was fond of saying.

Mary's mother took my hands in both of hers. 'You are welcome here,' she said. She hadn't guessed yet that I'd be staying. Mary would tell them later: when we had eaten the feast that was yet to be prepared, when the men had drunk the whisky that I'd brought, and dresses had been divided between aunts. The children would be shooed away and Mary and Muddy and the closest of the family would talk privately while I shared the washing-up with women I would come to know.

A proposition would be made, and they would accept.

'You will love her,' Mary promised them.

'She'll work,' Muddy said.

'It won't be a free ride,' he'd warned me many times, but I'd never have expected it to be.

'It's not a resort,' he'd told me in our very first conversation on the phone. 'It's bare bones basic.'

'I can manage that,' I had assured him.

Muddy and Mary left early the next morning. They'd be back in a fortnight, but it was more important than usual for them to enter the country straight away and properly in Manila, Muddy said. They took a long list from Mary's parents, and shorter ones from uncles, but no one gave them money except me. What would this new life cost? A good generator, two mattresses, a roll of lino, fuel and food and fishing nets, four dive masks and two spear guns, nails and chainsaw blades and a pair of gumboots.

I stood alone on the cool sand and watched *Muddy Duck* motor out and past the palm-tipped point. On a distant island, rising through low cloud, was the perfect triangle of an old volcano. I knew that I would learn its name and the language of its people. I would come to know the sounds and smells and tastes of this new place. I would get used to a thinner mattress, bitter coffee, cold water. I would join the songs and prayers and laughter that had filled the evening before. I would grow. I would have my baby surrounded by warm women with capable hands, and I would give her a name all to herself, tie no memory to her for threads to reach back and take root.

I knew it would not be easy every day, that I would need to work and try and there would be tears, and at times I'd wonder whether I had made the right choice.

I knew there'd be no going back to who I'd been before.

I knew that Rosemary Lamb was gone forever.

But I knew, too, that this would be a better life than she had ever dreamed of. A richer life than anything she'd conjured in the middle of the night. It would be fuller, and prouder, for my own dreams hitched behind it.

Sunrise spread before me golden orange, and *Muddy Duck* cut a clean line, smaller now and in silhouette. I stopped waving and turned towards my new home, where an aunt whose name I could not quite remember was stepping carefully around a net already cast and drawn and laid out for the early morning sun to dry. She came towards me with a smile so wide it raised the apples of her cheeks and crinkled the corners of her eyes.

'I have something for you,' she sang softly. 'Maybe you're a little bit lonely? Maybe you need a little friend?'

And she handed me the puppy in her arms.

'You give him a name,' she said, 'and you feed him, and you love him, and he will be yours.'

It was the last piece of a Cinderella jigsaw. I took him with tears in my eyes and I knew right away what I would call him.

'Hello, Richard.'

'Richard!' She laughed, but she was not laughing at me. 'Ooh-la-la, Richard Gere!' She fanned her face with one hand while the other tapped her chest. 'Richard Gere!' she sang again, walking away now with tilting hips and hands still fluttering. Laughter light on the early morning breeze, and shadows long as the sun broke the horizon.

CHAPTER FIFTY-FOUR

Meg

There is one more thing.

It is something I sucked on for a long time, the rough button of a peppermint that thinned before it cracked, an idea that had first come to me the night of Rosemary's twenty-first but had revisited since then, a dozen times.

A sock glimpsed beneath a washer.

Curiosity killed the cat, my grandmother used to say.

I called from a public phone in Roma Street Station, a thick perspex hood muffling last calls and platform changes. Someone had scratched *Slut* into the plastic with a knife or a coin, and the receiver smelled of disinfectant.

It took fifty cents to get me past the receptionist and then, 'This is Susan Haines.' A cheery tone. 'How can I help?'

'I'm interested in a house you have listed,' I said. 'It's up in Carney County, near Winifred but out of town. It's by the sea.'

She knew the place I meant.

'I'm a writer,' I told her tentatively, testing its tread like a pair of slippers. I gave a false name and pretended yet another life, as if I were a character in one of Rosemary's movies.

'Are you able to come into the agency?' Susan Haines asked. 'I'll be here until eleven.'

It was only three stops on the train, and a short walk.

She had suggested that I come in and yet seemed surprised when I arrived, and worked hard to swallow whatever it was she had just bitten into. Tucking what was left of it into a drawer, she offered me tea or coffee and the chair opposite.

'So, you'd like to know more about the Beach House?'

She'd never been there. If she had, she would have known there was no beach.

I'd told her I was a writer, thinking she would try to sell the light and space, but she didn't. 'You'll know a bit about its history?' she said. Its recent history, she meant. Its most recent occupants. *House of Secrets,* the newspapers had called it. It was a hard look she slid up, and I realised then that Writer sounded more like Journalist.

I shook my head and tried another lie: 'I drove past it once.'

No one drove past Lily's house. It was kilometres off the highway heading north, a shorter drive and hike from Magpie Beach, but it wasn't on the way to or from anywhere else. Susan Haines didn't know that. She'd only seen it in the pictures she was showing me, and I wondered who it was who'd been to board up all its windows and stick her signs there to weather in the sun.

The photographs were taken before the light was shuttered off. Windows were clean and open. It was the house I'd known well from the outside and briefly from within. For me it would always be Lily's house, though in the photos every trace of her was gone.

'It's incredibly spacious, really, for its size,' Susan said.

'How big is it exactly?'

She fingered a sheet of paper on her desk and spun it around so I could see, though what I'd come for wasn't where her cherry-red nail was tapping.

'May I?'

She pushed the paper towards the tips of my fingers, and there it was: *Owner/Builder: Paul Vale.*

There was only one P. Vale listed in the book I found pressed into the kitchen drawer back at the boarding house. Three men were playing poker at the table, and I stretched the cord of the phone around into the common room, where a fourth stood ironing orange robes.

'The Gallery. Paul Vale speaking.' (Vale pronounced *var-lay*. Emphasis on *var*.) He had a light accent, but it tilted at the end to say he'd been Australian for a long time.

I realised then that all I could do from my place at the end of a phone line was pose a question and accept whatever answer I was given.

It was not enough for me.

'Are you open to the public?' I asked instead.

'Of course.' And he reeled off his opening hours, and the bus numbers and train lines I could take from the city.

I waited until Wednesday, when he'd said he closed at twelve, and I timed it to arrive there at ten to.

It was a grey day. Cool enough for a cardigan, but warm enough for sandals. The Gallery was not far from the bus stop, and easy enough to find between a tattoo studio and a hair salon. It was less a gallery than an art supplies shop, and Paul Vale was just finishing with a customer when I walked in.

He was tall and slim and leaning on the counter, his left leg wrapped around the back of his right, laughing at something the younger man had said. His head was tipped back and there were feathers in the lines around his eyes.

I didn't clear the lump in my throat to get their attention, but the laughter petered out and the customer gathered papers and packets and said goodbye. Paul Vale lifted a hand to wave him off, and with the same raised palm he then acknowledged me.

He wore black jeans, worn sneakers and a loose shirt patterned with palm trees and flamingos and untucked. Shaggy hair curled a little where it touched his ears. Hair that was so black it was almost blue.

'Welcome!'

The shade and shape of his face. The tilt of his chin. I knew it was him.

I'd believed it when I'd seen the papers at Stilton and Haines, a printed P to match its softer cousins in the corners of two postcards.

Mark your diary!

Don't forget!

I'd first wondered on the night of Rosemary's party, when I'd seen the sketch of her mother in its frame. So much care in its creation, and that sense of something interrupted. The green strands in her eyes you had to sit so close to see, pencil strokes betraying something soft and secret.

I've always said whoever did that must have been half-pissed.

Or in love.

And Joanna: *By God, this place hasn't changed.*

She'd not once been out to visit them at Magpie Beach, Eddie had told me.

'Can I help you?'

He looked just like his daughter.

Lily was right after all, when she wrote that everyone tells someone.

'I only want to talk,' is how I began.

Acknowledgements

Tip of hat, and shout of round.

To the giants of my story, the tallest of my thanks. Sarah McKenzie, thank you for taking me on, for telling me, 'You did. It is,' and for finding a home for me with Ultimo. Thanks to all the good people there (I'm sure there are no bad ones), but most of all Robert Watkins. Thank you for signing me up, for loving *Rosemary* with such flag-waving enthusiasm, and taking such good care of her (and me). Thank you for giving us to Ali Lavau, and thank you Ali, for combing through our tangles with calm and careful fingers.

Without stories told, there would be no stories written. Thank you then to my dad, Bill Williams, for the grass beneath my feet. The making-up and the making-do. *The Crimson Cavern* and Gorilla Gudge, and Kathmandu at the bottom of the stairs.

Thanks to my brother, Simon Williams, for the *Omega Man*, and *Adventure in Forgotten Valley*; and to my sister, Caroline Huhncke, for reading me the *Moomins*, and always writing back.

Mr Bergin, who taught at St Robert's, thank you for reading with voices, while you sucked on your pipe. Because you loved books, I learned to love them too. Dr Michael Thurlow and Val Horner, thank you for your kind words of encouragement, no doubt long-forgotten. But not by me.

Thank you to my stepmother, Sheila Williams, for stories of the way things were and might have stayed. Aunties Phil and Jane, and

Aunty Mimi, there are diamonds in the details of your memories. Thank you for sharing so many of them, and bringing so much of what came and went, to life.

For all the years of letter-writing—for every envelope stuffed like a sausage and covered in stamps and last-minute questions—thank you, Lisa Noakes (it's your turn, by the way). You will hear me in these pages, because you grew my voice.

The warmest of my acknowledgements to my husband and my children. without your support, I would not have found the time or space to write this book. Thank you, Dorian, for the laptop which re-lit the fuse; for understanding the importance of having adventures, and for the stories that follow you home like mice. You are my best friend and my turkey-carver. Harper (who tells it like it is) and Paige (who plays it like she feels), thank you for your patience—for always waiting for me to finish (find my glasses, my keys, my phone). P, thank you for the company of your music, especially in closing chapter fifty-three. Thanks H, for adding to the kitty of weird things that could possibly happen, every time you leave the house. You are a born story-teller.

Few people knew that I was writing a book until *Rosemary* was done, but thanks to all of you who've championed my journey past *The End*. I have very much appreciated the asking-after, the champagne and the mint sauce.

Of course, to everyone who's read this far, thank you for trusting me with hours of your time. I hope I took you somewhere.

And finally, I would like to thank my husband's friends—the fishermen and surfers and dirt-bikers (you know who you are). In spending your weekends with him, you left me a quiet space to get this done. Keep up the good work!

Louise Wolhuter grew up in northern England, and moved to Queensland, before settling in Perth to raise a family. She currently works as an Education Assistant in a primary school, which leaves her early mornings, weekends and school holidays to write.